Getting It in the Head

Getting It
in the Head

Stories

Mike McCormack

Henry Holt and Company ▪ New York

Henry Holt and Company, Inc.
Publishers since 1866
115 West 18th Street
New York, New York 10011

Henry Holt® is a registered trademark
of Henry Holt and Company, Inc.

Published in Canada by Fitzhenry & Whiteside Ltd.,
195 Allstate Parkway, Markham, Ontario L3R 4T8.

Library of Congress Cataloging-in-Publication Data
McCormack, Mike, date.
Getting it in the head: stories / Mike McCormack.—1st American ed.
p.   cm.
ISBN 0-8050-5371-9 (alk. paper)
I. Title.
PR6063.C363G48   1998   97-43465
823'.914—dc21   CIP

Henry Holt books are available for special promotions
and premiums. For details contact: Director, Special Markets.

First published in hardcover in 1996 by Jonathan Cape, UK
First American Edition 1998

Designed by Michelle McMillian

Printed in the United States of America
All first editions are printed on acid-free paper. ∞

1   3   5   7   9   10   8   6   4   2

To my family and Noelle Donnellan—for keeping the faith

Contents

Acknowledgments

Some stories in this collection have appeared in the following magazines and anthologies: "The Stained Glass Violations" in *Passages*, "A Is for Axe" in *Brought to Book* (HarperCollins), "Thomas Crumlesh, 1960–1992: A Retrospective" in the *Sunday Tribune* and *An Anthology of Irish Comic Writing* (Michael Joseph), "Machine: Part II" in the *Connaught Tribune*, "Dead Man's Fuel" in *Conjunctions*, and "The Occupation: A Guide for Tourists" in *Ambit* and *Best Short Stories 1995* (Heinemann).

Getting It in the Head

The Gospel of Knives

When I opened the door and saw her standing there like an effigy, draped from head to toe in some fashion paraphrase of a chador, my mind flamed with a single, sordid thought: I wanted to get down on my knees before her in that sweetest of all acts of sexual worship and lick her out good and proper. I could see from her face—the swarthy skin, the too-even set of her teeth, the retroussé nose—that this was a woman of pent-up desires and trammeled passions and I fancied that I was the man to rectify all that. I glowed with confidence. Here was easy meat and it was as much as I could do to stop a predatory grin from spreading over my own teeth. However, when I invited her into my room and she spread out her collection of knives on the table I knew that I had made one of the bigger mistakes of my young and now bitter life.

"I'm a seller of knives," she said needlessly, arranging the gleaming pieces on the table, "and I'm here to sell you one of these."

I swallowed heavily, eyeing the array of steel which had so quickly covered the table. I would never have guessed that there were so many variations on the single theme of the blade.

"I'm sorry," I stammered, "but I've got all the knives I need. I've got a bread knife and a set of steak knives and a short blade for peeling. I live on my own, so you can see then that I'm not exactly in the market for a new one."

"No," she said quietly, "I think if you look closely at the circumstances of your life you will find that there is ample room in it for one extra blade. No one's life is so complete that they can afford to do without one of these knives."

"I thought you were selling encyclopedias or you were some kind of a Jehovah's Witness," I said plaintively.

"No, I'm a seller of knives. My work is to spread the Gospel of Knives because in the beginning was The Knife. All other versions are fiction. My job is to spread the redemptive word of The Knife. Answer me this, what is the greatest of man's inventions?"

"I suppose you're going to tell me it's the knife."

"Of course, there is no other answer. Taken unawares, most people say it's the wheel or fire. But they are wrong because the knife is at the source of all. When man picked up his first knife and started cutting and sawing and slicing it was the opening moment of his humanity, the instant of his divinity. Now in all my years in this ministry I've never met a man who did not need a knife. I've met men who have denied God's word out of face and I've met men who couldn't sign their name and they've all managed without any noticeable handicap. But all these people were bound together by their need for knives. And do you know why? The simple answer is that it is impossible to go through life without cutting or slicing; it wouldn't be human. If I met a man who didn't need a knife I'd just pack up my bags and walk away because it would be a sure sign that I had met someone who was less than human and a waste of words. But you're human, are you not?"

"Yes, I suppose so."

"Well, then it follows that you need one of these knives, it's unavoidable."

"I've already told you that I'm full up with knives."

"Have you a lover?"

"Yes," I lied.

"Good, because every lover needs a knife. I knew of a man once who woke up beside his beloved and saw for the first time how ugly she was, the scales had finally dropped from his eyes. And even though she was sleeping on his arm he was so panic-stricken he started to chew his own arm off, gnawing and tearing at it like a snared animal. And it took him so long that eventually his beloved awoke and looked at him. He got such a fright that he went into shock and couldn't move. She couldn't move him either and he died there in the bed within fifteen minutes. Now if he had one of these"—she held up a short, double blade, smooth and serrated—"he could have had that arm off in two minutes and made good his escape. You wouldn't want to end up in a situation like that, now would you?"

"That's a ridiculous story. Besides, it could never happen; my sweetheart is very beautiful."

"All beauty fades but with proper care and attention a good knife will last forever."

"I heard a story once of a child philosopher who couldn't get his penknife sharp enough and he spent all his time honing it until one day the blade disappeared altogether."

I will never know why I made up that story.

"That's the story of a fanatic," she said coldly. "The story of a man looking for irreducible truths. It wasn't the knife which failed him but his imagination. The knife was probably perfectly good within its set application. What he should have done was get another knife. There is no danger of that happening with these knives. Have you ever been to prison?"

"No, I live a virtuous and God-fearing existence."

"And is your life so blameless that you are utterly without fear of reckoning?"

"The truth is that I have no life. I have no qualifications or work. I have no future and I'm not old enough to have a past. Occasions for sin are severely limited."

"Nevertheless, the world is full of treacheries. One day you might find yourself incarcerated, walled up for a crime you didn't commit, mass concrete and iron bars between you and the blue sky. You might have exhausted all words and petitions and found no succor in prayer. Then these are the knives for you, they are absolute knives. This one can cut through any substance known to man, it has never been known to fail."

"That's ridiculous," I retorted.

"Knives are sacred," she replied. "I would not defile them with lies."

"You're serious about all this?" I said incredulously.

"Yes," she replied. "Because these are serious knives."

By now any notion of sexual conquest had fled my mind completely. Her unspeakable beauty dominated the room like a caryatid from some distant, ruined temple and her smile filled me with dread. I could almost hear her mind whirring through a set of instructions, sizing up the options before her face committed itself. It did not help either that my table was now laid out and glittering as if for some terrible, total surgery. I wanted my room emptied now, bare and empty as I had always loved it.

"I know everything there is to know about knives," she continued. "Anything I don't know about knives is a lie. Look at this one." She took up a short, curved piece and juggled it neatly from hand to hand. "This is a survivalists' knife, special army issue to the SAS, the U.S. Navy Seals, and other elite antiterrorist units. It's a tungsten alloy laid over with Teflon. It's hafted by a brass tang to an ebony handle. It's the sharpest knife in creation, strictly under-the-counter material and rarer than most gems."

Suddenly she hopped forward on one foot and her arm swung down like a scythe. The knife split the air and buried itself in the door at the other end of the room. The walls resonated with the terrific impact. She withdrew the blade cleanly and handed it to me.

"Now bid for it," she commanded.

"I've got no money, I'm on the dole. I can't afford to go throwing away money I don't have on things I don't need."

"Who said anything about money?"

"You're a saleswoman," I said. "Money is what you deal in."

"You're being presumptuous again. You've been that way from the moment you opened the door. I prefer to think of myself as a kind of beneficent society, like the International Gideon Society for instance. I leave people their knives and I walk away. I've left knives in hotel rooms and houses all over the world. Sometimes, however, I have to go door to door and get some remuneration, I have to keep body and soul together also."

"But I have nothing to give. Look around you, I've only these four walls and these four limbs. I have nothing to give."

"That is not true. When I opened the door you wanted to possess me, you wanted to get down on your knees and worship. We could settle for that. One knife against one loveless act of sexual possession. A fair exchange is no robbery and since I want you it would be an honorable transaction."

I almost squealed in horror. "I can't," I said, a dense wave of nausea swelling through my body. "It's crazy. It's the craziest thing I've ever heard. Why can't you just leave me the knife and go?" I could feel myself being reduced to a caricature of despair. I was on the verge of wringing my hands.

"I'm not a charity," she said coldly. "I want you and you need this knife. I really don't see any problem."

"I told you before I don't need the knife. Jesus, do I have to go on and on repeating myself?" Tears were beginning to well behind my eyelids.

"You've just told me that you own nothing. Ten minutes of sexual humility and you will own the finest knife in creation. What is there to be afraid of?"

I was suddenly sobbing, my whole body jerking like a string puppet, tears coursing down my face. Some nacreous light seemed to have spilled in the room and the walls had taken on a tremendous slant. She was now standing before me, sphinxlike and implacable.

"Are you being wilfully ignorant or do I have to spell it out for you? That knife-throwing trick is the least of my talents. I do not think you want to see my full repertoire."

I felt my legs collapse beneath me and I was suddenly on the floor, watching my tears spill onto the carpet. When I looked up she was hauling my face up by the hair, standing over me with her legs apart and holding her skirt up with her free hand. She was smiling down on me now without humor, flashing those perfect, too-even teeth.

"That's it, boy, on your knees. Be witnessed in the true faith of The Knife." She pulled my face in closer. "This is going to stay with you for the rest of your life. Like a good sharp knife in fact."

The Stained Glass Violations

Meats for the belly, and the belly for meats; but God shall destroy both it and them.

—I Corinthians 6:13

Oh, my mother, not again. Tell me it is not my time come round again. Tell me that I can stay here within you, cowering down, letting the whole thing pass over my head. Tell me you will protect and instruct me, bring me news about the world, its trials and convulsions. Tell me you will keep it at a distance from me, something abstract and objectified, never allowing it to touch me. That would make me happy. This time, all seeing, I would be the perfect spectator, casting a cold eye from the margins, suffering none of its humiliations and pains. Yes, that is the way I want it this time.

Oh, Mother, tell me it is a mistake, a momentary flaw in the structure of things. Tell me that if I close my eyes and hold my breath time will pass me over it and I will be able to consign it to those black pits of memory where we keep those dark and unspeakable things. And tell me also, Mother, that for fear of waking it we would never speak of it again.

Oh, my God, who am I trying to fool?

` ` `

She knows that if she can eat the Christ Child this terrible obsession will be at an end. That is why, in the darkness and humidity of this summer's night, she is up on the western nave of the cathedral, next to the canal, working on the window with her pliers. This is her second time here this night. On her first visit her nerve failed her and she was afraid to touch the Christ Child. She took instead a few of the pieces that surrounded Joseph and Mary, featureless squares that were tight up to the stonework. They were background pieces without detail and when she returned home with them, she knew that they would be useless; there would be no fulfillment in them. So now she has returned again and this time she knows that she will have to prize the infant from Joseph's arms.

Already she is nearly done. The seven white and amber pieces that make up the image of the Child have been worked from the lead strips and she has now only to crawl along the ledge, climb down, and walk home. Her thin body is vibrating from within with the energy of neurosis and starvation. On the ground, in the shadow of the buttress, she hunkers down like an animal to collect herself. Despite the narrowness of her obsession she has been careful. She has worn dark clothes and has kept to the shadows. She has made sure to wear something with pockets; she can hear the broken image rattle around in it now. She has been careful in her choice of pliers: it has long jaws like a surgical instrument, its inner surfaces have been milled for grip. Some of this knowledge she has researched— the pliers for instance and the structure of stained glass windows. But other details—the dark clothes, the pockets, and, oddest of all, the ability to climb the downspout on the cathedral wall—have been pure inspiration. She knows now that this is the knowledge of the violated—one part received wisdom and two parts black inspiration. She gathers herself now to walk homeward through the still city, hands deep in her pockets. She takes one last look up at the window and she sees that Joseph is left clutching a dark hole in his abdomen where once was the Child. Dimly, she remembers a biblical text: *Whosoever eats of the flesh of the lamb will have eternal life.* In the darkness she is not too sure why she should remember it and less sure what it means.

Walking through the silent city she remembers how this horror began one week earlier. At lunch hour that day she had walked into the city square already looking like a maimed thing. She had crossed the grass toward the one vacant bench that faced directly into the sun. She moved cautiously but with speed, threading her way among the coiled lovers who lay on the warm grass.

Already she was beginning to regret having come here. The whole place, the sun, the grass, and especially the lovers, made her feel alone. She reached the bench and sank into it with a feeling of relief. This, too, was a mistake. The sun, so bright, seemed to have singled out this one bench for special attention, falling upon it like a white blade. She would have liked to move but there was no other bench free.

All dowdy looks and no confidence, she had neither the nerve nor the style to sit and eat on the grass. And she knew it, too. She was now on the verge of tears and she felt bad enough without blighting the air, filling up the beautiful day with the gray substance of her loneliness. My God, she thought, why does it always have to be like this? Once, just once couldn't it be different?

She started. A thin man had loomed up before her. She hadn't seen him arrive.

"Greetings, favored one," he said.

Greetings. What a strange word, she thought. He placed his thin frame on the bench beside her and she appraised him. He was a startling old man, thin beyond belief and even on this hot day he carried a beige mac draped over his shoulders. But what was really amazing was that although he was undeniably there beside her with his legs stretched out before him, he projected not the clear lineaments of an identity but the mobile and blurred contours of a confusion; he looked like someone whose true identity had one day been smudged. She thought she could dimly make out a clean-shaven hawklike face with pointed features but she could not be sure. She felt that maybe deep within him there was some truer and stronger identity with sharper delineation biding its time until it saw the moment to come forth. He was a man who gave the impression of looking unlike himself, not out of some perverse desire to deceive but simply because this projected confusion was itself his true and inscrutable identity. Despite all this and the added fact that his presence beside her was a negative one, an absence, like a vacuum scooped out of the air, she was not afraid. She suspected he was one of the many vagrants about the city, one who at any moment was going to tell her that he was down on his luck, going through a rough patch, and had she a pound to spare to get him a cup of tea.

"Today is a beautiful day," he continued. "The sort of day which justifies the world."

She persevered with the smile.

"I suppose you're on lunch break," he said.

"Yes," she replied, "I'm a librarian. I have to return at two."

"Nice work I'd say, clean work. I haven't worked myself in twenty years." He was grinning now, well pleased with himself. "Imagine that, twenty years and I haven't done a stroke."

She liked him now and was well glad that he had sat down beside her. She flourished one of her sandwiches but he waved it aside.

"No thanks. A man of my age need only eat a couple of times a week. You're a growing girl, eat up."

She liked him now and she relaxed. "What did you work at?" she asked.

"I worked in a circus," he said proudly. "Was born into it and worked in it for the best part of thirty years."

She remembered the circuses of her childhood and her interest quickened.

"What did you work at? I'll bet it was the trapeze; you're very thin."

"No, not the trapeze, I had no head for heights. Guess again."

"Clown?"

"No."

"Ringmaster?"

"No."

"Knife thrower or animal tamer. They were my favorites."

"No, none of those."

He was smiling at her now, having teased her along like a favorite child. In all this there was something benign, something protective about him.

"I give up," she said. She had enjoyed the little game.

"Well," he began, "it was very strange. I was the only act of my kind in the whole of Ireland. England, too, if I'm not mistaken. I used to eat things."

"Eat things," she repeated. "What things?"

"Everything." He grinned, springing his surprise. "Bars of soap, small toys, metal, glass, timber, anything."

"Anything?"

"Yes, anything. Oh, it's not unheard of. People eat swords, frogs, and so on. I'm even told that in England there is a man who over the space of a lifetime ate a small aircraft. Still, though, the range of my consumption was something else. There was nothing I could not digest. Can you believe that toward the end of my career I was working on a way to eat a house?"

It may have been all a joke but she doubted it. He was too earnest, too obviously proud of his amazing craft.

"How did you start?"

He threw up his hands in a gesture of unknowing.

"I don't know. How does anyone start anything? One day you're here and the next you find yourself in the middle of something else. I remember thinking as a child that it was strange and funny that people should limit their intake to simple foodstuffs. I knew that the world was full of things waiting to be eaten. So I asked myself what would happen if I tried some of those other things. One day I sat down to a piece of timber, a piece of softwood. I wanted this first piece to be something organic, something that would not be too much of a shock to the system. I remember it well. I can see myself to this day under the caravan, tearing strips out of that piece of timber with my teeth as if it was a piece of meat. Three days it took me to finish it. But I kept it down and I knew then that my vocation had presented itself. I progressed on to metal then, small kitchen utensils that I sawed up into little, chewable pieces. It took me two weeks to eat my first saucepan and a further two months to digest it. But again I held it down. It was then that I set my sight on glass. You see, there is a precedent for eating metal. Copper and iron are part of our makeup. But glass is different, glass is taboo. Glass is a killing substance, not for internal consumption. I felt therefore that if I could consume glass I would be at the peak of my craft. Glass was to me what Everest was to Hillary. But first I had to prepare my constitution, toughen it up so to speak. It was at this time that my act became part of the circus repertoire: bleach, soap, timber, metal, that sort of thing. 'The Rubbish Man,' that's how I was billed. People flocked to see me. But in all that time I was only in training. I never once lost sight of my true goal—glass.

"One evening when I felt that my system had been toughened up enough I took a small piece of glass and ground it up real fine, like talc, and spooned it down with a glass of milk. I walked around with it for a few hours and then put my fingers to the back of my throat to see if I was bleeding. My vomit was streaked slightly with blood but not to a worrying degree. I was pleased. However, the trick was no use as it stood. Spooning down a white dust in the middle of a three-ring circus at thirty yards would never work; it lacked spectacle. So I had to work at consuming bigger and bigger pieces so that it would have the necessary visual impact. When the trick was finally unveiled I had graduated to the point where I could eat a four-by-eight-inch piece of unlaminated glass in under two minutes. People were amazed and shocked. In a few towns I was not allowed to perform. Priests denounced me from the pulpit and so on."

He raised a forefinger into the sunlight and began to hack the air like a zealot. "In the words of the Old Testament—in body and in Spirit and in the image of God was man created. Therefore it behooves us to act as God himself would have us act toward that which is his temple. Such mutilation is contrary to God's will." He lowered his hand and continued. "You know, even when I thought those Bible bashers were right my audience never failed me. Night after night they turned up to see me. People seem to find gratification in other people eating shit."

He suddenly brightened.

"Do you know that over the whole of my career I calculate that I have eaten enough glass to build a good-sized glass house?"

She would be late for work, very late. But it did not matter. She was now in thrall to this strange man and his extraordinary story. She wanted to take him home and listen to his tale forever, this tale which she was sure was for her and her alone.

The sunlight lay on them now like a dome and the day was so bright it seemed as if through some magic the air itself was polished. Already the square was emptying of people like herself who had to return to work. High on the side of the cathedral, prizing out the infant Jesus, she would remember this as the moment when she should have said good-bye and walked away. She could have walked away and been saved, retaining nothing of this incident but the memory of a strange old man with an extraordinary story. But she did not move. Instead she turned to him.

"So what happened? What do you do now?"

"Well," he continued, "audiences fell away in the seventies—television and all that. Our circus broke up in the mid-seventies and we all went our separate ways. Some even went as far as Eastern Europe; circus is a recognized and subsidized art form there. But I was too old so I drifted from town to town getting menial work, living hand to mouth. By then I was in my sixties so it was difficult to get work; there is not much call for a redundant glass eater. One day I was sitting here on this very bench, no work and sleeping rough, when a young man who recognized me came over and started talking. I told him my story, that I was out of work and so on. He told me to hang around the city for a few days till he saw if there was anything he could do. He was a student and the upshot was that I was offered a job by the university as a resident guinea pig. The university is contracted by pharmaceutical firms to carry out tests on drugs and other substances. Sometimes they find it hard to get volunteers for the more dangerous experiments. So that's where I come in. Seemingly I have built up an almost total resistance to poisons. I've even become an object of study myself. Sometimes they cut out parts of my stomach and digestive tract for examination. And"—he held up his hands in another gesture of resignation—"that is how I get by."

This was strange testimony and she felt weird hearing it. She had the eerie feeling also that it was meant especially for her. She imagined that this old man had held his tongue the whole of his life until this day when he had walked into the square and saw her, the perfect listener, the perfect receptacle for his story. For a short moment she thought about returning to work; the square was by now almost totally deserted. But she wanted to know more, she was convinced there were things she should know before she left. It would not do to leave with just a partial image of this old man. She turned to him again.

"So what's it like?" she asked. "Eating glass?"

"It's difficult to say. It's dangerous if you haven't got a vocation for it. It can cut up your stomach as easy as that and you won't feel a thing. One moment you're walking around and the next you feel light-headed and sit down. Then you keel over dead. You've been bleeding away internally all the time, unknown to yourself. Therefore any nourishment you gain from it is offset by the danger and poison of the thing. In short it's not much fun. I myself had to go through a long training before I could eventually handle it. Many a bottle of bleach and bar of soap I had to eat and puke up before I could handle it. It's like some sort of spiritual training, I suppose."

He was obviously struck by the clarity and truth of this last formulation and he furrowed his brow, presumably to make certain that he was not deluded. He seemed satisfied.

"Yes, that's what it's like—like doing some sort of penance or spiritual training that leaves you in a condition where you are capable of experiencing something momentous. But the experience is a dangerous one. If you survive it you know you have arrived at some limit within yourself and are almost godlike. But if you fail, it brings death and disaster and you are as well never to have started. I doubt that there are too many people in the world who would be able to survive it. It's a real discipline, an affliction, a thing of inspiration."

It made her smile to hear the old man explain his gruesome talent in such mystical terms. Did he truly believe that this was what lay at the center of his craft? She did not dare ask. Now that he had found sense and reason in it, it would be nothing short of wanton vandalism for a complete stranger like her to start picking holes in it. If he was happy with his explanation, and it seemed that he was, then so be it. Suddenly the old man seemed flustered. He began doing something complicated with the hem of his coat. She wondered had he forgotten something, had he told her the full story? Was there one more detail to reveal, probably a shameful one, before the story was complete? He rose up to look at her and he was very agitated, wringing his hands.

"I am sorry," he stammered. "I am sorry but I could not help it."

She was startled. A premonition rose within her that a pleasant experience was going eerily wrong. If it was going wrong then something of it had to be rescued so it could be remembered with joy.

"Don't say sorry," she pleaded. "I've enjoyed myself. Don't let it end like this."

He nodded his head with what seemed to her an odd type of respect and turned to make his way over the grass. She followed his thin back with her eyes until it disappeared off the grass and around a corner into a side street.

That night, for the first of many nights, her dreams were covered, structured, and dominated by glass. Beneath her feet the ground had the cold, intractable feel of a synthetic surface. Overhead the sky curved like a piece of engineering and her cries bounced back from it without release. Food was placed in her mouth but it splintered and crackled treacherously It made her mouth bleed and the droplets fell and clicked onto the ground as beads. But what terrified most was the feeling that she herself was made of glass, a glass that was warm and molten and pliable and that would continue that way until the day of her death when it would solidify and she would be struck rigid in that unyielding and unchanging topography.

She woke the next morning exhausted from a profitless sleep and when she faced her breakfast her whole being balked in revulsion. At work, the nausea continued all through the morning and at midday on the bench she gagged on the first mouthful of her sandwich. When evening came she pushed away her plate in disgust and decided to go to bed. A twenty-four-hour bug; come the morning it would be gone.

That night her dreams were more complex. Some of the fragmented images from the night before had coalesced into a decipherable narrative. She was attending some religious ceremony in a church which had the polished sheen of obsidian. A priest of some persuasion was berating his congregation from a pulpit, exhorting them to recognize the sacred in all about them and in the least among them. He harangued his congregation on this theme for a while and when the Eucharist came he raised the flesh of Christ into the air not as unleavened bread but as a scarlet disc of stained glass. He put it in his mouth and brought his teeth down hard to fragment it. He raised his head to the roof while swallowing. He then distributed similar discs to the faithful who came to the rails to receive the flesh of our Lord. All of them returned from the rails with blood seeping between their lips or trickling down their chins. When it came to her turn to receive, the priest bent over her and told her in blood-flecked words that it was not for him to give her anything. She would receive in another way and when she did it would be not just for herself but for the whole world.

Next morning, after refusing her breakfast again she made her way along by the canal to work. So early in the morning it seemed as if the colors and textures of her dream had carried over into the morning light. The sky was streaked with vermilion and the gold of the early sun was giving way to an all-pervasive blue. Passing by the cathedral she was struck by how queerly it was lit at this time of day. It seemed lit from within by some numinous presence and the light fell from its windows in great shafts which seemed to converge upon her. She wondered how the windows of the western nave seemed to be suspended there in the morning light, standing out from the stone structure, vibrant like elongated stars. She could see the Christ Child, the Virgin, and Joseph. The Child seemed to luminesce there in the silence with a life of its own. It seemed to reach out to her with some command, some imperative that would brook no avoidance.

With an effort she wrenched herself from the spot but for the rest of the day she was haunted by that image of the infant savior. It seemed to have scorched itself so deeply on the front of her mind that she could not get a focus on any of her work. Her indexing went badly. Nothing she touched fell into alignment and her mind wandered so much it was a relief when the day ended. But before leaving, on a dark intuition, she went to the reference section and took down a book, *The History and Origins of Glass*. She flicked through it and read how stained glass was manufactured and installed. She read for an hour and on her way home bought a hammer, a pliers, a mortar and pestle.

That evening, for the second day, her body refused food. Looking in her cabinets at the boxes of food a nausea rose within her and she had barely enough time to make it to the sink. Her stomach was so empty she suffered acute agony in retching. She sank to the floor in a fetal position, lathered in sweat. It was at this moment that an awareness formed that she was suffering from some sort of inverse inspiration. She could feel a hollow running the length of her whole being, waiting to be filled. Two days without food and she could already feel her strength ebbing from her, a tide that would leave her stranded like a dried fish if it continued. She would have to do something fast or she would be soon totally lost to this hunger.

She rose from the floor like one who had been felled, and gathered up her coat and tools and made her way into the night. She reeled through the streets like a drunkard until she came to the cathedral. In the gray streetlight coming off the nearby bridge she saw Joseph in the stained glass window offering out the Child to her with both hands.

She would have to be quick. Cars whizzed by on the bridge and it would be disastrous to draw their attention. How could she explain this excruciating hunger that had her refusing food and craving something fatal. She grabbed a downspout that ran in the shadow of a buttress, offered up an abortive prayer for its solidity, and began to climb up hand over hand. It was easier than she had imagined and she knew instantly that this newfound agility was part of the whole neurosis. In the darkness and her heightened condition she moved confidently, hand over hand, finding toeholds in the sheer limestone wall. She stopped for a moment on the ledge to draw breath and then moved at a crouch over to the window. She straightened up and was at last faced with the Child. It seemed now that in climbing the drainpipe, the concentration and physical effort had sapped away an essential part of her resolve. Either that or it was just shameful awe in the sight of the Child's gaze that persuaded her to avoid Him totally and remove marginal pieces instead, doing as little damage as possible to the window. She took out her pliers and began to prize out the lead strip from the framework close to the stone. Once she had a grip on the lead it tore out easily and she quickly managed to remove four lozenge-shaped pieces. Through the hole she could see into the dark interior of the church where the red sanctuary lamp glowed and the faint aura of the tabernacle door. But she did not wait, her hunger was crying out. Feeling the eyes of the infant on her back, burning his rebuke, she moved over the ledge and with the glass and pliers pocketed, shinned down the spout to the ground. Once hitting the ground she loped homeward like a released animal.

In her kitchen she laid out the pieces on the table. They were all one color and shape and with a scream surfacing within her she knew they were not what she needed. She swept them from the table in a quick frenzy, dashing them against the wall, and set out again into the night. This time, in front of the Child, she did not flinch. She set the pliers into Joseph's abdomen, gripped the lead, and prized it out carefully, trying not to let any of the Child fall to the ground—she felt bad enough violating the window without committing needless vandalism. Eventually, through the sweat that had begun to sting her eyes, she saw that she had wrung the Child totally from Joseph's grasp. All he had left now was a gaping hole in his abdomen and the lead came like dried veins curving outward from it. For the second time that night she pocketed the glass and the pliers and crawled along the ledge to the downspout. At the base of the cathedral she was consumed by a shaking fit. She squatted down in the shadows with her arms wrapped about her, flicking the darkness with her eyes as she tried to get a hold of herself. She saw the bridge opposite her and the cars upon it, plowing on into the night, and she wondered about the drivers. Did any of them ever have such a fixation as she had now? Did any of them suspect that so close by there was someone strung out on such an obsession? If one of them knew would he try to help? Would one of those drivers walk over to her in the darkness and say, it's OK, I'm your friend and I am here to help. Come with me and you will come to no harm. She continued to speculate like this until she felt steady enough to move off.

She is at home now, in her kitchen, and she is tempted to lay the glass pieces on the table and spend a few moments rearranging them into the image of the Child. But she cannot bear to look the Child in the eye. Besides, her body senses a nearness and has begun to cry out. She knows what she has to do. She empties the pieces into the dishcloth, lays it on the floor, and begins to hammer it methodically until she has a crude multicolored rubble. She turns the little pile into her mortar and grinds the debris until it is as fine as talc. It is difficult. Despite its lowly origins and ubiquity, glass is one of our more intractable materials. By the time she finishes her arm aches and her brow is sheened with sweat. She now has a little pile of powder in the mortar that looks for all the world like one of those similarly illicit powders that can be had for a price in the underbelly of any city in the world, patented for people like herself who have been ignored, cast out, shortchanged, or are just plain unable to cope. Somewhere within herself she can hear a counterpoint to this errant thought; yes, but this is the flesh of the Savior, the divine fix, the high without comedown. She lifts a spoonful to her mouth and something within her rises greedily to it. With a jerk of her throat it is gone. She spoons back the rest of it hurriedly and washes it down with milk. She stands still, waiting for some reaction. It does not come. She walks to her room and all the exhaustion of the evening comes to rest upon her. She falls face downward on her bed fully clothed and already she is asleep.

In the morning she wakes ravenous. In a gluttonous frenzy she hunches over a bowl of cereal and sloughs it back greedily. She thinks of animals and eats four bowls in succession with bread and an apple and a bar of chocolate. For the first time in three days she holds the food down. It is warm and weighs like ballast in her stomach and she walks to work with a solid step. Her fellow workers comment that she is looking much better; there is a bloom on her cheeks and she smiles shyly in return.

"I haven't been feeling well these last few days," she says. "Some kind of bug."

In the bathroom she checks to see if she is bleeding but there are no traces. Outside the sun is shining and for the first time in ages she feels a kind of happiness. At lunchtime she returns to the bench in the hope of seeing the old man but he isn't there. She eats with comfort and knows now that her obsession is at an end. She feels also that there has been a shift in the disposition of the world toward her. Several of her colleagues have come to her during the day and engaged her in jokes and silly games. She has laughed a lot, clasping her hand over her mouth like some shy schoolgirl caught in mischief. Even the sun has lost its oppression. It lies upon her now like a comforter, warming her, making her glow.

ˋ   ˋ   ˋ

The days which follow are the happiest of her life. She begins to enjoy her work and it seems that a genuine friendship blossoms between herself and her workmates. She goes for drinks after work with them to a little pub where she is shy at first but where the barman gradually comes to recognize her when it is her round. She goes to the cinema and one night at a club one of her colleagues kisses her, and tells her that now, when he has finally got to know her, he thinks she is great.

The next morning she wakes in her flat and rushes to the toilet, throwing up. On her knees she grips the toilet bowl trying to hold down the panic that is threatening to make her scream. Please, oh please, she cries. It is midday before she can hold down any food. And it is the same the following day and the day after that and the day after that again; sick and frail in the morning with her hand clasped over her stomach until the light midday meal that carries her over till the evening. And it is in these morning hours also that she is stricken with the crazed urge to eat things. In her flat she has to remove the detergents, the soaps, and even her bathroom sponge from out of her sight. At work she has her desk cleared of ink, correction fluid, and her eraser. And one morning in her nausea and weakness she realizes that her period, normally like clockwork, is three weeks overdue. She thinks of the days without food and the days of nausea and the glass, and wonders has all of this thrown her biology out of alignment. She waits another week, then two more, and at the end of four weeks she visits her doctor.

Her doctor is a kindly, middle-aged man who listens with his head inclined to his left side, a man hearing signals from a distant planet. He hears her list of symptoms and finally asks her does she herself have any idea what it could be. She skirts around the obvious, shaking her head, not wanting to face the incredible. He asks her about her love life and she tells him shamefaced that she has no partner, she is still a virgin. He shakes his head in mystification and tells her he will do a pregnancy test, otherwise he has no clue what it could be. Five minutes later she finds out that she is pregnant.

She remonstrates. "How can that be, I'm still a virgin?"

"It's very strange," he tells her. "I never thought in all my days of practice I would come upon such a case. It is a condition that is very rare, one in a million if I can remember the statistics correctly. There is no medical explanation which covers the case entirely. It's a form of parthenogenesis. What happens is that . . ."

He seems awed by her presence and he moves about the room giddily as he talks, keeping his distance and erecting a barrier of technical language between them.

"I find it unbelievable," he concludes, "totally unbelievable."

"Well," she counters, "it's happening, whether you believe it or not."

"It's not that," he says. "I've seen that. It's just that you're one in a million, one in ten million." He looks at her suddenly. "You are going to keep the child?" It sounds like an accusation, not the question it is meant to be.

She spreads her hands. "I don't know. This is such a surprise, such a shock. I hadn't thought about it."

He sits on his desk, making an effort to bring the situation under control. Despite the lack of frenzy and raised voices there is no doubt that the room has been visited by some disaster. He clasps his hands before his face in the manner of a penitent and seeks inspiration in the ceiling.

"All right," he says. He has finally come to some decision. "There really is nothing I can do for you at the moment. I could give you something for the nausea and vomiting but that is not the issue. What I suggest is that you go home, think about it for a while, and come back to me with your decision. Think it over. There are other options, things to be done and so on."

He is becoming flustered, his sentences are beginning to ramble. She unsettles him with her thin face and her eyes continually focused in her hands. He repeats himself again, almost pleadingly.

"There really is nothing I can do for you now. Call back in a few weeks when you have a decision."

She is glad to leave the room. She has difficulty in breathing there, the air seems filled with smoke. Outside in the sunlight she braces herself and it works its way into her, warming her chilled bones. She is marooned now, at a loss where to go. It strikes her that this world is stranger than she can ever imagine. She wonders is it always going to be like this, will there always be this cruelty at the heart of things. Will the world keep offering up jagged pieces of itself, not as a means to enlightenment but as a reminder that it will always have the upper hand? One moment it will seem solved, comprehensible, and full of sense, the next it will have heaved beneath her feet throwing up shapes and configurations without precedent, filled with terrors. She walks carefully through the streets now, unsure of her footing. People look strange, their skins have a funny pallor: she can see their veins. She fears that at every corner someone with a clown's grin will draw her aside and show her some new atrocity. She finds herself walking toward the canal and has to suppress an urge to stretch her arms ahead of her like a blind person. She feels like prey.

In the cathedral parking lot there is a crowd. Busy mothers and fathers fuss over children, straightening ties and fixing veils over angelic faces. Today is confirmation day and these kids have come here to sign up as soldiers of Christ, new recruits in His massive conscript army serving under assumed names. Standing on the edge of the crowd she notices that the Christ Child in the window has not been replaced. Part of the window has been blocked up with plywood from within. Earlier in the week she read in the local newspaper how the police are mystified by the breakage and how they have no clue whatsoever. She remembers the lines: "At this time we have neither suspect nor motive and we are led to believe that it was an act of wanton vandalism. We are looking for anyone with information, no matter how small, to please come forward."

She stands in the parking lot long into the evening and long after the crowd has gone, her hands clasped over her stomach. She has the same wish for herself: Would someone with some information please, please come forward?

I would like to think that from the beginning I put up a fight. Not some token gesture of disaffection with my terrible predicament but a full-blooded resistance. I picture myself rising to my knees in the afterbirth, eyes open and sharp—there is nothing of the doe-eyed lamb about me this time—my nose sniffing the air. And do I imagine it or is my slimy hand already reaching out to grasp some weapon? I see myself dark and primitive, grasping it by the hilt and marking a slow watchful retreat. I am not so much a child as a beleaguered rat. But my mother's legs are closed now and I am cut off, left stranded. Alone again. Just for that I wish my entrance had been marked by some carnage. I would give much to be able to say that on entering the world I killed my mother. But I cannot. Therefore did I hang my head and weep in despair. I did not. I filled the room with curses, dark occult sounds that shrieked out at the wretchedness and misery of it all.

Of course it was nothing like that. Instead, I lay stranded on my back choking in the amniotic fluid, my hands rising to my eyes to fend off the light. A nurse upended me with a quick slap across the arse and I drew some foreign but dimly remembered element into my chest, something upon which my young lungs scrabbled for foothold and having found it I rose quickly into myself with a wail. I was immediately aware of the hostile atmosphere, the uniforms, the searing lights, the physical abuse.

Oh yes, there is not much difference between birth and interrogation—both are issues of truth and identity.

I am young, very young, but I have the memory of aeons. I can remember clearly the last time and all I can say is that Father's work or no Father's work I am not going to let it happen like that again. This time it will be different. The world will be given an even chance this time and no more.

I am young and I am willing to admit that I am not in full possession of the facts. Maybe there are mitigating details that I cannot remember but I doubt it. Therefore my plan is simple. Bide my time quietly and keep my ear close to the ground, my eyes open and my mouth shut. I will hoard up knowledge. I have got a good thirty years before I make my entrance proper so I will be circumspect. But I do know a few things: I am and I have memory and this time it is going to be different.

A Is for Axe

A IS FOR AXE

Six pounds of forged iron hafted to a length of hickory with steel wedges driven into the end. During the autopsy the coroner dug from my father's skull a small, triangular chip which was entered as prosecuting evidence by the State. It was passed among the jurors in a sealed plastic bag like the relic of a venerated saint.

More than any detail of my crime it is this axe that has elevated me to a kind of cult status in this green and pleasant land of ours. I am not alone in sensing a general awe that at last, small-town Ireland has thrown up an axe murderer of its very own. It bespeaks a kind of burgeoning cosmopolitanism. At last our isolated province has birthed a genuine, late-twentieth-century hero, a B-movie schlock-horror character who is now the darling of down-market newsprint.

As I was led to trial several of my peers had gathered on the steps of the courthouse. Long-haired, goateed wasters to a man, they sported T-shirts emblazoned with my portrait and short lines of script. GERARD QUIRKE FOR PRESIDENT they read, or GERARD QUIRKE—A CUT ABOVE THE REST. My favorite is GERARD QUIRKE: A CHIP OFF THE OLD BLOCK.

B IS FOR BIRTHDAY

I have picked through the coordinates of my birth and I find nothing in them that points to the present calamity. I was born on the twentieth of October 1973, under the sign of Libra, the scales. It was the year when the sixth Fianna Fáil administration governed the land, added two pence to the price of a loaf and three on the pint. In human terms it was a year of no real distinction—if there was no special degree of bloodshed in the world of international affairs neither was there any universal meeting of minds, no new dawn bloomed on the horizon.

I have these details from a computer printout which I got from James, a present on my eighteenth birthday. He bought it in one of those New Age shops specializing in tarot readings and incense that are now all the rage in the bohemian quarters of cities.

I was named after St. Gerard Majella whom my mother success-fully petitioned during her troubled and only pregnancy.

C IS FOR CHANCE

Chance is at the root of all. 20, 10, 3, 12, 27, 8. My date of birth, my father's date, and my mother's also. These are the numbers my father chose on the solitary occasion he entered for that seven-million-pound jackpot, the biggest in the five-year history of our national lottery. And for the first and only time in his life the God of providence smiled upon him.

D IS FOR DEFENSE

I had no defense. To the dismay of my lawyer, a young gun hoping to make a reputation, I took full responsibility and pleaded guilty. I was determined not to waste anyone's time. I told him that I would have nothing to do with claims of diminished responsibility, self-defense, or extreme provocation. Neither would I have anything to do with psychiatric evaluation. I declared that my mind was a disease-free zone and that I was the sanest man on the entire planet. As a result the trial was a short(ened) affair. After the evidence was presented and the judge had summed up, the jury needed only two hours to reach a unanimous verdict. I was complimented for not wasting the court's time.

E IS FOR ELECTION

As a child, nothing marked me out from the ordinary, except for the fact that I had been hit by lightning. I had been left in the yard one summer day, sleeping in my high, springed pram, when the sky darkened quickly to rain and then thunder. All of a sudden a fork of lightning rent the sky and demolished my carriage. When my parents rushed into the yard they found me lying on the ground between the twin halves of my carriage, charred and blackened like a spoiled fruit. When they picked me up they found that the side of my head had been scored by such a perfect burn, so perfect in fact that, were it not for the ear it had carried with it, you could have admired the neatness and tidiness of it. While my mother carried me indoors my father stayed in the downpour, shaking his fist and bawling at the heavens, cursing God and his attendant angels.

In the coverage of my trial much has been made of this incident and the fact of my missing ear. Several column inches have been filled by popular psychologists who have repeatedly drawn parallels between the lightning strike and the axe. All have sought to deliver themselves of fanciful, apocalyptic axioms. It surprises me that at no time has a theologian been asked to proffer his opinion. I feel sure he would have found in it some evidence of a hand reaching out of the sky, a kind of infernal election.

F IS FOR FUTURE

My life sentence stretches ahead of me now, each day an identical fragment of clockwork routine piled one upon the other into middle age. I do not care to think about it.

Ten months ago, however, after my father came into his fortune, I dreamt of a real future. Hour after hour I spent in my room working out the scope and extent of it, embellishing it with detail. I polished it to a gleaming prospect of travel in foreign climes, sexual adventure, and idle indulgence. I mapped it out as a Dionysian odyssey, a continual annihilation of the present moment with no care for the morrow. It would take me in glorious circumnavigation of the earth all the way to my grave, ending in a fabulous blowout where I would announce my departure to the assembled, adoring masses— an elegant, wasted rake. I was careful enough to leave blank spaces in the fantasy, filling them out during moments of conscience with vague designs of good works and philanthropy. I confess that these were difficult assignments; my mind more often than not drew a blank. My belief is that I had not the heart for these imaginative forays. My cold and cruel adolescent mind was seized mainly by the sensual possibilities and I hungered cravenly for them.

G IS FOR GOD

My father stayed in the downpour to decry the heavens and my mother pointed out in later years that it was at this moment God set his face against us and withdrew all favor. Whatever about God, it was at this moment that my father turned his back on all religious observance, an apostasy of no small bravery in our devout village and probably the only trait in his personality I inherited when I entered my own godless teens. A steady line of self-appointed evangelists beat a path to our door to try and rescue him out of the cocoon of hunkered bitterness into which he had retired. But my father's mind was set. The God of mercy and forgiveness was nothing to him anymore and the community of believers were only so many fools. He could be violently eloquent on the subject. In black anger he would wrest me from the cradle and brandish me in their faces.

"There is no God of mercy and forgiveness," he would roar. "There is only the God of plague and affliction and justice and we are all well and truly fucked because of it. This child is the proof of that. More than any of you I believe in Him: I only have to look at this child to know. The only difference is I have no faith in Him."

These rages would reduce my mother to a sobbing shambles. She would recover, however, and then redouble her observance on his behalf, attending the sacraments twice daily to atone for his pride. Icons flourished in our house and the shelves and sideboards seemed to sprout effigies overnight. My father ground his teeth and reined in his temper.

H IS FOR HISTORY

I admitted my interest in killers at the pretrial hearings. However, even now, I maintain that it is nothing more than the average male teen infatuation with all things bloody and destructive. Like most young men of my generation I can reel off a list of twentieth-century killers quicker than I can the names of the twelve apostles. At school I listened critically to the tales of the great ideological killers—Hitler, Stalin, et al. I became convinced that the century was nothing more than a massive fiction, an elaborate snuff-movie hugely budgeted and badly edited, ending with an interminable list of credits. I came to believe that beneath this vast panorama of warring nations and heaving atrocities the true identity and history of my time was being written by solitary minds untouched by ideology or political gain—solitary night stalkers prowling alleyways and quiet, suburban homes, carrying their knives and axes and guns and garrotes. And I believed also it was only in this underworld that concepts of guilt and evil and justice had any meaning, this world where they were not ridiculed and overwhelmed by sheer weight of numbers. Bundy, Dahmer, Hindley, Chikatilo, Nielsen—the list goes on, an infernal Pantheon within which I will now discreetly take my humble place.

I IS FOR INDOLENCE

After my leaving cert I signed on as a government artist—I drew the dole. It was an issue of some scandal in the village; after all, my father was the possessor of probably the biggest private fortune in the county.

One evening after signing on I sat in a local pub putting a sizable hole in my first payment—I was quickly discovering the joys of solitary drinking. On an overhead TV I listened to the news and heard that the unemployment figures had topped three hundred thousand for the first time. The figure was greeted with equal measures of awe and disgust by the other drinkers.

"Christ, it's a shame, all those young people coming out of school and college and no jobs for them. The country is going to hell."

"In a hand cart," another added.

A third was not so sure. "I don't know," he said, a large, straight-talking man. "Half of those fuckers on the dole have no intention of working, they'd run a mile from it. And it's not as if there isn't plenty of it to do either. Look at the state of the roads or the grave-yards for that matter. A crowd of friggin' spongers the whole lot of them if the truth be told."

It was a brave thesis, particularly so in a townland surrounded by subsistence farms, the owners of which topped up their incomes with government handouts.

But he was right, at least in my case he was. I went home that night and for the first time in my life I knew what I was. I was a sponger, a slacker, a parasite, a leech on the nation's resources. Like most of my generation I had neither the will nor imagination to get up and do something useful with my life. And what was worse I took to my role joyfully, safe in the knowledge that I could fob off any queries by pointing to the statistics or by saying that I was indulging in a period of stocktaking and evaluation before I launched myself on the world with a definite plan. I could loftily declare that I was on sabbatical from life. Only in solitary moments of truth and pitiless insight would I speak the truth to myself: I had no worthwhile ideas and no courage; I was good for nothing.

J IS FOR JAMES

The only shaft of light in my childhood years was the presence of my friend James. Throughout my trial he was the one constant, sitting in the public gallery with his hair pulled back in a tight braid, chewing his bottom lip. I could feel his eyes upon me, placed like branding irons in the center of my chest. Now he comes to me every week, bringing me my record collection and my books: Hesse, Nietzsche, and Dostoyevsky, a young man's reading or so I'm told.

James was more than my friend, he was my champion. I would be at the center of one of those taunting circles, my tormentors wheeling about me, dealing out cuffs to the side of my head and insults. "Ear we go, ear we go, ear we go," they would chant. My defense then was to disappear down inside myself, down into that part within me that was clear and painless, a place lit by fantasy, ideas, books, and music. Almost inevitably James would round the corner. I would see in his eyes the dark fire that was already igniting his soul.

"Leave him alone, you pack of cunts," he'd yell. "Leave him alone."

Then he would wade into the center of the circle, shouldering me aside, his Docs and fists flying, working his surprise to the limit by scoring busted noses and bruised balls. Sooner or later, however, he would find himself at the bottom of a pile of heaving bodies, curling into a tight fetal position to ward off the kicks and blows that rained down on him. Just as suddenly my tormentors would scatter, yelling and whooping, leaving James bloodied and bruised on the ground like carrion. In those moments I used to think that James was the victim not of his love for me but of his own rampant imagination. Now I can see him rising from the dust, his face bloodied and running like a clown's makeup, and I curse myself for my cynicism.

K IS FOR KILL

The axe swung through the air and cleft my father's skull in two and he lay dead upon the floor.

L IS FOR LUG

When I reached my teens I grew my hair to my shoulders. By then, however, it was already too late to prevent me from being teased mercilessly and earning a succession of nicknames. My peers were never short of cruel puns and covert abuse whenever I was near. "Ear, ear," they would yell whenever I opened my mouth to speak or, "Ear we go, ear we go, ear we go," whenever we gathered to watch football matches. From national school my name was Lug and in secondary school the more technically minded tried to amend it to Mono. But Lug was the name that stuck and I hated them for it, hated them for their stupid wit and their lack of mercy. But I did not hate them as much as I hated my father on the day he discovered it. He returned from answering the phone in the hallway. It was one of my "friends."

"Lug," he said gleefully. "Christ, they have you well named there and no doubt about it. We used to have an ass with that name once— Lugs. Mind you, he was twice the creature you are. He could work and he had a full set of ears."

I burst out crying and ran to my room. I stayed there the rest of the afternoon, weeping and grinding my teeth. I eventually dried my eyes and took a look at myself in the mirror and I resolved then that no one would ever make me cry again.

M IS FOR MUSIC

Because of my impaired hearing my love of music has caused much wonderment. Again this has proved a fertile snuffling ground for those commentators desperate to unearth truffles of reason in this tale of blood and woe.

I am a metal head, a self-confessed lover of bludgeoning rhythms in major chords and rhyming couplets dealing in death and mayhem. My record collection, now numbering in hundreds, reads like a medieval codex of arcana: Ministry, Obituary, Bathroy, Leather Angel, Black Sabbath, and so on. My greatest solace now is that I can listen to these records in the privacy of my cell without maddening anyone. If there was anything certain to unleash my father's temper it was the sound of these records throbbing through the house. He would come hammering at my bedroom door.

"Turn that fucking shit off," he'd roar. "Christ, you would think a man of your age should have grown out of that sort of thing long ago."

But I never did grow out of it and I don't foresee a day when I will. This horror of this music is rooted within me as deep as my very soul and I would no more think of defending it than my father would his own lachrymose renditions of "Moonlight on the Silvery Rio Grande."

N IS FOR NEVER

As in never again. At the bottom of our souls all young men are sick. We do not grow sick or become sick nor is it some easy matter of hormonal determinism. This sickness is our very nature. Having suffered from the disease myself I know what I am talking about. It manifests itself generally as a disorder of the head, a slant of the imagination that preoccupies us with mayhem and blood, slashing and hacking, disease, waste, and carnage. There is not a young man of my age who, in the privacy of his own heart, has not thought of killing someone. Many times James and I would sit fantasizing about a kill of our own, our very own corpse. We weighed up the options like assassins and narrowed it down to a single, clean strike in an airport terminal bathroom where there is an abundance of unwary victims and suspects. We were armchair psychos, already tasting the blood. Most young men grow out of this sort of thing, taking to heart secondhand lessons in mercy and compassion, turning in wonder and revulsion from their former selves. Some never learn and continue to stalk the earth with weapons, amassing victims in the darkness. But the truly wretched ones turn away also, not out of principle or humanity but from the antidote at the heart of the disease itself, the terrible soul-harrowing and puke-inducing disgust.

O IS FOR OBSEQUIES

QUIRKE (MARY ELIZABETH) died suddenly at her residence, Carron, Co. Mayo, May 21st 1993, in her fifty-ninth year. Deeply regretted by her sorrowing husband Thomas, her son Gerard, and a large circle of relatives and friends. Removal to the Church of the Immaculate Conception, Carron, this (Wednesday) evening at seven o'clock. Requiem mass tomorrow (Thursday) at twelve noon. Funeral afterward to Cross Cemetery. No flowers. House private.

> *Your story on earth will never be told*
> *The harp and the shamrock*
> *Green white and gold.*

P IS FOR PATRIMONY

Four months ago James and I stood in a green field behind our county hospital, two unpaid extras witnessing a dedication. There was a small platform bedecked with ribbons, a few local politicians, the diocesan bishop, and my father. The field was populated by a motley collection of patricians, merchants, and outpatients; a few nurses stood at the fringes. Incredulity hung in the air like a fine mist. We were here to witness the sod-turning on the foundation of the Thomas Quirke Institute for Alcoholic Research, a laboratory annexed to our county hospital and funded in equal measure by European grant aid and the single biggest bequest to the health services in the history of the state—my father's entire lottery win. I listened as the politicians spoke on the straitened circumstances of the health services and on the pressing need for an institution of this sort in a province ravaged by alcoholism. My father was commended as a man of vision and philanthropy. I saw the bishop sprinkle holy water on the green earth and invoke the saints to guide the work of the institute. Then my father stepped forward to turn the first sod, his public awkwardness belying his easy skill with the spade. The audience whispered and shook their heads and as the earth split and turned I saw my fortune vanish before my eyes.

In honor of the occasion James and I left the field for the pub across the road and got sinfully and disastrously drunk.

Q IS FOR QUIETUS

We sat in the kitchen drinking the last of the whiskey. It was two in the morning and darkness hummed beyond the windows. James was slumped at the table, his head resting in his extended arm, clutching a glass. His speech came thick and slow.

"Every penny," he was saying, "every fucking penny gone up in smoke and pissed against the wall. I wouldn't have believed it myself if I hadn't seen it with my own two eyes. And every one of them bursting their holes laughing at him behind his back. The Thomas Quirke Institute for Alcoholic Research no less. Sheer bloody madness."

"Give it a rest, James, I'm fed up hearing it."

It had been a long day and I badly needed sleep. A monstrous headache had begun to hammer behind my eyes.

"Are you not mad, Ger? Christ, I'd be mad. A whole fortune squandered in one act of vanity. You're his son, for Christ's sake. It wasn't just his to throw away. You're his son and you could have been set up for life."

"I know, James. It's all over now, though, and there's nothing anyone can do about it. It's all over."

"I'd kill him," he said suddenly, rising up and swinging the bottle wildly. "Stone dead I'd kill him. He hadn't the right, he hadn't the fucking right."

My father entered at that moment, his face flushed with drink, the knot of his tie well over his collarbone. James sat down at the table.

"Hadn't the right to do what, James, hadn't the right to do what? Go on, you young shit, spell it out."

He was standing with his legs apart inside the door, the cage of his chest rising and falling. He looked like a man who was going to reach for a gun.

"I was just saying, Mr. Quirke, it was a real pity that all that money couldn't be put to better use where right people might benefit from it."

"Is that so? And I suppose if it was your money you'd know what to do with it."

James's head was lolling heavily, a wide smirk crawling to his ears.

"I'd have given it to the poor of the parish," he said, guffawing loudly and gulping from his glass. "Every last penny. And I'd have put a new roof on the church," he finished, now giggling helplessly.

"And I suppose you wouldn't have left yourself short either, James? You being one of these poor that weigh so heavily on your mind."

He was leaning with both hands on the table now, towering over James. He wasn't totally drunk, just in that dangerous condition where he could argue forever or loose his temper suddenly.

"Do you know what it is, Mr. Quirke? Something I saw today. Every one of those people were there patting you on the back with one hand and smirking behind the other. Telling you what a great man you were and then going away bursting their holes laughing at you. I saw it with my own two eyes."

James had lost the run of himself now; he didn't care what he said. I stood between them.

"Cut it out both of you. James, it's time you left. I need to get to bed." I began hauling him to his feet.

"He'll leave when I'm finished with him," my father hissed, squeezing out the words between his clenched teeth. "When I'm finished and only then. What about you, James, were you laughing?"

"I didn't know whether to laugh or to cry, Mr. Quirke, I was in two minds." He was swaying drunkenly now, bracing himself between the chair and the table. "I didn't know whether to laugh or to cry. I was standing there thinking that some people have more money than sense."

My father lunged at him, his outstretched hands reaching for his throat. James keeled backward spilling the chair and my father landed across him, bellowing in rage and surprise. They grappled wildly for an instant. I threw aside the chair and James's boot flicked up as he rolled over, catching me under the chin and knocking me sideways into the table. I fell down, grabbing the tablecloth and bringing the bottle and glass shattering to the floor. We scuttled to the end of the room and my father came off the floor clutching the neck of the bottle at arm's length.

"I'll cut the fucking head clean off you," he roared.

He moved toward James slowly, as if walking over broken ground. It was at this instant that the axe rose into the air, just off my left shoulder, and passed in a slow arc over my head. And it was at this instant also that there was a sound of breaking glass and the light went out. The fluorescent light showered down around our shoulders as the axe clipped it and there was a sudden rush of cold air in the darkness, a grim sound of something splitting with a soft crunch. I rushed to the wall and turned on the bulb.

"Oh Jesus, oh fucking Christ."

My father lay face down on the floor, his head split open and the axe standing upright in it as if marking the spot. He was dead beyond any salvation. James was doing some frantic, crazy dance about his head and there was a smell of shit in the room.

"Oh Jesus, oh fucking Christ, what are we going to do, what are we going to do?"

I was stone-cold sober then, hiccuping with fright but perfectly in control. I started dragging James toward the door, hauling him by the collar.

"Go home now, James, there's nothing you can do. Go home."

I pushed him out into the darkness and slammed the door. My breathing came in jagged bursts and I needed to sit down. I righted the chair and sat at my father's head, a four-hour vigil into the dawn with no thought in my head save that now, for the first time in my life, I had nothing.

When the gray sun rose I stepped into the hall and rang the cops.

R IS FOR RESPONSIBILITY

Not for the first time James was picking himself up off the tarmac, wiping the blood from his face. It was after telling him rather imperiously that his imagination was running away with him. He was having none of it.

"Those fuckers walk all over you," he sobbed. "When are you going to stick up for yourself?" He was near crying.

"I can take care of them in my own time," I said cryptically.

"Well, it's about time you started. Look at the size of you. You're well able for them. What the hell are you afraid of? And your father, too. Christ, you put up with so much shit, it's about time you started hitting back. You have to be every bit as cruel as they are. You have to meet every blow with a kick and every insult with a curse. You shouldn't take this anymore; it's not right."

"I never asked for your help," I said coldly.

"Well, this is the last time," he yelled. "From now on you can be your own martyr or your own coward. I want nothing more to do with it."

"No," I said, "you'll always be there. You can't help it, you have the imagination for it."

I walked away, leaving him sobbing on the ground.

S IS FOR SUMMARY

Even now, in the fifth month of my sentence, I still receive weekly visits from my lawyer. There are loose ends still in need of tying up, details to be put to rest. He informs me that public interest in my case has not waned—apparently its notoriety is being seen as indicative of some sort of widespread malaise in the minds of our young people, a kind of national tumor in need of lancing. He tells me that there is much probing of the national psyche in the media.

More recently he has presented me with a sheaf of proposals from publishers and film producers, all of them looking for the complete story, the first-person account. I have refused all of them, returned the documents through the wire mesh. I have no interest in the superfluities that necessarily accrue within the scope of the extended narrative. I have chosen this alphabet for its finitude and narrow compass. It places strictures on my story that confine me to the essential substratum of events and feelings. Within its confines there is no danger of my wandering off like a maddened thing into sloughs of self-pity and righteousness.

T IS FOR TRUTH

Under oath and on the Bible I swore to tell the truth. I confined myself to the facts, which may or may not be the same thing. I believe now that this preoccupation with the facts is exactly the problem with all kinds of testimony. A clear retelling of the facts, no matter how accurately they record actual events, is a lamentable falling short of the truth. I know now that the true identity of things lies beyond the parameter of the facts. It lies in the treacherous and delusive ground of the fiction writer and the fabulist, those seekers after truth who speak it for no one but themselves with no motive of defense or self-justification. This is the terrain in which someone other than myself will one day stake his ground.

During the days of testimony I saw James leaning forward in his seat, chewing on his bottom lip, which had blossomed out in cold sores under the stress. His eyes bore at me from the other end of the courtroom as I confined myself to the facts.

U is for unravel

The thin bonds of our family unit sundered completely after the death of my mother. On some unspoken agreement my father and I commenced separate lives within the narrow scope of our house and small farm. I rose each day at midmorning when I was sure he was about his business in the fields. I ate alone in the kitchen, staring in mild surprise at the creeping ruin that had taken possession of the house. Now that we seldom bothered to light any fires, paint had begun to peel from several damp patches on the walls. A light fur like a shroud clung to the effigies and icons all about and the windows scaled over.

Yet neither of us would lift a hand to do anything. We were now caught in a game of nerves, each staring the other down, waiting for him to crack. But neither of us did: we were too far gone in stubbornness and pride. The dishes piled up in the sink and cartons and bottles collected everywhere. The house now reeked of decay.

I came down from my room one evening and he was at the table, drinking a bottle by the neck. I stopped dead inside the door and continued to stare at him. We spoke at the same time.

"This place has gone to hell."

And still neither of us made a move.

V IS FOR VISIT

Now that I have all my records and the last of my books I have
begun to sense a distance opening up between myself and James. It
gets worse with every visit, a widening fissure into which our words
tumble without reaching each other. Most of the last few visits have
been spent sitting in silence, staring at the blank tabletop. We have
made sudden despairing raids on old memories, seeking frenziedly
among old battles and fantasies for warm, common ground. But it is
hopeless, it is as if we were retelling the plot of some book only one
of us has read, and not a very good book at that. I am surprised at
the different ways we have come to remember things. I tell him of
one of his heroic interventions on my behalf and he grimaces and
speaks dismissively of a rush of blood to the head. He tells me a bitter incident of crushed youth and violent temper and I wonder who
he is talking about. We are different men now and we hold different
memories.

This week he had a real surprise. He sat across from me with his
eyes lowered on his hands, the curious air of a lover about to confess
some long and ongoing infidelity.

"This is the last time I'll be here, Gerard," he mumbled. "I'm
going away. America." He had developed a twitch along his jawbone since his last visit and I noticed that his nails bled.

"When did you decide?"

"A few months back, seeing you in here and all that. Everything's changed, it's all different now. I've got the medical and a job
set up in New York. It's all set up," he repeated. He continued to
stare at his hands.

I was obscurely glad that it was going to end like this. James's days as my protector were at an end and my incarceration was his loss also. I knew our friendship had exhausted itself—consummated might be a better word—and I knew that I was looking at a young man whose mission in life had been completed.

"I hope it goes well for you over there. Make big money and meet lots of women. American women go mad for paddies, I'm told. It's the dirt under the fingernails. Tell them you live in a thatched cottage. I hear it never fails."

He smiled quietly. "I don't know what I'm going to do. Probably work for a while and save a bit of money. I'd like to go to college."

"That's good. It's good to have a plan if only to have something to diverge from." I rose from my chair and held out my hand. "Best of luck, James. I hope it goes well for you."

"So do I. And thanks, Gerard. You were the only real friend I ever had."

"It goes both ways."

"Good-bye."

"Good-bye."

I watched him leave and I tried to remember a time when I had ever seen him walking away before. I couldn't.

W IS FOR WISDOM

My father made it clear to me that life wasn't easy. It was his favorite theme, particularly in those drink-sodden days after my mother died. He would fall upon me roaring, snatching the headphones from my ears.

"I suppose you think that it will be easy from now on, ya useless cunt," he'd roar. "I suppose you think that it's all there now under your feet and all you have to do is bend down and pick it up. Well, let me tell you here and now that it won't be like that, it won't be like that at all, at all. No son of mine is going to be mollycoddled and pampered and I'll tell you why. Because you'll work for it, like I did when I was your age and every other man of my generation. Because, and make no mistake about it, you young cur, it's work and nothing else that makes a man of you, a real man, not like those fucking long-haired gits I see you hanging around town with."

He was well into his stride now, pacing the floor and breathing heavily.

"Started work after national school we did, every man jack of us, footing turf at two shillings a floor, nearly a hundred square yards. And damn the bit of harm it did us. It made men out of us, real men who knew the value of money. Now all this country has is young fuckers like you spending all day on your frigging arses, cunts who know the price of everything and the value of nothing, eating and drinking the quarter session with no thought of tomorrow. I'm sick of the fucking sight of you."

He would grab a hank of my hair then and lift my face up, his whiskey breath burning my skin.

"But if your mother was alive there'd be a different tune out of you, I'll bet. She'd have put skates under you and not have you sitting here all day like a frigging imbecile."

This was the inevitable point of breakdown, the moment at which all his vehemence would drain away, rendering him mawkish and pathetic. He would collapse by the stove, weeping and snuffling into his hands.

"Oh Mary, Mary my love."

I did not know which was the most terrifying, the honest and direct terror from which there was no escape or this genuine grief which was his alone.

X IS FOR XENOPHOBE

We watched the interview on television the following evening. A study in western gothic, it showed the three of us standing in the doorway, my mother staring into her hands, plainly abashed by the attention, my father square-jawed and sullen, glowering darkly at the camera. At their backs I rose up between them, a half-wit's leer covering my face. The bright young interviewer, all smiles and bonhomie, waved a microphone in my father's face.

"Mr. Quirke, you are the latest Lotto millionaire, the biggest in its history. It must have come as a complete shock to you."

Father avoided the bait skillfully.

"No," he said dryly, barely hiding his contempt. "When you have lived as long as I have it takes more than a few pounds to surprise you."

"How did you find out that you'd won?"

"I just checked my numbers on the nine o'clock news and when I found out that I'd won I went and had a few pints in my local like I always do."

"You didn't throw a party or buy a drink for the pub?"

"I bought my round as I always do. I've always had money to buy my own drink, anyone will tell you that."

"Now that you have all this money, surely it will bring some changes to your lives, a new car or a holiday perhaps?"

"The car we have is perfectly good," he answered bluntly. "It gets us from A to B and back again. If we wanted to live somewhere else we wouldn't be living here. There'll be no changes."

The interviewer hurriedly thrust the microphone to my face.

"Gerard, you are the only child of this new millionaire. No doubt you have high hopes of getting your hands on a sizable share of it," she said hopefully.

"My father has a sound head on his shoulders. He'll not do anything foolish with it," I said simply, barely able to keep from laughing.

The interview ended in freeze-frame, catching my father with his jaw struck forward in absurd defiance and the half-wit's leer spread back to my ears. In the news coverage of my trial it was this image that defined the tone of all articles. The national press barely managed to suppress a tone of there-but-for-the-grace-of-God righteousness. Their articles were snide exercises in anguished hand-wringing and between-the-lines sneering at their dim, western cousins. Some day soon I expect to read accounts of sheep shagging and incest purely for tone.

Y is for yes

Yes, I have my remorse. All that night I sat over my father's corpse and watched the blood drain from his skull over the floor. I was experiencing a lesson in how death diminishes and destroys not just life, but memories also. All that night I had trouble with my recollection. I could not square this overweight, middle-aged corpse with the towering ogre who had terrorized and destroyed my teenage years. That was a creature from a different era, a prehistory of myth and violent legend. It had nothing to do with this small, west-of-Ireland farmer, this lord of forty acres with his fondness for whiskey and cowboy songs.

There was a clear and horrible disparity in that room, a terrible and universal lack of proportion.

Z is for zenith

On the first morning of my detention a small deputation of prisoners greeted me in the exercise yard. I was amazed to see that they bore several gifts for me—a ten-spot of hash, a quart of whiskey, and a list of warders who could be bought off for privileges. I stood bemusedly trying to conceal these gifts in my baggy overalls, watching the bearers retreat diffidently across the yard. Evidently my reputation had preceded me, elevating me on arrival into that elite category of prisoner who was not to be fucked with. I had a secret laugh about that. This of course is on account of the axe. There is no doubt but that the nature of my crime has made it a transgression of a different order, even in here, where there are men doing time for crimes that are barely speakable. Knives or guns are understandable—they are the instruments of run-of-the-mill savageries. But an axe is something else again. It is the stuff of myth, the instrument of the truly sick of soul.

From the beginning I have received fan mail, curious and vaguely imploring missives from faceless well-wishers. *Dear Gerard Quirke, Not a day passes when I do not think of you alone in the isolation of your cell. You are in my thoughts every day and I pray for the deliverance of your wounded soul.* Today I received my first proposal of marriage.

I have begun to think again of my future and I have made some tentative plans. Yesterday I signed up for an Open University degree in English Literature and History; it will take me four years. Now my days are full, neatly ordered within the precise routine of the penal system, meals and exercise alternating between longer periods of study and my record collection. At night I lie in this bed, plugged into my stereo and smoking the good quality dope that is so plentiful here. The lights go down and peace and quiet reigns all about. I spend the hours before sleep remembering back to the final day of my trial and I acknowledge now without irony the wisdom of that judge when he handed me this life sentence.

Old Man, My Son

I have just returned from burying my son, I think. I say that not out of certainty but defiance. What is beyond doubt is that I have returned from burying someone and he was very small and a blood relation. To me and my wife he was our only child, our son Francis, nine and a half years old. But that is a minority opinion. To the greater world there seems no doubt but that he was my father, also named Francis, an aged hero of the War of Independence. The old men who came up to me on sticks as I stood by the graveside were in no doubt as to the identity of the corpse. Grabbing me by the arm with their clawlike hands they spoke fervently:

"I'm sorry about your father, John. He was the last of a breed of heroes. It's a shame the way time passes." Or a variation: "I remember him well, John. We all looked up to him. He was an inspiration."

I stood there on the graveside as the rain fell steadily, darkening the soil that the grave diggers were heaping on the coffin. I continued to receive this doddery procession of old men who made their way cautiously over the slippery ground. They shook my hand and offered their sympathies and I shook theirs and nodded in acceptance. But in truth I had not a clue what was happening about me. Here was the world, present on the twenty-eighth of March 1991, at the funeral of my father while my wife and I could have sworn that three years previous to the day we had buried him and now we were here at the graveside of our only son, Francis.

My wife, surrounded by the emotional scaffolding of her brothers and sisters, is in the next room grieving. She does not have a clue either; we seem to be all alone in this horror. And it is precisely because of this aloneness that some sense has to be made of the whole thing, some sense no matter how small. It is this lack of sense that has me here writing.

Let me be clear. When I have finished writing I do not expect to have achieved some all-explaining insight into the unique horror that has held sway in our home for the last six months. That onus of explanation seems to me an almost intolerable burden to place upon any writer. Even before I start, I know I will never be able to write an explanation and even if by some miracle I were to achieve one I do not think that any written one would satisfy my heart. A written explanation, lying on a page, bloodless and incapable of making itself felt in my heart—the only place where an explanation has any validity—is no explanation. Therefore my task in this writing is more modest. All I hope to do is lay down the facts so that in these at least there will be some clarity. From the whole debris of this horror salvaging the facts is the least I can do for my wife and myself.

I will start with my father. The relevant thing about my father is that he was a hero of the War of Independence and probably of the Civil War also although he rarely spoke of this second adventure. In one of the few Risings outside Dublin in 1916 my father, as a very young man, commanded a small company of volunteers based in the Mweelera mountains above Killary harbor. From this redoubt they attacked and occupied the police barracks on Westport. In an incident that has gone largely unchronicled my father then stood in the smashed bay window of the station and read out a self-penned version of the Proclamation of Independence to the bewildered township who had gathered in its square. The occupation of the barracks lasted till the weekend when military intelligence informed them that a Royal Irish Infantry detachment with artillery backup was being deployed from Galway military barracks to lift the occupation. By this time word had come through of the almost total failure of the Rising outside Dublin. There was nothing for it but to withdraw. In the dead of night the volunteers stole westward along the Louisburgh road toward Killary harbor and refuge. Rounding a corner somewhere between Westport and Louisburgh they ran through a British Army checkpoint but not before Father, a frontseat passenger in the truck, stopped a .303 bullet with his chest. Somewhere in the Mweelera mountains a makeshift medical post was panicked by a wound classed somewhere between serious and critical. When the torrent of blood welling from his chest had been stanched it was quickly realized that there was not one among the volunteers with the skill needed to remove the bullet. It was decided to cleanse the wound as best they could, bind it, and hope for the best. In nervous agitation, an effort to kindle some hope in those about him, a young volunteer recalled how he had heard stories of soldiers who'd carried bullets and shrapnel in their bodies for the whole of their lives with only minimal discomfort.

It was as if the telling of this story acted as a template for subsequent events because this was exactly what happened. After lying in a fever for ten days, during which time he was to rise in his bed several times, screaming and flailing his arms in the air, physically fending off death, the fever broke and my father lay on his back with steel-blue eyes gazing into the sky above Mweelera. His first words were, "So where am I?" He carried that bullet in him the remaining seventy years of his life until on the two occasions of his death when my wife found him in the room lying on his back, staring at the ceiling, his eyes calmed like blue metal.

Up to the sudden change that took place in him six months before his death, nothing distinguished my son Francis. When he was born over nine years ago it seemed the right and symmetrical thing to do to name him after his grandfather. Now I ask myself was it here, in his naming, that the damage was done? As I have said, the child was ordinariness itself. Small, with his mother's blond hair, he had the energy and cheer of any child his age. He was admired by visitors as a dote and spoke easily with them, never cheekily and even if so only to the extent that could be passed off as childish spiritedness. He was bright but not exceptional and his interests were similar to those of any child his own age and to the same degree: his bike, football, sweets, and mischief. Up to those last six months he was a child like any other and we loved him as only a single child can be loved. I say that so no one can accuse us of having given our child reason to reject us. As you shall see—and remember I am putting down the facts—his change never consisted in a rejection of us. Never once did he accuse or express dissatisfaction. In fact, in a more world-weary way, he seemed as happy with us as he had ever been.

Lastly, before I speak of the change, I must talk of his relationship with his grandfather. It was quite simple. To Francis, Grandfather was a hero of some distant and, in his young mind, awesome conflict. He saw him as a solitary giant, a war hero who partook in great adventures, a treasure trove of great stories. Night after night he would sit at his feet and worry him with incessant questions till bedtime. In this he was the envy of his school friends. It also pleased my father. "He's a good listener," he would say fondly. I ask myself again, was it here in the avidness with which he was listened to that my father found renewal? I do not know but as we shall see he did find a renewal of sorts.

About the change. Despite its surreal banality the incident itself is easily remembered. Six months ago we sat here in this kitchen eating. At this point I am tempted to speak of the weather, the time of day, the type of meal it was, and so on in order to mark the incredible incident against a background of particular detail. But would that explain anything? I do not think so. It will suffice to say that the three of us were in the kitchen eating and Francis was carrying his mug from the table to the sink where my wife was preparing to wash up. As he approached the sink the cup slipped from his grasp—it will be the last time in this account that I will call him child with any certainty—fell to the floor, and spun to a stop before the sink. My wife turned, on the verge of telling him to pick it up, but was struck silent by the intensity of the gaze with which Francis was looking at the mug. She would describe it later as a mixture of amazement and agony, the composite reaction of an old man who has seen many such troubled things in the past and the incomprehension of one to whom it was all totally new. My wife opened her mouth to speak but Francis took her forearm as one would a passing child and, in an unforgettably leaden voice, as if the memories and fatigue of a lifetime had come to rest upon him in that moment, he told her, "Bend down and pick that up like a good girl."

In that moment and with those astonishing words he changed the whole complex of relationships in our house.

My wife, seconds before having been a mother on the verge of rebuking her child, was changed in an instant into a woman worried about the health of this old man. It is a measure of how complete and successful this reversal was for her because she picked up the mug in silent awe and handed it to him. After depositing it in the sink he returned to the table, and lowered himself gently into his chair, one hand on the table, groaning heavily, his bones apparently suffused with stiffness. A look of horror and astonishment passed between my wife and me. Despite ourselves we sensed some momentous change in our fortunes, some new beginning. Francis had resumed eating with a slow thoughtful relish far beyond his years. I decided to venture a question into the incredible silence that now reigned in the kitchen.

"Are you feeling all right, Francis? You're not sick or anything?"

"A man of my age is always sick," he replied dryly.

Again it is indicative of how completely he had changed that I did not dare rebuke what I thought might be left of the child in this now old man—one does not reprimand someone for saying something that is in all probability true. I had not a clue how to handle the situation. In fact it took all my powers of concentration to recognize exactly what was happening. The child Francis in outward appearance was still recognizable before me but his deeper identity had been supplanted entirely by the character of an old, jaded man. For a dread instant I toyed with the notion that there were actually two people before me. My wife stood at the sink, her mouth slung open and her eyes staring wide. Francis, or more correctly whoever it was that was now within Francis, sat spooning up the last of his meal, apparently heedless to the great change that he had brought about in his house. I realized instantly that for him there had been no change—one moment had been perfectly continuous with the previous one, there had been no slip sideways into someone else. It would therefore be ridiculous to start asking him what had happened. In any case he put an end to my thinking at that point by speaking grimly.

"You're right, I am tired. I'll lie down for an hour. Wake me up when it's time for the news." He walked stiffly from the room.

My wife broke immediately from her trance and began to sob hysterically. I went to her and held her in my arms.

"What's happened?" she cried. "What has happened?"

"I don't know."

"But he's changed," she protested. "One minute he's my son and the next I'm his daughter. What caused it? What do we do?" Her voice was climbing higher, nearing a thin note of hysteria. Something frantic was moving within her like a current. I tightened my hold on her.

"Let's wait and see," I said. "Maybe when he wakes it will be all over." These words were solely for her benefit. I did not believe for an instant that something that had come upon us with such resoluteness and completion would not end in some disaster.

He woke from his nap a few hours later and entered the kitchen, his eyes glued over with sleep. He asked for tea and when it was brought to him he supped fervently at the table. Previous to this Francis never drank anything but milk.

"Is the news over?" he asked presently.

"Yes, it's over," I replied. "There wasn't much on it."

"What did it say on the weather?" He was seated by the window, looking out at the sheets of rain that hopped in the tarmac-covered yard.

"It said there would be no change. It would be like this till the end of the week."

"I suppose there's no use going for a walk then. I was going to go to town for fags."

This was incredible. Could he really be so oblivious to the change that had taken place or to the silent turmoil which roiled about him? I could see my wife at the sink and the almost superhuman effort it was taking her to keep from breaking down was visibly marked on her face. Francis sat at the table, fair-haired and smooth-skinned, but with all the mannerisms and fatigue of an old man. He seemed to be the still center of a small cyclone that was rampaging silently through the room. Now I was sure that he saw nothing different in himself. To him there had been no change: he was as he had always been. But to me he was my son turned in an instant into an old man. And there was the problem. I was already willing to admit that he was now an old man but who exactly was this old man? I decided to wheedle his identity from him gently, to proceed with caution. I feared that waking him suddenly to the change would plunge him also into a crisis. At that moment two crises in the one room were more than enough.

"When did you take up smoking?" I spoke very gently.

"What do you mean, when did I take up smoking?" he repeated testily. "You know very well that I've smoked since I was twelve, smoked all my life except for twice at Lent when I couldn't go the distance and was back on them inside two weeks. Thirty Woodbine a day and nothing less." Looking out the window he changed tack slightly. "I can't go anywhere in this rain."

As I listened to these words a dim germ of horror and recognition began to flower within me. "Here," I said. "Have one of mine." I proffered a red box with one fag extended toward him.

"John," my wife hissed, "you can't go giving the child cigarettes."

"It's OK," I said, "I know what I'm doing."

This was brave talk indeed for in truth I hardly dared recognize what I was seeing come ever clearer into focus before me. Francis took the fag with gentle ease and raised it to his mouth. With one movement he bit off the filter and spat it into the fire. He took a light from me and angled his face backward for the first drag, tipping the lighted end into the air. With his eyes closed he drew fearlessly on it as if he'd been doing it all his life.

"That'll do," he said, picking a scrap of tobacco from the tip of his tongue. "A bit weak but it'll do." He sat and smoked the rest of the cigarette, sunk in such silent contentment that my wife rushed from the room choking back sobs.

"So the weather's going to stay like this. It's just as well then we decided against planting spuds. They'd be washed out of the ground with this rain."

He talked on like this into the evening, taking an avid interest in the news and most particularly a current affairs program that dealt with the BSE scare that had affected so many cattle in the west.

"The price of cattle will go to hell," he declared solemnly, twitching his nose. "We won't get a pound a kilo by year's end if this keeps up." Despite his youthful looks he spoke with the certainty of one who was laying down the law and anticipated no dissent. "It will be the end of the small farmer," he pronounced. "Only the big ones will be able to afford quarantine and the small ones like ourselves will have to sell off at below cost price. Isn't it always the same?"

I could take no more. I staggered from the room in a daze.

The following morning we had our next big shock. He appeared in the doorway of the kitchen done out in a perfectly fitting black suit and a black hat that scooped down over his child's face. Across his waistcoat was slung a watch chain. He stood in the doorway, framed like a portrait, consulting his watch with eyes that were surely failing.

"Not that a man of my age has much business knowing the time," he concluded grimly before turning to me. "Has the post come yet?"

"There's no post on a Saturday," I said.

"That's right," he conceded, "I completely forgot. The memory is going on top of everything else."

As on the previous day he lowered himself gently into the chair beside the table. I was glad my wife, who had not yet risen, was not there to see him. Despite the almost comic contrast between the clothes and his face he seemed even older in essence than the day before.

After breakfast our neighbor came in on an errand. I was glad to see her because with her by the hand was her daughter Anne, one of Francis's classmates. My immediate hope was that he would recognize some kinship in her that would snap him out of this terrible persona. But his first words crushed any such hope. He put his hand out to ruffle her curls.

"You're getting bigger every day, Anne. What class are you in now?" An immense weakness came over me as I heard him speak.

"I'm in second class," she simpered, pleased to be the center of this old man's attention. Her mother picked her up in her arms.

"You're looking well yourself, Francis, getting younger every day. This damp weather must suit you."

It was now his turn to simper. "It's a good job it agrees with someone," he said. "This country will be washed out from under our feet if this rain keeps up."

"When it hasn't been washed away in all these years it's not likely to happen now. Say good-bye to Francis, Anne." She turned to me. "We'll be on our way, John, it will soon be time for the dinner." And they left.

And so I knew the incredible truth. The change in Francis had taken place only before our own eyes: for the rest of the world nothing at all had happened. Worse than that, my neighbor had spoken to him as someone she had known all her life. By now my own recognition of him was beginning to take fuller shape and that night I decided to test it to the full. As the nine o'clock news ended I suggested we go into town for a drink. My wife's mouth fell open in disbelief but I frowned aside her silent protest. We traveled in my car and he sat beside me in his black suit, his young features heedlessly radiant under his black hat. If at this point I could have overcome my horror at the dawning recognition that was now nearing a certainty I would have been able to see the Chaplinesque comedy in our situation; I was definitely able to see the horror.

I entered the pub behind him and immediately my recognition was confirmed. The three or four men leaning over pints at the counter turned around and saluted Francis as if it were the most natural thing in the world.

"Evening, Francis. It's a wet one."

"It's always a wet one in these parts," he replied dryly.

"What will it be, Francis?" asked the barman, throwing aside the damp cloth.

"The usual, two pints of Guinness," he replied with a certainty that was fast becoming the mark of his character. He was even sure of what I drank.

And the night went on like that. On the one side, between him and his friends, a complete and unsurprised recognition of each other; within myself, a descent quickened by alcohol into a deepening pit of despair. Talking back and forth among his friends that night Francis left me to flounder in this pit. Only once during the night did he turn to me.

"Cheer up, son," he said. "It could be worse."

I had not a clue what he meant.

That night when he had gone to bed I stayed up alone sorting through all the documents that had made their way into our home. By the early hours I had two separate piles on the table. On the left, among others, there was a pension book, a will, a death certificate, and a coroner's report. All these testified to the existence and death of my father. On the right, in a much smaller pile, there was a birth certificate, a christening certificate, and a small collection of school reports. All of these spoke the existence of someone who at one time had been my son. Yet now I could neither be sure of my father's death nor of my son's existence. Now the only certain thing was that in some ghastly way they were both present in the one person at the same time, my father's character in the body of my son whom the rest of the world seemed not to remember. I felt the room beginning to reel about me, becoming a vortex, pulling me down. What was I going to do? In my confusion and misery I had a wild notion of taking my shovel and driving into the night toward the graveyard and digging up that documented and three-year-old corpse. I could see myself already in the graveyard, the rain suitably pissing down as I dug furiously, a decent and honest man driven to hideous deeds by some presence in his life that he is neither responsible for nor capable of making any sense of, a character in a cautionary tale, a black-and-white movie illustrating how the dark shapes of the unspeakable rise up to shatter our lives. I dismissed the idea with a groan. This was no black-and-white movie and, after all, what would it prove to dig up a skeleton that I would never be able to identify?

My wife, red-eyed and sleep-disheveled, entered the room. She sat down beside me at the table and I noticed with alarm that she too seemed to have aged. But would this disaster not age anyone? I put my arm around her, as much to comfort myself with her solidity as to steady her now that I had decided to tell her what I knew. I turned her face toward me.

"He's come back," I started. "I don't know how or why but the Francis we have now is my father."

"Yes," she said, "I know. I've known since the moment he started talking about smoking." She began to sob. "Where is our child, John, where did he go?" I held her toward me and made some useless comforting noises. Presently she pulled away from me. There was a sickly gleam in her eyes.

"John, what if we're mad? What if the whole world is right and we're wrong? What if our son never was?"

"That can't be," I retorted quickly. "How are all these documents explained, birth certificates, christening certificates, school reports? Where did they all come from?" I drew to a halt suddenly, aghast at what I was saying. My hands clutched my head. "What the hell am I talking about? Forget these documents, forget these school reports. Remember the child, remember the things he did. Christ, we still even have his things."

This was true. His schoolbag stood in the hall by the hotpress piled high with his clothes; at the end of the hall was a room decorated with posters of football teams and motor bikes, a small boy's room. Earlier that day I had noticed his bike in the garage. More correctly, I had woken from a reverie, aware that I had been standing and staring at his bike for a long time. But it was a spell in which I found no clue where my son was nor even where to start looking.

These were the first days of the six-month horror that dominated our lives like some waking nightmare. And as the nightmare continued it fleshed itself out, became more complete as the days went on. That following Monday, as he had expected, a new pension book arrived for him in the post. His friends began to call on him as if he had never been gone and one day a student came to interview him as part of the research he was doing on the history of the Rising. He spoke most often of the past, his military adventures, departed comrades, and even, in glancing references, of his marriage. More and more of his speech became prefaced with remarks like, "I remember when," or "In my day," or "God be with the days when." It was a unique horror to see this young face reaching down into an impossible reservoir of experience for these memories and then lay them there before us blithely like dead things. But the worst of it was that, while in our eyes he retained his childlike looks, his manner became so jaded and crotchety that a time quickly came when it became difficult for us to summon up the image of our son Francis. One day, walking into the garage, I found my wife running her hands absentmindedly over his bicycle. She had been using it as a prop to try and prompt her imagination. I knew it because more than once I had come to my senses in his bedroom, staring in the same way at his pile of toys in the corner, trying desperately to visualize our child playing with them. Once Francis, or whoever he was, happened in on me as I sat there.

"You don't want to spend too long staring like that. Life passes you by quickly," he said.

That day in the garage my wife looked at me with her eyes brimming.

"I'm losing touch with him, John. I can't see our child anymore."

The child Francis was receding from our imagination like a story told to an infant, a small boat drifting away on an infinite sea of loss.

What was our attitude toward Francis during those six months? Did our initial horror and confusion turn to outright hatred and bitterness? Did we treat him as we would some monster in our midst? Hand on my heart I can say that we did not. There was a continual hope in our heart that our son Francis would one day reassert himself from out of this composite being, one day emerge completely from beneath the character of my father, shiny and new like a small, eclipsed moon. Built upon this hope was a genuine attitude of concern that this Francis be nurtured. As long as he lived there was a real chance that our son would return.

In the month before he died a real bitterness entered into Francis. There was a political reason for this bitterness and although I have said I will confine myself to the facts I would like to speculate that the reason for his recurrence was a simple, unbelievable vanity.

It was the run-up to Easter and this was the year of the seventy-fifth anniversary of the Rising. As we remember, the celebrations this time were contentious. Over twenty years of bloodshed in both nationalist and unionist communities in the north had put paid to any idea of repeating the innocent pageantry and procession that had marked the fiftieth anniversary. In those years the IRA had stepped forward into a political void claiming to be the true heirs to the legacy of 1916. And in those twenty years no one had been able to completely discredit their claim. But now that the commemorations were coming around again a new tactic was devised by those who wanted to deny the historical legitimacy of the IRA. The tactic amounted to a tacit denial that 1916 had ever taken place at all. Prudence, caution, and sensitivity were counseled by our revisionists as a pretext for not offending the northern, unionist tradition. Deep down, however, more than a few people suspected that some massive denial was taking place. It was easy to believe so: anguish and embarrassment hung everywhere like a curse. Francis was incensed.

"Have we lost our nerve altogether?" he raged. "Are we that afraid of ourselves that we're going to allow the birth of our nation to be held ransom by a crowd of thugs?"

And as the time of the commemoration drew near it became obvious that the celebrations would be only a token affair. Francis's disbelief turned to rage.

"What the hell are we embarrassed for? Can you imagine this sort of thing happening in any other country of the world? Christ, the French or the Americans would never stand for it, and damn right, too."

But beneath the bluster and anger a deep undercurrent of betrayal was affecting him deeply. And it was this undercurrent that eventually sucked away his health and resolve. On Easter Monday we watched the televised ceremonies from outside Dublin GPO. Despite the presence of the Taoiseach, the president, a few foreign ambassadors, and a handful of wheelchaired veterans, the ceremony itself lasted little more than half an hour. It was a craven, threadbare affair. When it ended I knew something vital had been drained from Francis. He seemed paler and sunk even further into his chair if that was possible. His voice came from a long way off.

"Is that it? Is that all there is to show after seventy-five years—embarrassment and a government policy of amnesia?" His disappointment filled the room like smoke.

How ludicrous is it to say that it was for these celebrations that Francis had returned? How ludicrous is it to say that the chance to relive his most glamorous moment had proved too big a temptation for his restless soul? Did he have it in mind to step forward and take one last bow even if only in the privacy of his own imagination? Whatever the truth, the fact is that the next day Francis was late to breakfast. After looking at me, my wife went to his room where she found him dead, lying on his back and staring at the ceiling in the same attitude of repose he had worn on the morning of his first death three years previously. She returned to the kitchen, confirming in a quiet voice what I already knew.

Now that the great event was upon us we were at a loss as to how we should react. On the one hand a horror had been lifted from us and we were free in all respects to continue with the rest of our lives. We could refer to the whole thing from now on as a mutual nightmare. On the other hand, a death is a death and a family death calls for some form of grieving, particularly so now that the return of our son was obviously impossible. It was this confusion then that dictated that we put grieving on the long finger until some indefinite point in the future when we had it clear in our mind what it was exactly that had gone from us.

Our reaction then was one of stunned efficiency. We telephoned the hospital and although it was irregular they said they would come and take the corpse away for an autopsy. Two hours later as the corpse was being lifted into the ambulance my wife's fortitude collapsed. The driver, no doubt meaning well, turned and sympathized with us, told us that death was always a trial but wasn't it great that someone so old went so peacefully? It was at this point that my wife broke down. She started to pummel the man's chest and shriek:

"He was my son, my son, do you hear?"

The driver took an embarrassed step backward as I tried to restrain her.

"Death is always a trial," he finished lamely.

Later that evening I went to the hospital to finalize details on the removal of the corpse. I received the autopsy report from a middle-aged man dressed in what looked like butcher's overalls. He got to the point briskly.

"A thrombosis. Your father was killed when his blood flow was hindered by a foreign object coming to rest on his cardiovascular system."

He held out a small, shapeless mass and placed it in my hand. It was surprisingly heavy and its true shape was barely discernible.

"A bullet," the coroner confirmed simply. "A very ancient one, too. He must have carried it in him for the most part of his life because nowhere on his body can I find any scar tissue." The note of amazement was obvious in his voice. "In fact, but for the bullet, there is no reason to believe that he would not have gone on living another fifty years. He was in amazingly good shape."

So this was how he'd died. The coroner's report on Francis's first death stated that he had died from a deterioration of his whole organism; old age in other words. There had never been any mention of a bullet anywhere. Walking from the hospital I was aware that I was still clutching it in my hand. I threw it in the nearest bin; I wanted nothing more to do with it.

So this is how it ends, the physical substance of the horror passing on but leaving in its wake the pure essence of the problem itself. There is absolutely no doubt but that Francis existed. But who was he? Was he my father or my son? How could he be both at the same time? Is it possible that in some way I could have had a hand in the birth of my own father? If he was my son how could he have so resembled my father? All these questions and there is no doubt but that they are the real residue of the last six months. My mind is a whirl.

But now, even though it is just over two days since he has died, I can sense an idea taking shape in my wife. On the night of his death as I held her in our bed she spoke quietly.

"John, maybe we could start again. Maybe we could try for another child."

I had an immediate sensation of falling, the feeling of some unyielding surface rushing up to meet me at a terrific speed. I shut my eyes and clenched my teeth till my temples ached. I eventually managed to speak.

"We'll see," I said. "We'll see."

But I don't know. I've got to get this sorted out before I can have another child. I keep wondering to myself, how can a man bring a child into the world when he hasn't a clue who he is himself?

Thomas Crumlesh 1960–1992: A Retrospective

My first contact with Thomas Crumlesh was in 1984 when he exhibited with a small artists' collective in the Temple Bar area of the city. His was one of the many fringe exhibitions hoping to draw the attention of the international buyers who were in Dublin for the official Rosc Exhibition at the Guinness Hops Store. It was July, just four months after Thomas had been expelled from the National College of Art and Design for persevering with work that, in the opinion of his tutors, dealt obscenely and obsessively with themes of gratuitous violence.

His exhibition, *Notes Toward an Autobiography,* had been hanging less than three days and already word had got out and excited quite a bit of outraged comment. It consisted of four box frames with black silk backgrounds on which were mounted his left lung, the thumb of his left hand, his right ear, and the middle toe of his left foot. Crumlesh was present also and easily recognizable—he was standing by the invigilator's desk with his head and left hand swathed in white and not-too-clean bandages. He was deathly pale and carrying himself delicately; like most young bohemians he was badly in need of a shave. After I got over my initial shock I ventured a few words of congratulations, more by way of curiosity than from any heartfelt belief in his work's merit. He surprised me with a lavish smile and a resolute handshake, contradicting completely his frail appearance. This was my first experience of the central paradox in his personality—the palpably gruesome nature of his work set against his unfailing good spirits and optimism. He surprised me further by telling me in conspiratorial tones that he planned to leave the country that very evening. Some criticism of his work had found its way into the national press and already a few people with placards had picketed the exhibition. He had even heard word that the police were pressing for warrants to arrest him under the obscenity laws. He confided further that what really worried him was that he might fall foul of Ireland's notoriously lax committal laws; he quoted an impressive array of statistics on secondary committals in the Republic.

I ended that encounter by buying his lung. His enthusiasm and verve convinced me of its worth and his whole appearance told me that he was in need of the money. Before I left he outlined the program of work he had laid out for himself—a program that would take him up to 1992, the year he hoped to retire. I offered to check his wounds—his bandages looked like they had not been changed in a few days. He declined the offer saying that he did not have the time; he needed to cash the check and he was afraid of missing the ferry to Holyhead. We shook hands before parting and I did not expect to see him ever again.

Our paths crossed again two years later. I was in London, attending a symposium on trauma and phantom pains in amputees at the Royal College of Surgeons. By chance, in a Crouch End pub, I picked up a flyer advertising the upcoming festival of Irish culture and music in Finsbury Park. Near the bottom of a list of rock bands and comedians was mention of a small exhibition of avant-garde work to be shown at a tiny gallery in Birchington Road. Thomas's name was mentioned second from the bottom. When I eventually found the gallery it was nothing more than two rooms knocked together on the third floor over a Chinese restaurant. Among the second-rate paintings and sculptures Thomas's work was not difficult to recognize. It stood in the middle of the floor, mounted on a black metal stand, a single human arm stripped of skin and musculature leaning at an obtuse angle to the floor. The bleached bones of the hand were closed in a half fist and the whole thing looked like the arm of some nightmare robot. As I approached it the arm jerked into life, the fingers contracted completely and the thumb bone stood vertical. It looked eerily like a ghost hitching a lift from some passing phantom car. It was untitled but carried a price of two thousand pounds.

Thomas entered the room and recognized me instantly. I attempted to shake hands—an embarrassing blunder since I had to withdraw my right hand when I saw the stump near his shoulder. As before, he was in good spirits and he entered quickly into a detailed explanation of what he called his "technique." He had bleached the bone in an acid formula of his own devising to give it its luminous whiteness and then wired it to electrical switches concealed beneath the carpet that would be unwittingly activated by the viewer whenever he got within a certain radius—he admitted borrowing this subterfuge from the work of Jean Tinguely. He then circled the arm and put it through its motions, four in all. Firstly, a snake pose that turned the palm downward from the elbow and extended the fingers fearsomely, then the hitching gesture, then a foppish, disowning gesture that swiveled the forearm at the elbow and threw the hand forward, palm upward, and lastly and most comically an "up yours" middle finger gesture that faced the viewer head on. He grinned like a child when I expressed my genuine admiration. I had no doubt but that I was looking at a postmodern masterpiece. I little suspected at the time that this piece would enter into the popular imagery of the late twentieth century, reaching iconic status through exposure on album covers, T-shirts, and posters. I only regretted at the time that I had not the means to acquire it.

But Thomas was not without worries. He confided that he had found it extremely difficult to find a surgeon who would carry out the amputations; he had to be extremely careful to whom he even voiced the idea—the terror of committal again. It had taken him three months to track down an ex-army medic with shellshock who had been discharged from the parachute regiment after the Falklands War to where he ran a covert abortion clinic in Holloway. In a fugue of anesthesia and marijuana Thomas had undergone his operation, a traumatic affair that had left him so pained and unnerved he doubted he would be able to undergo the experience again. This fright had put his life's work in jeopardy, he pointed out. He was looking me straight in the eye as he said this; I sensed that he was putting me on the spot. Then he came straight out with his request. What I need is a skilled surgeon I can rely on, not some strung-out psycho. He spoke evenly, without the least hint of hysteria in his voice. He will of course be paid, he added coyly. I told him that I needed time to think on it—it was an unusual request. He nodded his agreement, he understood fully the difficulties of his request, and he would not blame me if I refused him outright. We shook hands before we parted and I promised to contact him the following day after I had given his request some thought.

In fact I had little to think about. I very quickly resolved my fundamental dilemma: the healing ethic of my craft set against the demands of Thomas's talents. One parting glance at the arm convinced me that I had encountered a fiercely committed genius who it seemed to me had already made a crucial contribution to the imagery of the late twentieth century. It was obvious to me that I had an obligation to put my skills at his disposal; the century could not be denied his singular vision on grounds of arbitrary scruples. My problem was how exactly I was to make my skills available. That evening in my hotel room I gave the problem much thought and I returned the following day with my plans.

I found Thomas in high spirits. The lead singer of a famous heavy metal band had just bought the arm and Thomas was celebrating with champagne, drinking it from a mug, trying to get the feel of his newfound wealth, as he laconically put it. He poured me a similar mug when I declared my intention to help him. I explained my plan quickly. Before every operation he should forward to me exact details of what he needed, then give me two weeks to put in place the necessary logistics and paperwork at the clinic where I worked. I believed I would be able to perform two operations a year without arousing suspicion. He thanked me profusely, pumping my left hand with his, telling me he could rest easy now that his future was secure. In a magniloquent moment that was not without truth he assured me that I had made a friend for life.

He contacted me for the first time in November of that year telling me that he planned to exhibit a piece during the Paris Biennale. He needed six ribs removed: when would be the most convenient time for me? I wrote in reply that I had penciled in the operation for Christmas Eve and that he could stay with me over the festive season and into the New Year while he recovered. The operation itself, an elaborate thoracotomy carried out in the witching hour of Christmas Eve, was a complete success and when, on New Year's Day, I presented him with the bundle of curved, washed bones he was thrilled; it was good to be back at work, he said.

It was during these days of convalescence that our relationship moved onto a more intimate footing. Mostly they were days of silence, days spent reading or listening to music in the conservatory that looked out over Howth to the sea beyond. Sometimes a whole day would go by without any word passing between us. Neither of us was awkward in this. The looming, inexorable conclusion of his art ridiculed any attempts at a deeper inquiry into each other's past. He simply gave me his trust and I gave him his bones and internal organs. That was enough for both of us.

On the third of January he returned to London; he wanted to get to work as quickly as possible. Five months later he sent me a photograph from a gallery in Paris, a black-and-white close-up of a piece called *The Bonemobile,* an abstract, lantern-shaped structure suspended by wire. His letter informed me that although the piece had excited the inevitable outrage among the more hidebound critics it had also generated some appreciative but furtive praise. Nevertheless, he doubted that any buyer would rise to the fifty thousand franc price tag he had placed upon it. He understood the fear of a buyer ruining his reputation by buying into what some were already calling apocalyptic voyeurism. Still, he lived in hope.

That was the first of twelve operations I performed on Thomas between 1986 and 1992. In all I removed twenty-three bones and four internal organs, eighteen inches of his digestive tract, seven teeth, four toes, his left eye, and his right leg. He exhibited work on the fringe of most major European art festivals, narrowly escaping arrest in several countries and jumping bail in four. In his lifetime he sold eight pieces worth a total of fifty thousand pounds, by no means riches, but enough to fund his spartan existence.

Inevitably, by 1989 his work had taken a toll on his body. After the removal of a section of digestive tract in 1988 his body slumped badly and following the amputation of his right leg in 1989 he spent his remaining years in a wheelchair. Despite this his spirits never sank nor did his courage fail him; he was undoubtedly sustained by the tentative acclaim that greeted his work in avant-garde circles. For the first time also he was being sought out for interviews. He declined them all, pointing out simply that the spoken word was not his medium.

His deterioration could not go on indefinitely. In March 1992 he wrote telling me he planned to exhibit his final piece at the Kassel Documenta. He traveled to Dublin the following month and spent a week at my house where he outlined the procedure I was to follow after the operation. On the night of the tenth, after shaking hands with appropriate solemnity for the last time, I administered him a massive dose of morphine, a euthanasia injection. He died painlessly within four minutes. Then, following his instructions, I removed his remaining left arm and head—messy, dispiriting work. I then boiled the flesh from the arm and skull in a huge bath and using a solution of bleach and furniture polish brought the bone to a luminous whiteness. I fixed the skull in the hand and set the whole thing on a wall mount; *Alas, Poor Thomas* he had told me to call it. Then I sent it to Kassel at the end of the month, Thomas already having informed the gallery as to the kind of work they were to expect. In critical terms it was his most successful piece and when Kiefer singled him out as the genius specific to the jaded tenor of this brutal and fantastic century his reputation was cemented. This last piece sold for twenty-five thousand deutsche marks.

When, as executor of the Thomas Crumlesh estate, I was approached with the idea of this retrospective I welcomed it on two accounts. Firstly, it is past time that a major exhibition of his work be held in his native country, a country that does not own a single piece of work by her only artist to have made a contribution to the popular imagery of the late twentieth century—a prophet in his own land indeed. Secondly, I welcomed the opportunity to assemble together for the first time his entire oeuvre. My belief is that the cumulative effect of its technical brilliance, its humor, and undeniable beauty will dispel the comfortable notion that Thomas was nothing more than a mental deviant with a classy suicide plan. The rigor and terminal logic of his art leaves no room for such easy platitudes.

Several people have speculated that I would use this introduction to the catalog to justify my activities or, worse, as an opportunity to bewail the consequences. Some have gone so far as to hope that I would repent. I propose to do neither of these. Yet a debt of gratitude is outstanding. It falls to very few of us to be able to put our skills at the disposal of genius: most of us are doomed to ply our trades within the horizons of the blind, the realm of drones. But I was one of the few, one of the rescued. Sheer chance allowed me to have a hand in the works of art that proceeded from the body of my friend, works of art that in the last years of this century draw down the curtain on an entire tradition. His work is before us now and we should see it as an end. All that remains for me to say is, Thomas, dear friend, it was my privilege.

Dr. Frank Caulfield
Arbour Hill Prison
Dublin

The Angel of Ruin

From the beginning they called him the kid, sometimes the Irish kid but mainly just the kid even though he was eighteen and taller already than any of the men in the crew. But he was thin, desperately thin and pale and he looked like a stricken tree standing in the gravel yard fronting the warehouse. He was wearing black jeans and a T-shirt and his hair hung lank in his sunken face. He was a detail in misery, looking as if at any moment he was going to burst into tears.

His new boss, now striding from the warehouse toward him, was John Cigali, an Italian American in his mid-thirties, a self-made man with a broken coke habit and four years' military service abandoned after amnesty was handed out to Vietnam draft dodgers. He now eyed the kid with unhidden skepticism.

"Have you worked with fiberglass before?"

The kid shook his head wanly.

"Never mind, you'll learn. From now till the end of summer you'll be eating and sleeping fiberglass." He peered more closely at the kid. "Is there no sun at all in Ireland? You look as pale as shit." He then turned on his heel and returned to the office.

Mike, the kid's cousin, emerged from the office clutching a sheaf of pink forms. He was in his mid-twenties, over six foot tall and with his head cropped to the bone. He thrust the pink forms at the kid.

"Signatures," he said. "State and federal tax, insurance, that kind of shit." He took a pen from his shirt pocket. "Welcome to America, sign up and piss away your soul."

The kid signed the forms on the hood of the Oldsmobile nearby while Mike fiddled with the locks of the loading bay doors. When they were opened the kid saw tools and buckets stacked neatly on the metal apron.

"All this shit has to go in the truck," Mike said. "Start loading while I finish writing up these documents."

The kid began loading up. There were several rolls of fiberglass matting, buckets of chemicals, paintbrushes and rollers, a giant vacuum cleaner that looked like a huge reptile, several hand tools for the tool rack, and, lastly, two massive jackhammers weighing nearly a hundred and twenty pounds each. The kid could barely lift them; he staggered rigid-legged to the truck and dropped the first heavily among the other tools. His face was flushed and a pulse throbbed frantically on his jawbone.

"Out of the way, kid."

Mike had come quietly up behind him. He was carrying the second jackhammer, handling it easily before lowering it lightly into the truck. He grinned at the kid.

"This is as good as it gets," he said, making no concession toward the kid's embarrassment. "From here on out it's all downhill. We're ready now so let's go. We have to be there by midday. The others are there already and John's going to follow us in the car."

The kid took his seat in the front of the truck and they moved off, driving for two hours through the claustrophobic New England landscape where beech forest grew right to the margins of the road, through the small cities of Holyoke and Springfield and on into

Connecticut where the terrain rose steeply and his ears popped, past intersections in the middle of nowhere where no traffic flowed but where traffic lights still swung from overhead cables and finally onto the interstate hewn from raw rock. While they drove the radio blasted out retro rock, Lynyrd Skynyrd, Led Zeppelin, all classic seventies music. When the kid asked him did he listen to any post-punk music, The Smiths for instance, Mike told him bluntly that he didn't listen to faggot music.

Beyond the suburbs of New Haven, where the country opened up into a gray wasteland that spread as far as the sea, they pulled in at the entrance to an immense, wired-off compound. Over the entrance hung the logo of the CHEMCON company. After Mike signed in the truck and two men at the security booth, the red barrier lifted and they drove up the pitted road to the plant. To their left, in front of a warehouse complex, a small, vile lake spread itself out over two acres, bordered on one shore by a multicolored refuse tip. All about its edge yellow drainage pipes had their ends uncovered, all carrying spill-off and waste from the plant beyond; on the lake's surface floated languid clouds of gray scum.

Mike motioned to the lake. "Nothing in that sewer but two-headed fish and unspeakable things. It's a real cesspool."

They rounded the farthest shore of the lake and pulled in between a decrepit warehouse and a series of brickwork laboratories. Up ahead a battery of chemical tanks blocked off the end of the alleyway. The kid got out of the car and stood in the silence: silence like a coma.

"How come it's so quiet?"

"The whole plant is on shutdown, three weeks of it. Bar a skeleton crew to keep it ticking over, there are no other workers here but maintenance and repair crews. That's why we're here; we have a heavy schedule of work to complete before they get back from their holidays." Mike's voice trailed off in fatigue. "It's a waste of time if you ask me. This place is only a shit hole."

The kid looked about him. Corrosion and decay seemed to work in the air like a virus. The metal storage tanks raised on concrete platforms stood like shabby monoliths, their seams and rivets weeping with rust. Pipes dripped from cracks that needed sealing and some of the entrances to the laboratories gaped blankly without doors. All around, the brickwork added a terra-cotta tone to the corroding metal and some of the brickwork itself had been graffitied over with obscene hieroglyphs, a lurid psychedelic detail.

Mike was handing him a yellow hard hat and safety glasses.

"See those pipes? Last year we lagged every one of them, tried to dry them off and coat them with fiberglass. We said at the time it was useless, told them that the resin would never take to the corrosion and that the whole thing needed replacing. But it was no good, that was what we were contracted to do. Look at the mess now."

Around the storage tanks the lattice of supply pipes was hung with a filthy bunting. The fiberglass matting had come away from the corroded metal and hung in strips, flapping lazily in the warm breeze and streaked through with a green hue from the acid; it was an unspeakably doleful sight.

A car approached behind them and slouched to a halt beside the truck. The boss got out. He was already wearing a hard hat and glasses and he spoke directly to the kid.

"Go nowhere without that hat and those glasses. We don't want you going back to Ireland with a patch over one eye or daylight showing through your head. No smoking either," he said. His voice then lowered to a note of fatigue. "This whole place might go up in a bang any second."

He was holding a massive torch, inserting batteries and flicking it on and off.

"OK, if we're ready I'll show you the work." He paused for a last moment in the sunlight to look around him. The ruin and decay of the plant seemed to find a raw spot in him. He spoke softly to himself. "I hate this fucking place. It burns a hole in me every minute I'm here." Then he was making strides toward a darkened doorway in the warehouse, calling in his wake for them to follow him.

Inside, out of the sun, the kid couldn't see a thing: he just followed in the wake of the boss's torch. Underfoot he could feel the concrete crumbling wetly, slewing sideways into treacherous pools. All about was a kind of serpent hissing and a heavy dripping of liquid. In front, high up beyond the torchlight, a red neon sign pulsed, DANGER TOXIC. The kid slowed and clamped the hat down further on his ears. He had a feeling that terrible shapes and creatures were straining out toward him in the darkness, trying to lay mangled claws upon him. But worse still was the total presence of decay which seemed to agitate the darkness, working in it as it worked in every pore of the concrete and metal.

"This is it then," John declaimed, swooping the torch in a low arc. "One thousand square yards of corroded concrete, eaten away by acid and God-knows-what shit. It all has to be lifted down to the subfloor and replaced. That's all there is to it."

The kid's eyes were now attuned to the murk and he had a dim view of the shambles all round. On all sides the floor was breaking down into pools of sludge, the acid raining down from the web of overhead piping feeding the phalanx of holding tanks ranked against the opposite walls. A flooded conduit ran the length of the floor and against the farthest wall a massive fan chopped the air lazily.

"This is hell," the kid breathed.

"Not at all," the boss retorted, his voice ringing off the metal. "This is smokestack America, a piece of living history." He turned to the floor. "I have to go and get those pipes emptied. We need those lights fixed as well and I want to get that fan moving properly.

We need some air in here or we're going to suffocate. Mike, take the kid to the canteen and show him the rest of the crew. I'll get you when everything's set up."

Mike led the way from the warehouse, out past the brickwork labs where no one worked, and past the silent workshops littered with discarded tools toward a raised timber shack that may at one time have been painted. Inside, seated in a booth, he was introduced to the rest of the crew. There were three in all. Jeff, the boss's younger brother, a heavy slob in his early thirties with none of his brother's military bearing. He was sprawled out blowing smoke rings at the ceiling, his Adam's apple exposed. Kevin and Leo were in their early twenties, friends of Mike and both bearing the gray hue of a binge that had not entirely been purged from their systems; both were drinking black, unsugared coffee. In true American fashion he shook hands with them all and they made room for him in the booth. Jeff was curious.

"So what brings you to America, the land of the fee and the home of the bribe?"

"A student visa." The kid tried to smile but gave up when the corners of his mouth wouldn't work. He lowered his eyes. "For three months." It sounded like an apology.

"No need to be ashamed, boy, we're all doing life here. What are you studying?"

"English and philosophy. I hope to graduate next year."

"We're all graduates here, too," Leo said. "Honors students from the University of Budweiser, doing postgrad in booze and beaver."

"You know Jack shit about beaver," Kevin said. "Pam and her five sisters is your limit. Leo is all talk, kid, all talk and no tackle."

The kid finally managed a smile, a thin, composite expression, more pain than mirth.

"One thing's for sure, you'll find no women or booze in this fuck of a place. You're not likely to learn much either."

"Is it as bad as it looks?"

"No, it's a lot worse. This place is the devil's asshole, kid, once you're here there's no getting away from it."

"Do you not go out after work, for a beer or something? It's real hot in that warehouse."

Jeff shook his head. "There's no time. We work nearly eighty hours a week on this contract, anything to get it finished. Take it from me, you're not fit for much when you've done a day's work in this place, you just crash into bed. Pussy will be the last thing on your mind."

They talked and smoked awhile longer, downing more coffee to kill off the deep-rooted hangovers. The kid learned quickly that there were only two topics of conversation in blue-collar America—sex and money—and it wasn't always obvious which of the two was at issue. Presently the boss arrived, carrying a clipboard, all business.

"Are we ready?" he asked. "Have we scratched and smoked enough? If we have then it's time to rock. I've got lights set up and the fan working so let's go." He swung his arm in a beckoning arc and the crew got up and followed him.

In the warehouse two carbon arc lamps had been mounted on stands and were casting a lunar glow over the floor. Against the farthest wall the fan now moved at full speed, tumbling heavy wads of warm air through the length of the room. The pools glistened blackly all around, heavily cast over with fleeting rainbows. John was handing out rubber moccasins and heavy gloves.

"Pull these on; those boots will fall off your feet in two days if you don't. Keep these gloves on, too." He turned to the floor. "First thing we do is unblock that conduit, see can we get as much of this fluid as possible to run out into the manholes. Mike, you and Kevin get shovels and work through its length. The rest of you, get squeegees and start moving that slop toward the door." As the rest of the crew moved off he turned to the kid and gave him one last appraisal.

"OK, kid, this is your chance. Now we get to see what you're made of."

Working under the carbon lights, in the sharp reek of the acid, they spent the rest of the day drying out the floor, slopping the heavy sludge with the rubber squeegees, and then using the vacuums to suck up the residue from the pools. By the end of the day the floor glistened like a sand flat and they brought in a series of blowers to continue the drying overnight. As they were leaving the kid was standing by the truck, inspecting his blistered hands.

"Piss on them," the boss said, coming up behind him.

"What?"

"Piss on them," he repeated. "It will wash them out and the salt will harden them. You'll get no infection either."

"Yah, sure," the kid replied.

"Have it your way then."

But as they drove to the motel they made a stop at a drugstore and the boss presented him with a small package—a bottle of meths, some cotton wool, and a roll of lint.

"Thanks."

"Don't thank me; it's an investment, not a present. I'm not losing any time with those hands."

"You won't."

"Damn right I won't."

The real work began the next day, breaking up the floor with the massive jackhammers and barrowing out the rubble to the refuse tip near the lake. The kid vied gamely for his turn on the jackhammer and then caused much guffawing among the rest of the crew when he was thrown off balance in a heap by its first surge of power. But he got up and tried again, gritted his teeth, and hung on for twenty minutes before handing it over to Mike. He stood clenching and unclenching his numbed hands, shaking from the vibrations. In the canteen his hands still shook and he slopped his coffee at the first gulp. So, for a time he drank from a straw, and for long after it was necessary, just for the clown value of it.

But very quickly, after a few days, he found nascent muscle in his arms and back and he was able to take his full turn. He stood with his legs braced apart and his arms stiffened, the massive vibrations shaking every bone in his torso, his head pounding with rhythm and his whole being running with adrenaline. A definite change had come over the kid: he was happy and he had begun to smile and his hands were healing fast. Best of all he knew that he had hacked it, knew it in his heart, and knew it from Mike that the boss was well pleased with him. He had no worries about holding down the job for the rest of the summer.

By the end of the first week the kid was having a feeling of almost total rejuvenation. The chemical plant became his element and he thrived in it like a hothouse orchid. He began to flex the new-born muscles in his arms and back and they were wondrous as wings, and he took to walking around at every opportunity with his shirt off, singing crazy fragments of songs, his white torso glowing in the pale light. The boss was unimpressed.

"Put it back on," he told him curtly. "You're not Charles Atlas yet."

Beneath the arc lights, with the compressors and blowers working, the warehouse grew baking hot. After the first hour's work their bodies ran with sweat and their shirts clung like second skins. They took it in turns to foray into the daylight for fresh air. The kid preferred to walk to the refuse tip on the waste ground behind the warehouses and stand on its low peak where he caught the thin breeze that blew in over the lake. He would stand there on the summit for the duration of a cigarette, slick and steaming like a newborn thing.

He was finding himself enchanted by the place. Like a child his mind took in the palette of decay spread all around him, the green murk of the lake, the copper tones of the rusted metal and faded paintwork, the blackened chimney of the incinerators; all these colors fixed his imagination into a coherent spectrum of ruin. The kid now knew that there was no other fact in creation, no other dynamic in the world except this corrosion and wearing away, this attrition which seemed to level everything down to a uniform plane of ruin and which had this chemical plant as its center and origin. And he stood there in the middle of this desolation, a newborn god, lithe and keen-eyed, ready to spread his wings.

He never stayed long in the open sunlight anymore; he would stub his cigarette and return quickly to the sanctum of the warehouse. Sunshine no longer had anything to offer him.

While he worked the kid developed a theory about the plant; it became a pet project. One evening at the motel, sprawling among the empty pizza boxes and beer tins, he spoke about it. It was his longest soliloquy so far.

"The way I see it, the whole plant is a kind of monument, a cautionary symbol of waste and deterioration, emblematic of all the piss-poor aspirations and materialist dreams of the century. The whole place is a work of art, a piece of kinetic sculpture."

"Is that so?" said Mike, his voice thick with doubt and hash. He was lying on the bed blowing heavy smoke rings. "Then what am I doing here? I'm not an artist, all I do is work with fiberglass. I'm a repairman."

"That's just it, you're not a repairman." The kid was real excited now, his eyes like two pitch bores in the middle of his skull. "This place is not broken, it does not need repair, and no matter how it looks it's not falling apart either. All it's doing, day after day, is refining itself, coming more clearly into its own identity. And its identity is one of rot and decay and corrosion. That is why we lay down a new floor or lag a few pipes every year. It gives it something new to feed off."

The kid was aware that the rest of the crew was looking at him in slack-jawed amazement; the boss seemed to be staring at him with special intensity. He could feel the flush on his cheeks from the fervor of his words and he had the horrible feeling that he had made some sort of fool of himself. Then he saw Mike grinning at him, shaking his head as if he had caught him doing something obscene.

"I think you're full of shit," he said, without losing his grin. "Full of shit like a whore's outhouse."

The kid sighed with relief.

"Fuck you, too," he said, well glad of his escape.

They now had the entire floor lifted down to the foundation and they spent most of their time vacuuming the uneven surfaces, preparing it for the readymix. They spent three days shoveling the concrete, three days of backbreaking labor bent close to the ground with short shovels carrying massive blades. Then they got down on their knees and moved over the floor, section by section, with a two-by-four on its edge, screeding it to a smooth finish. When they had finished the last section more time was needed for it to dry out completely.

"We'll give it two days," the boss said. "Two days and no more. Till then I've got work set up in a few places. Mike, take the kid to the opposite warehouse. Inside you'll find a series of flues. Their inner surfaces need relining. Show the kid how to work with fiber-glass, give him his first taste of it."

In the warehouse they found the flues, four of them dismantled and mounted on trestles, their inner surfaces black and pitted. There was an assortment of paintbrushes and fiberglass matting among the other tools on the ground.

"There's only a good day's work here," Mike concluded.

"Well, maybe at last I will get to work with some fiberglass. I haven't seen one bit since I started this job."

"We'd better make a start then," Mike said. Reaching for one of the grinders he handed it to the kid. "OK," he said. "Grab a hold of this."

The kid was shown how to clean out the inner surface of the flues and how to use the grinder smoothly and lightly in long, curv-ing strokes and how to sweep out the dust and apply styrene. He was shown also how to cut the fiberglass mat with a minimum of over-lap and how to lay it seamlessly within the curved surface before coating it with chemical resin and finally how to get a smooth finish by carefully laying down the thin veil of gossamer fiber on the glis-tening surface. The kid relished this change from the brute labor of the floor. He had proven himself in that sweat and muscle arena, now was the time to pick up a skill. The kid learned fast and the work went well; by midafternoon they had nearly half the flues completed.

"Let's take a break," Mike said. He was wiping his hands on a rag steeped in acetone. "We're well ahead. There's no hurry. Let's get some coffee and a cigarette."

The kid shook his head. "I'm going to take a walk around the plant, have a last look at it before I go. We've only got a few days left." He jammed the hat on his head and walked from the warehouse. Mike watched his stark form disappear through the brightened entrance of the loading bay and for one instant he could have sworn the kid exuded all the light about him.

The kid walked beyond the tool crib and canteen, past the lab complex that sidearmed round one shore of the lake, and onto the waste ground that ran as far as the perimeter fence. It lay strewn with fragments of brick and timber: saw grass grew heavy over treacherous lengths of abandoned piping. From the perimeter fence he had a full view of the plant. It was laid out like some childish construct of cubes and cylinders. From its center the blackened chimney sent up a plume of heavy smoke that curved out over the far perimeter, a beacon to the wider world. At the base of the plant the lake reflected the sky like a tarnished mirror.

The kid felt a sudden pain in his chest. To his amazement he found himself on the verge of tears. He began to talk to himself.

"I love this place," he said. "This is my home and I belong here. I know everything it says about decay and ruin and corrosion and they are all truths to me. And now look at me: have I not grown strong by them?"

At the far end of the waste ground he saw the boss walking toward him, picking his way cautiously as if he were walking on marsh land.

"Having a last look?" he asked when he finally drew up.

"Something like that," the kid said. "A kind of overview before I leave. I'll miss this place when I leave. I've learned things here."

The boss nodded. "When I saw you first at the tool yard I didn't think you could hack it in this job. But I was wrong. You've thrived in this place, you've got stronger, and you even talk more. In all my years of working with different men I have never known anyone to be so affected by such a place."

"It's this place all right," the kid replied. "I think it's beautiful. This place is a work of art and I've reacted to it as I would to a work of art. I've been transformed by it, I've been inspired by it." The kid seemed to glow in the sunlight, his face and arms luminescing against the scorched color of the grass—for a moment the boss had a vision of insect larvae. The kid was staring vacantly at the plant, lost in some idyll of ruin and decay, totally unprepared for the vehemence of the boss's attack.

"I've heard enough of that shit," he said suddenly. "Enough of that crap. This whole place is a death trap, nothing more and nothing less." He swung the kid round by the arm, facing him into the perimeter fence. "Two miles down the road from here there is a small village called Wickhurst, no more than a hundred people. Three years ago it buried four infants, all of them with skin blued over from arsenic poisoning. Groundwater contamination was traced to this plant. On the far side of this plant a dairy farmer opened a pit on the margins of his land and buried a third of his herd in it, all of them asphyxiated by windborne emissions. Their carcasses couldn't be used for dog food. So no more shit about this place being some sort of monument; it's a death trap and that's all there is to it. No more theorizing or philosophizing. You work for me now so just make sure that you do good work and check once in a while to see that your head has not run away with your ass."

He threw his cigarette to the ground in a lavish gesture of disgust and strode away heavily through the grass.

The kid needed the isolation of the perimeter fence to get over his shock. The boss's words and violence seemed to have sprung from some personal wound. The kid could not believe that he harbored any resentment toward him. He found himself trembling, unable to account for the vicious turn of mood. He stayed a long time at the perimeter, leaning against the wire, feeling the lattice pattern imprint itself in his skin. Presently, he pushed himself away and returned to where his work was among the cylinder and cube abstract.

ˋ   ˋ   ˋ

As he worked the rest of that evening he thought over what the boss had said about the deaths and contaminations. He was not surprised to find no revulsion or horror within himself, just a clear forensic curiosity prompting him to seek more information.

"Do you know about the deaths and contaminations that this plant is supposed to be responsible for?"

Mike nodded. "Sure, we all know. This plant has paid out over five million dollars in environmental lawsuits during the last decade, spillages, groundwater contamination, emissions, the works. Even now it's tied up in more court cases than you can count. Why do you ask?"

"Just now I met John and he gave me a fucking about my attitude toward this place. He thinks that I'm besotted with it and he told me to get a grip on myself. Then he told me about the dead babies and the dead cattle. He wasn't pleased. How do you feel about working here?"

"I hate this place. I begrudge every moment that I have to spend here; I wonder what it does to my soul. I imagine it corroding away every minute I spend here like one of those pipes or tanks." There was no trace of irony in his voice, just a dark knife edge of bitterness. "But it's work," he continued, "and that's why I do it. I've worked for John for six years since the mid-eighties, the boom years when we could pick and choose work. But it's not like that now. Work is real tight and we need this contract. It can get us over three slack months and all the winter months are slack ones. Besides, if we didn't do it, someone else would."

"And John doesn't like it either?"

"Not a bit. He took over this contract from another company who abandoned it after those kids were killed. This contract saved his company from going under. John used to employ ten men back in those peak times. Now his crew is down to us."

"Have you ever thought of doing other work?"

Mike shrugged. "I like this work. Besides, I owe John, he took me on first and I became his foreman. Now he's over a barrel. He hates this contract but he needs it to keep his company. He's got kids and alimony as well so he can't afford to let it go. But I think he worries about his soul also. And he's worried about you, too. What he does not like is your enthusiasm for the place. You've been working and singing and talking your head off since you've come here like a man possessed. I think it scares him. I think he believes you might have caught some sort of bug here."

"Maybe he's right," the kid said. "Look what's happened to me since I've started working in this place. I've never felt happier or stronger. I'm sure if I checked I'd find that I've put on weight. Now I'm told about all these deaths and pollutions but it doesn't change a thing for me. I don't feel any different toward the place. I'd be telling a lie if I said I did."

"You can't deny what you feel," Mike said dryly. He had just tidied away the last of the tools and the flues now glistened like split fruit. "Just remember that you are the only one who feels that way. Unlike you, most of us would give a lot to have this contract somewhere else. Remember that when you start eulogizing next time."

During the final days, as they laid the fiberglass covering, the kid seemed to reach a new peak of well-being. His body now soared with such energy he seemed to have difficulty just standing still and despite Mike's cautions he could not stop himself singing as he worked, bawling out isolated phrases and choruses over the clamor of the fan, making the others grimace, not entirely in mock pain either.

Pour shame all over us
Harden it into a crust-cement

The boss did not hide his annoyance. "Shut the fuck up," he yelled. "Thank Christ we're moving out of here in a few days. Maybe then you'll calm down and quit acting like you've got a belly full of amphetamines."

"I can't help it," the kid said. "I've never felt better in my life. Look at this." He held out his arms from his body and bunched up his biceps and pectorals like a bodybuilder posing in a competition. "Charles Atlas or what?"

"Only a sick fuck could thrive in a place like this," the boss retorted.

"Then I must be a sick fuck," the kid said. "Where do we go after this?"

"Maine, one week at an Ocean Spray plant. Good clean outdoor work relining concrete containers. You might get some sun on that white ass of yours."

"Or I might fry. I'll be sad to leave here. Home is where the heart is."

"It's news to me that you have one."

The kid just shrugged.

The fiberglass was laid quickly, the glistening strips advancing over the floor, slick and heavy like an oil spillage, drying finally into a dull sheen. On the third day they laid down the final veil covering, bonding it down with a last coat of resin. Then they stood back at the doorway, taking a last moment to appraise their work. The floor shone with nocturnal radiance, like a pool seen in a dream. From above, the metal containers were reflected in its illusory depths.

"How long will it last?" the kid wanted to know.

"It should last forever," the boss said. "But nothing lasts forever in this place. Too much heavy chemical will be spilled on it and too many heavy weights will crash down and crack it. Probably next year whole sections of it will have lifted up and ruined, like every other piece of work we've done here." He turned quickly in disgust. "Come on," he yelled. "Get these tools rounded up and let's get the hell out of here. I'm sick to death of this place."

It was only thirty minutes' work to gather up the tools and place them in the back of the truck. They worked quickly, rejuvenated at the prospect of leaving. As he came out of the warehouse the boss squinted in disbelief when he saw the kid walking to the truck carrying the last pieces, the two jackhammers dangling at the ends of his arms, his whole torso a knotted cartography of muscle. He lowered them gently into the back of the truck and then turned with a wide grin on his face.

"When I started this job I couldn't lift one of those hammers. Now I can measure my well-being in pounds and ounces."

"So now you're twice the man."

"Not twice the man. Just different, different altogether. Listen, I've even developed a singing voice." For the last time the kid broke into song.

> *Forget the glamor*
> *And mumble a jackhammer*
> *Under your breath.*

The kid was dancing now, too, prancing by the side of the truck in some improvised step, swinging his arms in the failing light to hold his balance. The boss watched him carefully and for a fleeting moment he had a vision of the kid taking flight, his fingertips finding some impossible grip on the air and hoisting him higher into the gloom, up by the warehouse wall and out over the lake like some cancerous angel. It was an epiphany of beauty and ruin and the boss was lost in it for a few moments until Mike rounded the side of the truck, an unlit cigarette jammed in his mouth. He gazed for a long moment at the dancing kid.

"That kid needs his head seen to," he said solemnly.

The boss nodded, moving his head slowly, as if supporting a great weight.

"His head among other things."

They stood looking awhile longer and all the time the kid continued dancing, his broken image soaring in the curved surfaces of the holding tanks. And he continued dancing, dancing, dancing even after he had stopped singing.

Machine: Part II

The relevant clause of my grandfather's will reads thus: "I, Christopher Monk, being of sound mind and body, do bequeath to my grandson Peter that which has become my life's work, 'The Machine.' " That is as simple as it was, how by death and documentation I came to possess "The Machine" and as a consequence my vocation as a mechanic.

I will attempt a description of my grandfather since descriptions of all other things are more problematic. In brief, he was a tall, ancient man with wild hair and white teeth, a man much given to grim laughter and forgetfulness. At least that was how he looked to me in the crucial six months toward the end of his life when he would fill me with unease by looking down from his great height and, placing his hand on my young skull, intone softly, "Peter my boy, one day it will all be yours."

As a young man Grandfather was the first in the parish to have a motorcar—a 1938 black Humber that roared its way over the unsurfaced roads of West Mayo to dances in Newport, Kilmeena, and, farther north, Ballina. The car conferred on him such prestige and eligibility that nobody was surprised when he married shortly after he bought it and well within the year had an only son, Christopher Junior, my father. It was then that Grandfather set up the small garage that was to be his livelihood until he signed it over completely to Dad in the early eighties. This garage was born with a flourish that would typify Grandfather's style for the rest of his life. Undeterred by the absence of trade and his near total lack of technical knowledge, Grandfather erected over the doorway to his workshop a carefully painted sign: CHRISTOPHER MONK AND SON LTD. ENGINEERS.

But by perseverance and trial and error, Grandfather did develop a real feel for the steadily growing number of stalled and defective machines that staggered to his workshop. Initially it was cars suffering from dirty carburetors, blown gaskets, and bad steering alignment, but gradually the great, truculent hulks of agricultural machinery made their appearance. These were the machines that he clasped to his heart, these machines that came out with the sun and the crops and that, in such a few short years, signified by their presence and absence the cycles and times of the years: turf cutters in early spring with long arms awry in need of welding jobs, mowing machines in late summer needing teeth, and threshing machines with broken spindles in late autumn. These were the machines that enamored Grandfather, these yearly machines of birth and renewal that lumbered along the still unsurfaced roads, a proud and kingly species.

How he began work on "The Machine" no one can remember. All any of us can say is that shortly after signing over the garage he rose one morning at dawn on a sudden inspiration and locked himself into an abandoned workshop at the end of the yard. He stayed there the entire day and emerged only at nightfall, haggard and drawn from some occult exertions upon which he would not be brought to speak. My mom remarked that Grandfather in fact never emerged from the workshop that evening but was replaced instead by some jaded version of himself. And my father agreed, saying dryly and to no effect, "He was never the same."

What happened from then on in the shed was a mystery. There was never any noise or commotion from it but the place was locked and out of bounds. From time to time he would wander out into the main workshop searching absently for an angle grinder or welding rods and retire with them without a word into his lair as if he had never emerged. His routine was now to rise at dawn and after breakfast make toward the workshop, clutching in his fist the mug of tea that would be his sole nourishment until he emerged toward nightfall, spring and summer, gray and distracted, to wolf down a huge feed of milk and spuds and meat. At the table he would make some mechanical inquiries on the weather for the following day, business in the garage, or the health of some ailing neighbor. But these were futile inquiries, incapable of bringing this strange, preoccupied old man back into the circle of his family. No sooner would he have uttered his queries than he had forgotten about them, risen from the table, and gone to bed where he lay in a sleep so deep and dreamless it might have been a coma. I now know him to have been a man suffering in the maze of an inspiration, the inspiration of his own death. But in those last months he had become such a complete stranger that our house could not have been more discomfited if an Old Testament prophet, crazed and engodded, had come to live with us. Therefore I must shamefully admit to a feeling of relief on that autumn evening when, on his return from the workshop, I saw his thin frame stricken down in the yard by the hammer blow of a heart attack.

But now and again there were diversions. Some days, instead of going to the workshop, he would ask me to accompany him on what he termed "metal forage." We would raise the generator into the back of the truck and get out two angle grinders, then we would travel into the boglands and up the side roads to where almost inevitably, as if waiting for us, we would come upon the marooned hull of some abandoned Ford or truck. Then, donning our dust masks and goggles, we would set to dismantling it. Toward night we would return and dump these mangled and rusted pieces of metal at the door of the workshop: in the morning he would begin hauling them in.

One day, a few months before his death, we went on a major expedition. With spare discs for the grinders, a flask of tea, and a bag of sandwiches beside us we set off in a northwestern direction, out onto the Erris peninsula, onto a topography where bog stretched away on all sides to the horizon. Driving down a side road we came upon a huge resource of abandoned machinery. There was an antiquated diesel engine with its windows smashed and the fuel long since gone plus a stricken bulldozer without tracks looking like a felled beast. A small railway track led off into the bog carrying the skeletons of a few carriages, the timber stripped from their frames. But the dominant machines were two massive turf cutters. They stood there like becalmed ships, the toppled mainmasts of their cutting arms extended out over the bog. They were cloaked in rust and they were obviously what we had come for.

Grandfather explained to me that this had been a state project that had been abandoned in the late sixties when, after years of cutting away the overlying bog, the granite beneath had suddenly surfaced and put an end to the whole thing. By that time the machines were so run-down and outdated they were simply left there to the corrosion of the wind and the rain and their slowly deteriorating identities.

I was moved by the place. With its lunar stillness and the rust covering everything like a winding sheet and the heather clawing its way up into the engines, it seemed to me a place of tragedy. My heart ached for these noble and now abandoned machines, left sightless and immobile, sacrificed to principles of efficiency and performance. And yet, despite all this and the birds of prey that hovered overhead, this was not a place of death. These machines had about them the poised and breathless quality of things that waited in anticipation of some momentous arrival, something that would come forth and be so new that it would disturb both the living and the dead—leaving nothing the same ever again. Some fundamental and irremediable adjustment would be affected in the fabric of things when it made its appearance. This was the kind of resonance that was in the air.

We set to dismantling the turf machines and it was then that I learned the first law of metal forage. I had in mind to amass an impressive pile of gear boxes and transmissions, all complex, three-dimensional structures, when Grandfather came over to me shaking his head: "No, no, no, go for the straight lengths and the curved ones, the simple pieces. That's where the secrets lie." He pointed to his own pile, a tidy collection of straight lengths and curved pieces lying within each other. "Those pieces," he said, pointing to mine, "are too used."

In our dust masks and goggles we bent over the machines for the rest of the day like surgeons—or was it priests?—and by evening we had a huge pile of corroded metal loaded on the truck. I took a final look at the now ravaged machines and saw that Grandfather was moving among them, stroking their pitted surfaces as if they were living things, offering some compensation for his pillage. I saw him stop and then extend his hands out over the machines in a hieratic gesture. He was intoning softly, as if they had ears:

"Come unto me all you who labor and are burdened and I will give you rest."

With that said he climbed into the truck and we journeyed homeward in silence. Things returned to normal the next morning. He was up early unloading the metal into the dark womb of the workshop. I left him to it—he made it clear that my help was no longer needed.

When the small catastrophe of his death had subsided and his will had been read out I went to the workshop to appraise my inheritance. Switching on the light I first reacted with awe and disappointment. At this point it may be of some use to inquire what I thought lay behind the great timber door, for surely I must have had some preconceptions. Yes, I did. I had long been familiar with the strange fruit of Grandfather's errant imagination, but this time my preconceptions were without definite form. All I could think of was some strange and utterly unprecedented machine that would perform a function no one had ever dreamed of, but as to the shape this machine would take I had no idea. And now that I was faced with it finally I felt both awe and disappointment; awe at the sheer size of the thing, for, from a base of ten feet square, it rose to a jagged pinnacle the full height of the workshop, a good twenty feet; disappointment in that it conformed in no way to any previous machine I had ever encountered. Roughly speaking—very roughly, for it defied, and still does even now, any descriptive ability or category that I can lay my hand on—it was a skeletal structure of pyramidal shape, a welded structure of rusted metal and jarring colors that was so big it was possible to climb inside it, rather like an elaborate and decrepit child's climbing frame. Within its structure were recognizable all the component parts we had collected.

What I am describing is obviously not a machine but a work of art, a thing of craftsmanship and, most of all, inspiration. But even in those first moments, I knew that this was to simplify it, to reduce it to the lowest form of its identity and meaning while allowing its greater truth to remain concealed. Oh yes, even then I knew that it was much more than a work of art. It was then that my mother came in behind me and raised me toward some insight when, wringing her hands in a mixture of grief and exasperation, she said simply, "Whatever it is it's not natural." Then she pointed toward an outcrop of suspension near the base upon which lay a sheet of paper covered in my grandfather's tight script. It was headed "MACHINE: PART II" and it continued:

Dear Peter,

I will set you straight from the beginning since you have been led astray by the relevant clause in my will. What you are looking at is not my life's work but is in fact something much more important: it is my death's work. The inspiration for it came to me slowly over all the years I have worked in the garage and seen all those limping and broken machines come to me for repair. It came to me slowly that, like our-selves, these machines were essentially religious beings who exist as we do ourselves according to religious principles. As we live in accordance with those laws of love and worship that have been revealed to us, so we have handed to these machines the principles of efficiency and performance. And like ourselves, being both fallible and finite, they will fall from these principles into obsolescence, disrepair, and break-age. And so they were brought to me for a form of redemp-tion. With a few repairs, a spot weld here, a new gasket there, I would restore them to the principles of their rightful being—I was in fact offering a form of forgiveness.

As time went on and the number of machines increased, I realized that what was needed was not this grudging and piecemeal form of forgiveness but a lavish gesture that would rescue these machines for all time, such a gesture as we our-selves had been rescued by. Having found my obsession my mind was set. Now all I had to decide upon was in what realm I would work out and achieve this forgiveness. It would obvi-ously have to be in some field of human endeavor since we were responsible for these machines and their ultimate failure as God is for ours. When the idea came to me finally, I was pleased with its symmetry and irony, its general fitness for the task. Working within the realm of art, I would erect a symbol of forgiveness, a symbol of God's love for all his creatures and artifacts, a symbol in which those to whom it was addressed would have participation. Thus, a piece of sculpture that would incorporate the very things it was meant to save. As for the necessary sacrifice, God in his own time and wisdom would provide.

It worked better than I had imagined. There was no shortage of material and after a few exploratory models to perfect the design the sculpture flourished beneath my hand. And so, too, was a sacrifice provided. As I worked I felt the strength draining from me. Day by day it ebbed till toward the end I feared I would not be granted enough to finish the task. But now that I have finished I see God's wisdom and economy and realize that I was granted strength enough and no more to finish and provide this explanation. I know that when I walk out of here tonight it will be for the last time. At this moment my work and my life are completed. Therefore, Peter, forget the structure and the design—it is after all only the visible symbol. Focus instead on the suffering and the intention, for it is there that its true identity lies. And finally, remember one last thing: it is no accident that your name is Peter and such a name is a destiny.

Your grandfather
Christopher Monk

And that is how I was left with this mysterious, corroding symbol, this symbol that I have never moved nor altered, and how also I received my vocation as a mechanic. A few days after reading the script, I got in the truck and traveled out once more to the abandoned bog project on the Erris peninsula. When I got there everything had changed—there were no machines, just bogland stretching in a continuous vista with nothing but blue sky overhead. In the middle of the bog a new metal sign had been erected by the authorities: THIS AREA HAS BEEN CLEARED AND PRESERVED AS A WILDLIFE SANCTUARY BY THE BOARD OF PUBLIC WORKS. DUMPING STRICTLY PROHIBITED.

That made me smile because deep in my soul I know it is a lie. I know that those machines were not simply cleared away to municipal dumps to disintegrate and die among other machines, but that they and others like them were reconciled with their savior, Christopher Monk, my grandfather, in the new kingdom of heaven.

Materials Grant

Any day now, any day.

It's going to happen any day now and when it does I'm going to be there, pouncing on him from the shadows, my teeth bared and my claws spread. I've been watching him these last weeks like a hawk and, as he's predicted, all the signs are falling into place. All the signals point to a massive breakdown of his whole psyche, the collapse of his weak, attenuated soul. And when it does I'm going to be there, sleek and poised, my muscles straining. The minutes are falling like knives, this time of waiting is at an end. My instruments are clean and ready to hand—I am ready.

He's in bad shape. He who was such a tower of strength, I wouldn't have thought he could sink so low. He now inhabits the house like a revenant, blundering from room to room with no purpose in mind. He can't sleep, he hasn't eaten in four days, and he bears all the signs of it. A blue, almost translucent hue has entered his skin and the veins of his temples stand out like purple knots. There is an inconceivable tension within him: when he moves I can hear the plexus of his entire nervous system chime like a misstrung harp. Every ashtray in the house is full and sometimes in the middle of the night I hear him sitting here in the darkness carrying on a monologue with no one but himself. These are bitter times.

And it's not as if he doesn't have labor enough to occupy and distract him. Each day new tasks pile up to either side of him and each day he is stricken in disbelief. Each morning I find him transfixed in terror, clutching his hair, marveling aloud that the world can be so lush with vexations.

Yes, I could do something for him. After all he is closer to me than my own brother. I could extend a helping hand, make speeches of reassurance, bolster his confidence and self-esteem but that is not my job. My job now is to bear witness, to idly stand by, to harbor him silently into his ruin.

There is no telling what form it will take or how it will leave him. A gibbering wreck or a blade-wielding psycho, all that is in the gift of the future. There is no past form against which it can be anticipated, he has no previous history of anything like this—he was always so quick to boast of his spiritual health. Consequently I have taken no precautions or protective measures.

Without shame or guilt I assert my moral right. I have been granted salvage rights over him and I will exploit them to the full. I will pick through the rubble and debris and I will single out those pieces that are mine. My instincts will not betray me and it is not in his nature to disappoint: I trust him completely. He only asks that I stay by his side and never leave him alone. He is committed to meeting the calamity head on. I am humbled by his courage.

He is moving again. I must follow.

The Reach of Love

Five months into my mom's second pregnancy Dad began working out the details of my sister's immortality.

On the evening of the amniocentesis that confirmed finally that I would at last have a sister, he arrived home from town joyously drunk. In the sitting room where Mom and I sat watching telly, he stood clutching a bottle of Bushmills in one hand and a glass in the other, swaying back and forth in the middle of the floor like a man bracing a small boat. He gulped back a mouthful of whiskey and began to treat us to a long speech dealing with history and the state of the world. He touched on several apocalyptic themes—the dwindling ozone layer, the pillage of the earth's finite resources, the declining western economies, and the continuing population boom among others. Finally he tied up the threads of his discourse by slopping more whiskey and announcing boldly that, as of this moment, he was renouncing the procreative urge; after the birth of my sister and his daughter there would be no more babies in the Monk household. There was a pause here for more whiskey before he continued. His life had been enriched by marriage to a beautiful woman who had borne him a fine son—his words, I swear—and now fortune had seen fit to extend to him the daughter he had longed for. He had his health and a roof over his head and all in all it would take the fingers of both hands to total up his blessings—a man could ask for no more. He paused again for more whiskey and continued on a cautionary note. Yes, it was true, a man could ask for more and the sorry state of the world was testimony to the fact that more men were asking for more every day of the week, but he, Christopher Monk, would countenance no such greed in his own heart. He had consequently decided to burden the world with no more expectations. In short, to use his own phrase, he was going to tie a knot in it. He continued swaying and slopping the whiskey as he refilled his glass. He then proposed a toast, heedless to the fact that he was the only one in the room with a drink.

"Life," he said, raising his glass. "And plenty of it."

He then nearly keeled into the fire before Mom grabbed his hand and both of us dragged him off to bed and took off his boots. His fifteen stone bulk rid us of any notion we might have had of trying to get him beneath the covers. We threw a quilt over him and left him there, sprawled out diagonally on the bed, snoring like a felled giant. For the first time in her marriage Mom slept alone in the spare room.

Next day Dad returned from town with a box of Solpadiene and a new telescope. He announced that he was going to examine the heavens. We took the announcement in our stride: Dad had always been a dabbler. Once it had been local history. In a rush of enthusiasm he had compiled a neat index of all the neolithic and megalithic monuments in our parish, marking them out on an Ordnance Survey map that had covered an entire wall of the kitchen. This map became a major talking point among the men who came to our garage to get their cars seen to. Then this historical map had been replaced by a geological one that mapped out the rock formations of Clew Bay and the surrounding Mweelera mountains. His immediate interest had been the news that these mountains were yielding up six ounces of gold to a ton of limestone, the richest strike in Europe since the Bohemian mines of the seventeenth century. Dad was worried.

"A total and utter disaster," he had opined grimly. "Do they not know the damage extensive mining could do to an area like this? All that pounding and grinding down of rock, not to mention the amount of cyanide needed to wash it."

These words marked Dad's entry into public life. Later, he had become something of a local hero when, as head of the antimining lobby, he had taken their case through the length and breadth of the legal system and finally, in the Supreme Court, wrung a concession from the government to ban all mining in the area till well into the next millennium. Till the arrival of the telescope the geological map had hung on the wall, a frayed monument to his tenacity and that glorious victory for local democracy.

The day the telescope arrived the map was taken down without ceremony and replaced with color plates from *The Philips Book of Astronomy*. The pages of the book covered the entire wall between the kitchen sink and the window facing onto the backyard. From his place at the head of the table, Dad had a full view of the entire northern sky, its planets and constellations, nebulae and meteors. The room itself seemed to open out into space now, out into those far galaxies where the stellar winds blew and the music of the spheres chimed. The visionary in Dad was well pleased with the effect.

After the wall was papered he took the telescope onto the flat roof of the garage and bolted down the tripod against the winds that blew in from the sea. He then switched off the light in the yard and spent a long time peering through the lens, sweeping back and forth through the heavens and taking down notes with the help of a flash-light in one of my foolscaps. Mom and I just looked at each other and shrugged; Dad had another bee in his bonnet, no doubt we'd find out about it soon enough.

One evening, after some time writing and scanning, he came into the sitting room and called Mom out to the garage. I watched from the kitchen window and saw them talking at the foot of the ladder that led onto the roof. Evidently Dad wanted her to climb up. I saw Mom protest, a look of consternation on her face. She was pointing to her swollen tummy. She turned to come back to the house but Dad grabbed her wrist and seemed to plead some more with her, holding her face between his hands and leaning his forehead onto hers until she finally relented. She mounted the ladder cautiously, making her way heavily, rung by rung with Dad behind her, his hand on her waist. When they were together on the roof he stood close to her and swept his hand over the sky, pointing out constellations and vivid stars, then finally bringing it to rest open-palmed against one sector of the heavens. He kept it there and talked closely to her for a few minutes, his mouth almost on her ear. Then she turned and kissed him deeply, embracing him tightly for a long moment. What was going on? I was then mortified to see Dad stand behind her and lift up her sweater and T-shirt, exposing her swollen bump to the night sky. She leaned back into his arms with her eyes closed and he continued to stroke her exposed flesh. I turned from the window, deeply embarrassed.

When Mom came in minutes later she was smiling and shaking her head, looking real pleased. She saw my agitation.

"That man is daft," she said. "Pure daft. As daft as a ha'penny watch."

"What's he doing?" I could hardly contain myself.

"You'd better ask him yourself. Coming from me it would sound crazy, coming from him it just sounds daft. A good daftness though," she said. "The daftness of love." Her smile broadened now over her entire face—she was gently enjoying my disadvantage. "Go out and ask him."

On the roof Dad was taking down more notes. I didn't know how he stood the cold—I cursed for not wearing a jacket. The night was clear and the sky glistened heavily; I could hear the sea booming onto the pier a quarter mile distant. To the west I could see the lights of Louisburgh, our little town.

"Dad, what the hell are you looking at?" I sounded gruffer than I felt.

"What does it look like I'm looking at?" He spoke without lifting his head from the copy.

"You can't be just looking at the stars."

"That's true," he said, "I'm not. I'm not looking *at,* I'm looking *for,* I'm looking for your sister." He was looking at me now without a trace of mockery.

"I didn't know that the stork flew at night; besides, it would be four months early."

He ignored my witticism and left down his copy.

"Have you ever thought of how much death there is in the world?"

I swallowed hard. I hated these man-to-man talks. I remembered a similar feeling of trepidation as a ten-year-old when Dad had tried to instruct me in the facts of life. That discussion had been abandoned by mutual consent after a few minutes, when it became obvious that I, a voracious and indiscriminate reader, knew more about the ins and outs, dead ends, and cul-de-sacs of twentieth-century sexuality than he did himself.

"Why should I think about dying? I'm only sixteen. I don't plan on dying for sixty years yet."

"You're dead right," he said. "It would be a sorry theme for a young man your age. But I think a lot about it myself."

I was worried by the turn the conversation had taken. I could see that Dad was going to climb onto one of his soapboxes.

"What is the greatest gift that one person can give to another? It says in the Bible, John's Gospel if I'm not mistaken, that no greater gift can a man give than to lay down his life for a friend. A typically martyred view of friendship, a curious inversion, having your friend shoulder the burden of your death. I say that the greatest gift is life and that there can be no greater gift than infinite life. So that is what I am going to give your sister—immortality, a place with the gods. I'm going to have a star named after her."

"I'm lost. I don't have a clue what you're talking about."

He pointed to the heavens. "Over twenty-five years ago the Voyager space probe set out to map the Neptune and Pluto systems. It has now gone beyond those systems, out onto the margins of new galaxies where it has discovered new stars and planetary systems, so many in fact that NASA has a problem finding names for all of them; the old mythologies have been exhausted. A new program has been launched whereby ordinary people can nominate someone instead. The only criterion is that they have to be dead and distinguished people. So, I'm going to have one of those new stars named after her."

"But she's not even born yet, never mind dead." I felt uneasy talking about my sister like this—fate was being tempted, I felt.

"That's true," he said. "But when she is born there will be a star there for her carrying her name."

"But I thought she had to be dead and distinguished. They're not going to hold a star aside for her till she does something with her life."

"That's true. What we're going to do is make a few nominations and see what happens at the end of the year when the first names are published."

I quickly saw the flaw in that. "But that's getting it back to front: you're naming the child after the star, not the other way around."

He shook his head. "Not at all. The nominees are published at the end of this year, six months after your sister is born. They do not name the stars officially until the new year. All we have to do is pick a name from the list of nominees and we can be pretty sure that the child will have a star all to herself. Besides, it's not a matter of chronology—the child, the living being, has priority over the star no matter what the naming sequence."

"And all this will give her more life?"

"Yes indeed. Up there in the company of gods and angels, deep in the bosom of the goddess Nut, a talent for eternity is bound to rub off on her. She will live forever, I have no doubt of that."

I was stunned in disbelief. I no longer felt the cold. I had heard Dad come out with some prize nonsense in his time but right then he was setting a new standard.

"Well, what do you think of the idea?"

I gave it to him straight, a mixture of anger and disbelief. "I think it's a load of bollocks. I've never heard such shit in all my life. Why can't we just name her after Mom?"

"It's no use naming her after Mom. Mom is having her life now and your sister will have hers. You have to remember that a name is more than a handle—it's a pathway, a route. We have to be careful how we go."

"Do you have any idea then what you intend to call her?"

"No, I haven't given it much thought yet. But there are bound to be plenty of names: nineteenth-century writers, politicians, scientists, and so on. The options are wide open," he said breezily. "Can you think of anything offhand yourself?"

"No, nothing comes to mind, I think I'll leave it up to you. You seem to have it all figured out."

He continued taking down notes and I left him shortly after.

So, for the next four months Dad kept an eye on the heavens. With the aid of his wall map and navigating carefully between constellations he got a fix on the general area of the star's location. It lay directly overhead at the farthest reach of the sky, a tiny spark of light harbored within the cusp of the Corona Borealis. I could not distinguish it from any of the other stars that thronged the vicinity but, as usual, Dad knew no doubt.

Six weeks before the birth he began his letter-writing campaign, sending off hundreds of nominations covering a handful of eminent women, using names and addresses he lifted from the telephone book—he wanted no one suspecting that there was a concerted campaign. I was persuaded eventually to send off a few of my own, more to keep him happy than anything else. I still had my doubts.

I watched Mom carefully. Now that she was carrying this celestial being I half expected her to take on a kind of starry radiance, a numinous glow. But I saw no change in her whatsoever—she maintained the lush beauty of her pregnancy and her ankles remained visibly swollen right up to the end. She did, however, develop a ferocious thirst. A continual supply of clear water from a nearby spring was always on hand, particularly at night when she sat watching telly. Glass after glass she drank until finally Dad brought the bucket in and left it between her feet. She dipped her glass into it as the night wore on, lowering its level by a truly jaw-dropping amount.

"She'll thank me for this later when she has nice clear skin," she said.

My sister is now six months old and she has yet to be baptized. In the meantime we call her "The Child" and we're comfortable with it. But it's something of a scandal in our village and people have begun to talk.

Last week the parish priest came to our house, something I can never remember happening before. He sat for two hours in the kitchen, beating around the bush with useless gossip and drinking enough tea to drown a man of lesser perseverance. Mom put him out of his misery by assuring him finally that yes, The Child would indeed be baptized, it was just a matter of time, a few more weeks. What she did not reveal was that we were waiting for the list of published nominees from NASA. I don't think he would have understood.

To pass the days we spend our time speculating over The Child's cradle, lowering names gently onto her sleeping form, seeing how they fit. I've always wanted to be able to sing but since I'm nearly tone deaf a singing sister would be the next best thing. Therefore, I'm holding out for Maria Callas: Maria Callas Monk. I had wanted Janis Joplin but I'm smart enough to know that her death is too recent and troubled, not highbrow enough. The philanthropist in Dad has his hopes pinned on—believe it or not—Emily Pankhurst; Emily Pankhurst Monk, another piece of daftness. I don't think he has a hope with it, however. Mom says nothing, she just lets us get on with it, but I think we both know that her choice will be decisive.

But what's strangest of all is that I think Dad may have started something. Last night I saw him on the roof with a couple of newly-weds. They stood close together with their arms around each other, the young woman holding her skirt down in the breeze. These December skies are huge and jewel-strewn. Dad had just finished mounting the telescope and he was starting to point out the heavens.

Estrogen

I could have sworn I heard my jaw hitting the floor. I had no need to look at myself to know that my eyes were definitely out on stalks. I had heard him talk some crazed shit in his time but right then he'd said something that sailed beyond the bounds of all reason. I mean this was an idea from a different planet, a different language. He was sitting there in a three-quarter-length chiffon skirt with his hair falling over a V-neck blouse that reached to his thighs. Black tights and ten-hole Docs completed the ensemble. This was my brother Pete, newly arrived on my doorstep with a jar of synthetic estrogen and a desire from hell: he was after telling me that he planned to grow a pair of tits.

"I can grow them here in peace and quiet," he elaborated calmly as he sat down, turning the jar of pills over in his hands. "A nice thirty-two B, taking into account my svelte figure. I don't want udders, just a nice demure pair to finish off this Pre-Raphaelite look, nothing too concupiscent."

The room reeled before me and I grasped the table for support.

"What the hell are you talking about, Pete, just what the hell are you talking about?"

"Well, you don't expect me to grow them at home, do you?" he snorted derisively. "A nice how-de-do that'd be. I have it difficult enough there without making it any harder for myself."

I was making an effort to keep in control.

"When did all this happen, this idea about tits—breasts—Jesus, and where did you get those clothes from?"

"The clothes are yours, from your old wardrobe. There's not much of a selection but I like these."

The room reeled a couple more degrees and I gripped the table tighter. Pete crossed his legs and the skirt fell away to his knee, exposing the curve of his thigh. I closed my eyes and breathed deep, trying to get a grip.

"And if you grow breasts is that going to be it? I mean, how far are you going to take it? Do you know just how far you want to take it?"

"I don't know. Look, I haven't got a lifetime supply of these tabs, only about another three months. I've been taking them since November so the effects are due to kick in any day now. When breasts start to grow it will take them about two months to fully form. So that's all I want—two months here, three at the max, just time enough to get the feel of them, so to speak. Then I'll see how it goes, if I want to hang onto them or take it further. Either way I'll be out of your hair in a few months. Promise."

"But, Pete, Galway isn't Amsterdam or Rio. Men don't wander about in broad daylight cultivating breasts under Aran sweaters."

"Who knows me here, Amy? No one, I've no friends here, I'm not likely to embarrass anyone. I don't even know your friends, you've made sure of that."

Oh, I saw it all then, or I thought I did—the cunning of the bastard.

"Oh, so that's it, so that's what this is all about," I snarled. "Some stupid plan to come here and make me feel guilty for getting out, for leaving the only son at home to look after his parents and some crappy little farm. Well, fuck you and your little guilt trips, fuck you."

I was well angered. I took a short turn around the table to calm down, I was breathing heavily. Pete was looking at me with a raised eyebrow.

"No, Amy, this isn't some guilt trip. I'm going to say it for the last time—I'm not jealous of the way you got out and left it all behind you. I could have done the same. Remember, Amy, I was the bright one. But I didn't leave because I didn't want to. Strange and all as it is, I love the home place. I love the fields and the animals, the cows and the sheep and the pissing rain and everything about it. And I want it; I want to see it grow, I've got plans for the place and I want to see it thrive. But I'm here now because I want to do this one thing also and this is the only place I can go. Where else can I go to?"

I sat down, momentarily defeated.

"I don't understand, Pete, I just don't understand. Growing breasts, for Christ's sake. I'd known you were gay but . . ."

It was his turn to pounce.

"You knew it in your head, Amy, just the way you know that liberal some-of-my-best-friends-are-gay shit, but you never knew it in your heart. When you were faced with it in your own brother you just fobbed it off like it was some sort of sexual fad. You weren't one bit supportive, you just turned your back and walked away."

"It was a shock to me."

"It was a fucking shock to me, too," he yelled suddenly, losing his temper. "There aren't many role models for the likes of me in west Mayo, in case you haven't noticed." He quieted down then and continued. "Amy, we're not here to talk about my being queer, that's all out in the open. I just got on with it and made the best of it.

I took the abuse and the stupid jokes and pretended not to notice that parents walked out of shops with their kids whenever I entered. But now that you've brought the subject up, I'd like an explanation. You were the cosmopolitan one, Amy, the one with the university education and degrees, and what did you do? You turned your back and walked away—my twin sister. How did you think that made me feel?"

I sighed and stroked my forehead. I could feel a momentous headache coming on.

"I know I let you down, Pete. I know I did and I'm sorry for it. But even with all that, how is growing breasts going to make it any better?"

"It's not going to make anything better, Amy, it's not about making anything better. I want to grow breasts because I want to grow breasts. That's all there is to it."

"No," I said, waving my hands. "No, that's not all there is to it. You don't just up and decide one day at the drop of a hat that you want to grow tits." I winced immediately when I realized my awkwardness.

"Thank you, Amy, that old lump-hammer sensitivity again. Amy, this isn't some drop-of-the-hat decision as you so sensitively put it. I've wanted breasts since I was a teenager. It didn't make sense to me at first, I thought I was crazy. It was only when I started coming out and seeing how different I was that it made any sense. Wanting breasts was always part of me."

"But that tells me nothing, Pete. Where did the idea come from— the first inkling or desire or whatever?"

He stubbed the fag and stared at the ceiling for a long moment.

"OK," he said. "I had a girlfriend in my teens—Sharon Crean— remember her? One night we were at the pier drinking a flagon and we started fooling with each other, kissing and everything. She was well into it but it was hopeless for me. I didn't exactly rise to the occasion. I was all over her and eating the face of her but nothing was happening and I couldn't understand it. I was beginning to panic, I didn't know what was wrong with me. And then she got on top of me and rammed my hands up under her T-shirt. I went rigid with fright but I was rigid also with something else. Her breasts were in my hands and I couldn't move; I was feeling her skin and her heat and I just couldn't move. And then I knew why I couldn't move. It was because I wanted those breasts so much—not to kiss or caress but for my very own. I wanted them for myself, in the same way I wanted to grow up with muscles and stubble on my face. I wanted their bulk and warmth for myself. And when I realized this I got such a fright that I threw her off there in the sand and I ran all the way home."

I made tea and sat down, lit another fag. Everything Pete was saying had the ring of truth about it. I knew him too well, knew his flighty imagination and passion, to know that he couldn't be flippant about something like this. And I'd lived a long time with my betrayal of him also; lived through the nights and fantasized about the number of ways I was going to make it up to him. Now that the opportunity was here I was finding myself wanting yet again.

"Can you not see, Pete, why I'm finding it so difficult to understand? It's just so off the wall I can't get my head around it. You must see that it's difficult for someone when you come in here and spring this kind of thing on them. You have to give people more time."

"No, Amy, not time, people like you need to learn a bit of humility. People like you are so far up on the high moral ground you can't hear a word that's spoken to you. I meet do-gooders like you every day of the week. It's the new national industry—a conscience for every crisis. I'm sick of going to meetings chaired by liberal do-gooders like yourself talking about the decline of the West as if it were solely to do with services. It's no good telling you people that the West isn't dying because it doesn't have post offices or because cop stations are closing down. It's dying in people's hearts and imaginations, that's where it's dying, Amy." He sat forward in his chair, in full flow now. "Listen to this: I talked to Marie Quinn over Christmas. She did her leaving in eighty-seven with me. She told me she worked for six months in St. Theresa's in Castlebar dealing with outpatients from the country. And did you know they get busloads of these patients, whole busloads of patients who can't eat or sleep, depressed or hearing voices in their head. But the thing is she can't find out what the hell's wrong with these people. She's running all sorts of tests on them and everything but she can't pin it down. And these people are genuinely sick, you only have to take one look at them to know that they're fucked—there's no light in their eyes. And all Marie can write down now for a diagnosis is loneliness— loneliness as the root and sole cause of their sickness. It has no med- ical or scientific standing but that's what she's writing down. And Marie thinks these people are lonely for company, or wives or chil- dren or lovers. But that's not it; it's closer to the bone and worse than that. These people are lonely for their dreams and what they might have been, these people are lonely for their own imaginations. And that's where the West is dying, Amy, in the hearts and minds of the people, not in some raft of statistics about dwindling services and emigration and shit. But the point is, Amy, I'm fucked if I'm going to be one of these dead people. I'm not going to end up another corpse in this graveyard of dreams. I'm not going to end up shuffling along a psychiatric ward in a suit of clothes two sizes too small for me or sitting in some pub in London crying over bad Guinness, singing 'Take Me Back to Mayo.' I'm not going to be like that, Amy. This is where I belong and I'm not going to be pushed out by anything. Crazy and all as it sounds I love the place and I'm going to see it thrive. I've got plans and they will happen."

Pete was leaning forward in his chair. The color had risen in blotches along his cheekbones and he was stabbing the air with his cigarette, driving home each point with the reddened tip: there was no arguing him out of anything now.

"OK, Pete, get down off your soapbox. I don't know what half of that has to do with growing breasts but go ahead then—I give up—go ahead and grow whatever you want to grow. Stay here for a few months. Stay here as long as you want."

He sat back in the chair grinning a bit sheepishly, turning the jar of pills over in his hands.

"Sometimes I just rant, sis, I get so heated up that my tongue runs ahead of my brain and I get all up in a heap. But that's not to say I'm wrong, I know what I'm talking about."

"Not like us liberal do-gooders?"

"I didn't mean that, it was just a rush of blood to the head. So I can wait here then, you're prepared to put up with a fledgling hermaphrodite in your flat for a few months?"

"Let's just say I'm prepared to put up with my brother for a few months."

In the following days I questioned Pete as to where he was getting his supply of estrogen. He was popping 150 milligrams a day, twice the recommended dosage for any application. He just waved the query aside blithely, talking about the old man's prostate cancer and HRT, the pill, other sources. I was led to believe that if you had the right contacts then the female hormone was not exactly the most difficult thing in the world to get your hands on. And then he came out with one of those curious pieces of apocrypha that I will always associate with him; one of those pieces of information that stop you dead in your tracks irrespective of whether they're true or not: did I know that the falling sperm count in the western world was thought to be directly attributable to the increased amount of female hormone in the atmosphere and foodstuffs? The androgens were being overpowered on all sides. On the surface, the feminine might be suffering an ideological backlash, but down in the trenches, at the biochemical level, there was no doubt as to who was gaining the whip hand: the planet was being slowly emasculated on the q.t.

"I'm only signing on the winning side," he said. "Getting there ahead of the rush."

He stayed over three months in my flat and he thrived in it like a bird of paradise. He spent his days reading from my bookshelves while the hormone worked in his body, taking the opportunity to improve his mind. He went out a few times and trawled through the second-hand shops for a new wardrobe. He brought back a series of flowing skirts and floral print blouses and went through the permutations of them three or four times a day. Unbelievably, I found myself taking a hand in his metamorphosis. One night as he fiddled with his hair in front of the mirror I took the brush from him and gave him a complete makeover. I trimmed away the scraggy ends of his hair and layered it, then blow-dried it upside down to give it body. I smoothed out the weathered patches of his cheeks with foundation and used a blusher to take the focus off his jawline. I then used a warm kohl pencil on his eyes and finished his lips with clear balm. Gazing at himself in the mirror he pursed his lips and blew himself a kiss.

"Jesus, if I didn't know I'd fancy the ass of myself."

"How do you feel?"

"Good."

"Just good, nothing more than good?"

"Just good: comfortable, like a man living a warm dream. Happy I'm doing it."

"Can you see yourself walking out milking like that some day?"

"I don't know about that. I think that might be in the future yet."

"You don't talk much about your plans, Pete, you keep hinting at them but that's all you do."

He turned from the mirror and sat down to light a fag.

"I've given them so much thought, Amy, so much thought you wouldn't believe it. I sit in your room at night smoking and dressed in your clothes and I hear the same old solutions going through my head, the same old talk of increased quotas and subsidies and headage, the same old solutions that have us fucked the way we are. But I've got ideas for the place and my ideas are very different— they have imagination and fire and I know they can succeed. I don't want to talk about them though—they're so wild and fragile they might shatter in the light of day." He paused to tip his ash. "The first thing I have to do, however, is get my hands on the place. I can't do a thing until the place is signed over to me. I have all the forms and I keep shoving them under the old man's nose but he won't go for it; he's too set in his ways. I wouldn't mind but there's a pile of money in it for the fucker."

By now his voice had risen a few octaves and he'd stopped shaving a couple of weeks. It was obvious also from the slope of his chest that his breasts had flourished. When the great moment came he stood in the room naked but for a skirt with his arms crossed over his chest.

"OK," he said, "the great unveiling."

He closed his eyes and pushed his arms wide and his newborn breasts popped out, shimmering slightly as if they were going to take flight. And they really were breasts: warm and curved like small moons and tipped off with pink areolas. He pinched them between his thumb and forefinger and brought up two tiny nipples, no bigger than sucked sweets.

"See," he said proudly. "They work perfectly."

"They're marvelous," I said, genuinely awed. "Any woman would be proud of them."

"What about any man?"

"I wouldn't know anything about that."

"Do you want a feel?" he said impishly.

"No, I'll take your word for them."

"I think you're jealous already."

He preened himself a while longer, testing the curve of them in his cupped palms and checking out his profile from both sides in every mirror. He lifted his hair from his shoulders and held it above his head, turning this way and that so that he could get a complete view. His pleasure was obvious and I couldn't but be affected by the quiet joy with which he regarded himself. Over the following days he marveled at them continually. He changed the flowing blouse to stretch tops and spent all day parading from one room to the next, relishing his appearance in the light of each mirror. I came in one evening and found him washing dishes at the sink, naked but for the skirt. He just blushed demurely and walked away to his room.

I got up one morning shortly after and found him standing in his jeans with his bag packed. I thought he'd put weight on overnight but then I saw that he was wearing three or four sweaters.

"OK, Amy," he said, "I'm off. Thanks for all the tea and hospitality but it's time I was out of here."

"Where are you going to go?"

"I'm going home; it's spring now, time to get back to work, the quickening earth and so on. Besides, I've got plans, remember?"

"But what about, what about . . . ?" I was pointing.

"My tits," he interjected. "I've used up the last of the tabs so that's the end of it. They'll subside in a few weeks and I'll be back to normal, whatever that is."

"How are you going to explain your shape and voice?"

"I don't know. I'll tell them I put on weight and that it affected my voice. Something like that. Don't worry, I'll think of something. I usually do." He picked up his bags. "Amy, thanks a lot, I'm very grateful. It's not often that people are given the time and space to fulfill a dream. I'm very grateful for it."

"No problem, Pete. I think I enjoyed it. Do you think you'll do it again?"

"Yes, definitely."

"How far next time?"

"I don't know. I don't know if I have the nerve or inclination."

"Whatever you do, look after yourself."

"I will. You take care of yourself, too."

And he was gone.

Last time I was home there were big changes around the farm. I sensed them the moment I got out of the car. The concrete yard was scrubbed and the slurry pit was cleaned out completely. The shed doors swung open and there was no sign of the dogs or hens or geese that usually swarmed the yard.

Pete came through the doorway of a shed in jeans and T-shirt. I saw straight off that his breasts were gone and that a two-day-old stubble shadowed his face. He stared blankly for a moment and then ran toward me, a huge smile spreading over his face. He held me at arm's length after kissing me and shook me gently. His face was wide open with joy.

"Don't tell me," I said. "You finally got your hands on it."

"Finally. Lock, stock, and barrel, the whole fucking shooting gallery."

"Well done. What brought him round?"

"I don't know and I didn't query it. Maybe it was the money. He just shoved the forms under my nose one night and he had the whole lot signed. Do whatever the hell you want with it, he said. So that's exactly what I'm doing. Come on. I want to show you my big idea."

He dragged me by the hand around the back of the sheds where the open pasture began. I saw he had the biggest field sectioned off into paddocks—six in all, about one acre apiece. Each of them was wired off with two rows of sheep wire reaching to about six feet in height; the whole field was completely covered in sand.

"This is it, Amy, the wave of the future. This is where I am going to plow all my money."

"Into covering good grazing land with sand?"

"No, into ostriches."

"Ostriches?"

"Yes, ostriches. I've sold off half the herd and I'm importing six ostriches from England. And this is going to be their home."

"Ostriches, Pete, in this climate?"

"It's not so crazy. They've been farming them in England for the last couple of years and in Donegal for the last ten months. By all accounts they're thriving up there."

"And what are you going to do with them?"

"Export them, on the hook or the hoof. There's a ready market for them in Belgium and Holland. Ostrich meat sells for thirty pounds a pound in restaurants over there."

"Christ, you won't be eating too many feeds of that then. It seems a shame that those creatures should end up on tables though."

"You're just being squeamish, Amy—the old bleeding heart again. Squeamishness has no place in farming; this is a survival thing."

"I suppose the old man is thrilled with the idea."

"He just shook his head and walked away when I told him. I think he suffers from nightmares now—the hills of west Mayo overrun with ostriches."

"And your shape's back to normal."

"Yes, and my voice, too. It took about two months. I went around clutching my throat for weeks, telling them I had a throat infection and trying to keep my mouth shut. I wore a pile of sweaters, told them I'd taken a chill with the infection."

We were leaning on the fence posts, gazing out over the sandflats where they ran away in a single stripe to where the gradient steepened at the base of the hills and then became covered in gorse and heather. On the higher slopes black-faced mountain sheep flocked and on the low-lying pasture cattle grazed in the neighboring stripes.

"For the life of me I can't see ostriches swarming over these hills."

"Well, that's what it's all about, sis—seeing things, imagination, the future."

"I hope the whole thing doesn't blow up in your face and leave you looking an idiot."

He smiled quietly and rested his chin in his arms.

"You mean look more foolish than I already am—a cross-dressing queer, part-time hermaphrodite, and owner of a subsistence farm. Things would want to get wild bad for me to look more foolish than I already am. No, I've got a good feeling about this, Amy; I know I can make it work." He straightened up suddenly. "Look at this." He undid his jeans and pulled them apart. I could see that he was wearing tights beneath them over a pretty pair of French knickers. I burst out laughing and he grinned. "This is what the well-dressed young queen is wearing in this weather. It's called the rustic simplicity look. Have you ever thought of all the farmers there are out here and all the secrets they might be hoarding under their clothes?"

"No, Pete, I can't honestly say that small farmers hold much sexual fascination for me."

"You shouldn't limit your horizons, Amy. Keep an open mind. All those eligible young farmers, hard manual labor. I'm sure they'd be well able to cater to your every need."

"Shut up, Pete."

"Sometimes I get up in the middle of the night now and I put on all my favorite things—skirts, underwear, blouses, makeup, the whole thing—and then I go out and walk through these fields and hills, prowling the darkness, singing and dancing like a dervish or something. And I can see everything in the dark. I can see what this place was and what it is and what it's going to be. I have 3-D vision in the dark sometimes. And it's wonderful, it thrills me beyond belief. Some night, though, I'm going to meet someone who knows me and then I'm going to have some explaining to do. But I really don't give a damn. This is my land now and I just don't give a damn."

The wind was rushing through his hair now, casting it in a swirl about his face. The spark in his eyes shone through the murk and even his teeth seemed ablaze with a kind of joy.

"I'm full of hope for this place. I'm so full of hope for it because I've got a vision and like all visions it's a bit crazed. I love this place so much, some night I'm going to lie down and fuck it."

"Jesus . . . Pete!"

He was just staring out over the hills.

"Keep an open mind, sis, an open mind."

Dead Man's Fuel

Like the legions who have gone before and the legions who will
come after, I met him on the lip of his own grave a split second after
he came over from the other side. He was standing on the edge of
his grave, looking down at where he had lain beneath the trampled
earth and the whitewashed emblem of his savior. He was wringing
his hat into a shapeless mass between his hands, a look of anguish
and disorientation drawing his features. Not for the first time did I
think that if I had a penny for every time I had seen that look I
would long ago have indentured an apprentice and handed over my
trade at the first opportunity, then taken my chances with those
other pilgrims in the wastelands that lie beyond this graveyard. But
I am not running a business and no money changes hands in this
land without value; such dreams are only torment.

   Their anguish, their torment—so much of it have I seen through
the years that I admit now without shame that my soul is totally cal-
lused over with indifference. I do not give a damn for their sensibili-
ties anymore and because of that I have been freed to develop an
attitude of cold efficiency. It is an attitude that spares me and profits

them—previously so much time was wasted in grief and this rictus of foreboding. Now I come upon them suddenly, stalking among the crosses and mausoleums and startling them with my abruptness. I tell them straight out that if they value what is left of their lives then they had better follow me; if they choose to stay where they are and curl up and die, as they inevitably will, then that is a matter of no consequence to me. All I ask is that they decide quickly and not waste my time. Their choice is simple: they take their chances with me or they stay there and die. It's not much of a choice but then this is a world without mercy.

Thankfully he was not the argumentative sort. He was sharp enough to mark closely the piles of bones that stood at the head of several graves around; he drew the relevant lesson, then remolded his hat quickly and followed me from the graveyard outside to where the stores were situated. On entering, I informed him quickly that he was here to pick up provisions and instructions for a journey he was to make alone and that the sooner he was kitted out, the sooner he would be on his way, taking steps toward his destination.

First I relieved him of his suit and replaced it with a pair of jeans that were riveted and double-stitched in heavy fabric, styled more for endurance than comfort. He turned in his shirt and tie for three cotton shirts with long sleeves, one white to ward off the summer heat and two black to hold body warmth when the snows fell. He was given three jerkins woven from new wool and a long poncho of alpaca that could be belted at the waist and that would serve well as a blanket in the innumerable nights to follow. His shoes were replaced with heavy boots of Portuguese leather, laced above the ankles with leather thongs and lined also with kidskin. He was urged to work them continuously with animal fat and to set by a store of thongs from cured skins, cutting them in a spiral fashion from the edge of the hide to the center to maximize length; thus was the pilgrim clothed.

Nor did he go without armaments. I took down a shotgun and sawed four inches off the barrel and made up the loss in weight with fifteen extra cartridges. I told him that when he reached open ground he should fire off a few practice rounds to get the feel of the gun and write the loss off against experience. I showed him also how the thongs of his boots would double to string a bow from the hickory ribs beneath the canvas tarpaulin of his wagon, and how bull reeds and willow rods would make serviceable arrows—he would have plenty of time to practice the art of fletching using the feathers of grounded birds he would encounter on his route. And I gave him also a curved blade with three different edges for the various types of cutting and scraping he would do. It was bolted to a wooden handle, and with a piece of sandstone and a measure of linseed to keep it whetted; thus was the pilgrim armed.

I took down a book then, a compendium of all the beasts and flora he was likely to encounter. I pointed out those creatures that were good to hunt and eat and those that were carriers of contagion—rabies, anthrax, and brucellosis. I familiarized him also with the reptiles and snakes that would lie in his path and the various types of corrosion they bore; those types that could be sucked out without difficulty from a crossed incision at the wound and those that were so potent it would be better for him to lie down on the spot and pull a blanket over his head so that he would not forfeit his eyes to the crows before his breath left him. I pointed out also that it is in the balance of the universe that there is not an illness nor an ailment likely to befall him but that there is also an herb to counter it; an infusion of lungwort will ease diarrhea and chest complaints while a decoction of yarrow will aid blood clotting; powdered mullein is a good sedative and a poultice of burdock will clear most wounds. Against that, hemlock and camus are to be avoided for they are an antidote to no known illness and bring a fever and sickness all their own. I pointed out also that in time of catastrophe he might have to trade a limb to save his soul and that the serrated edge of his blade was plenty sharp enough to saw through any of his bones if he had the nerve for it. It would be a good index of his electedness if he could endure this calamity and continue the length of his journey without a full set of limbs.

We spent some time also poring over maps that are torn now and barely legible. I marked out for him the general direction he should take, his only choice being whether he should walk east or west. In fact this was no choice at all, since his destination was equal distance in either direction from the exact spot on which he stood. My advice was that, so early in the morning, he should set out on his strongest foot and walk east into the rising sun, putting its furnace behind him as quickly as possible for the greater part of the day. I showed him on the maps also those sands wherein it was possible to sink wells and find oases, and those parts that were lush with water-bearing cacti. I inscribed, too, those salt flats that were without beasts or vegetation and that were to be avoided at all costs. I marked off the narrow defiles between mountain ranges and the stone revetments that were the probable strongholds of brigands and felons and likely sites for ambushes. I counseled caution in these areas and when I had done so I rolled up the maps and put them aside, heedless to his protest that he needed them for the journey. I informed him that such maps did not come in duplicate and that there would be other pilgrims in his wake.

On the question of companionship I warned him against falling in with strangers on his journey. Once he had taken the measure of his own stride he would make better time at his own pace rather than breaking or lengthening it to suit others. But if these strangers were unavoidable then he should stand at all times with the sun and wagon to his back when addressing them and on no account was he to enter into games of skill or hazard where there was a possibility of his losing face or his cloak, for, whatever price he put on his dignity, he could ill afford to part with the latter. And I told him also that if the opportunity arose in the darkness, when no moon rose and no stars flecked the sky, it should not conscience him to take out his knife and open that same stranger's throat, particularly so if that man's boots were sturdier than his own and his oxen had wintered heavily on crushed oats. When first light came, he should hitch up his wagon and move off with no backward glance save to take an alignment from the carnage for he was unlikely to be called to account for it.

I told him further that of all the gullies and ravines and valleys on his journey none would have such depths and sheer sides nor be so lacking in footholds as the vortex of his own solitude, that pit wherein there is no progress that is not circular. Against it I taught him a handful of songs that were of no consequence save their melody and one canticle against sleeplessness; all of these to keep his mind supple and his tongue from falling into a rictus of disuse. In the days ahead without partners the gift of speech could readily flee him and it would be a fatal thing indeed for him to arrive at his destination and be unable to speak his name or give an account of his actions. I showed him also how a simple reed organ could be fashioned between his two thumbs with a blade of grass. It would give a range of two octaves and a fifth and two reeds blown in tandem would allow him to play simple harmonies and extend the range a further octave. I warned him against laughing upon such toys for he would be well glad of them in the night when wolves and predators moved beyond the light of his campfire. I told him that time spent crafting instruments of dissonance and percussion from hollowed bone and cured hides was time spent girding himself against idiocy: all travelers need time out to catch their breath and play.

And to give the vortex of solitude a wider berth I furnished him with a series of mind games to keep him thinking, for, like every human enterprise, death is something you have to continually bring your mind to bear upon. Along with a series of puzzles and conundrums I gave him also the ontological argument and the argument from design. I told him their history and significance and made him repeat them before me till I was assured he had their structure and progress committed to memory without flaw. And then I gave him a series of counterarguments and objections with which he could interrogate them, build them up or break them down as he saw fit. But because of the unique misery it afforded I omitted the teleological argument altogether and hoped fervently that he would not chance upon it of his own volition for it has a pitilessness and desolation without recourse.

Before we moved into the yard I spoke to him of how the terrain and cartography of his own mind would engender many rogue epistemologies and deceptions on his route, how calenture and hallucinations and mirages and tinnitus of the ears would raise up many fraudulent cities and oases in the desert and populate the night with the voices of friends long since departed and not yet conceived. More than on the plains or in the desert, the pit of despair is quarried in the mind and I cautioned him to look to it with the same vigilance he tended to his blade and his boots. I recommended an attitude of doubt and skepticism toward everything that did not glow with self-evident truthfulness except in those extreme circumstances of pain and desolation when wagers of faith were the only way forward.

All this done I took him around the back of the stores where the joiners were putting away their tools and the painters were finishing the last coat of creosote on the wagon. I told him the wagon was crafted in seasoned maplewood and that with proper maintenance it would take him the entire length of his journey. From this day out he was to look to it as he would to his very soul, keeping it clean and balanced with the weight distributed evenly over the four wheels and keeping also a sharp eye to the desert heat that it would not wring the last sap from the timber and sunder the mortices on rocky ground. Every opportunity should be taken to submerge the wagon in streams and in lakes to let the timber swell to a tightness. As I hitched up the oxen he voiced the inevitable preference for horses but I informed him that the desert floor was well littered with the bones of horses struck down by the brunt of the sun and that these same bones would make good cleaning and scraping instruments; oxen are the draught animals par excellence, creatures of fortitude and huge resilience. I told him how best to fodder them and I showed him the spot of their necks from which, in times of privation, a quart of blood could be syphoned and drunk steaming in the cold night without fatally weakening the animal, provided the incision was cauterized with a hot blade and the ox was allowed to rest at the first opportunity.

He was about to climb on the wagon and move off before he remembered a last thing—how would he recognize his destination? I told him that of all his worries, and he would have plenty, this would be the least of them. He would recognize it without error in the same way he would recognize his own simulacrum if it came walking toward him out of the desert with the self-same sins of his birth; keep striking a line due east into the rising sun and he would not miss it. I remembered then to take from him his timepiece and cast it in a pile with the others: in the days and months ahead it would be nothing but a torment to him. All he would need to know of time from this moment forth could be read from the elevation of the sun and felt in the slackness of his belly. My final instruction was that if in his life it had been his habit to petition saints or martyrs with prayers or offerings then now was not the time to neglect these rituals; small sacrifices of birds and game should be offered up when he had enough to eat and sufficient stores set by.

Finally he chucked the reins and moved off out of the courtyard without valediction or further query. I did not offer my hand in goodwill nor did I accompany him any step of the way but I kept watch until the wagon had disappeared below the curve of the horizon. Then I went inside and took out his bundle of clothes and set fire to them for he would not be returning to reclaim them.

And as they burned no breeze moved and smoke began to fill the yard and I fell to thinking of all the pilgrims I had instructed and equipped for this same journey, more pilgrims through the years than there are stars in the firmament or ants on the ground. I remembered how I had sent them out, one after another into the wastes, armed with those few chattels and instructions against blind chance and those nameless contingencies that lie in ambush at every step of the road, ready to waylay and leave them bloodied and broken on hot sands or in cold snows, their souls lost forever in this oblivion without any reckoning. I thought of the wisdom I had passed on to those travelers I hoped might profit from it and how easily this same wisdom is ridiculed by circumstances that refuse to reveal themselves; circumstances that bide their time and sneer like sentient beings from behind positions of strength, invisibly watching the pilgrims who pass by heedlessly with the backs of their necks clear and exposed. And I thought also of the confidence and certainty with which I speak out my instructions—whence did I get such authority? I am, after all, a man who has never moved beyond these perimeter walls and I have no experience whatever of the things on which I speak with such eloquence. I have never fired a gun or strung a bow, my food is handed to me on a plate and in the evening I play cards with the other craftsmen. Now the terrible truth is that I have no faith anymore in my work nor, if I search deeply enough within myself, can I remember a time when I did. I seem to remember it always as a performance, a soothsayer's carnival act, where I flourished these vague conjectures for the astonishment of some rude audience. All I can hope for now is that somewhere in my charlatan's eloquence some of these pilgrims will find material enough to make a fight of it; after that they will have to take their chances.

The fire is dying down now and the yard is filled with smoke. I can see no farther than the perimeter wall. Pretty soon now I will walk to the graveyard and bring back another pilgrim. I will go through the same ceremony of outfitting and instruction and with the same air of confidence—I know it well by heart. All I wonder at anymore is the difficulty I have with putting in words just how much I have grown to hate this job.

The Terms

On the very evening I burned down the left wing of our house my father told me that he hated me. He just stood there in the shadow of the gutted roof thumbing a shell into the rifle, making no bones about it nor putting a tooth on it in any way, just telling me quietly and for the last time that everything about me made him sick, everything: the massive dome of my head with its lank fringe, my useless legs and piping voice—most of all the lack of shame and outrage in my heart. He told me again that all the cruelty and misshapen ugliness of the world was summed up in my body and that he could not suffer it a moment longer. Then he told me that he was going to kill me. Frankly this wasn't news to either of us. Somehow we seemed to have always known that our relationship would come to this; it had been fated from the beginning to end in some swift settlement of accounts, some bloody reckoning. Putting it another way, neither our house nor our world was big enough for two people such as us.

Lately, however, and for some reason I could not fathom, I had begun to dream of something else. My sleeping hours had been filled of late with shapeless images of truce and acceptance, compromises, it is true, that fell a long way short of love and redemption but nevertheless something to be getting on with. However, when I saw my father thumbing home that shell I realized that he knew nothing of my dreams.

"I'm going to shoot you stone dead," he said evenly. "And what's more, I'm going to shoot you in the back."

"It's not going to be a fair fight then. I don't have any weapons at hand."

"I'm going to give you a fighting chance," he said. "You're going to get a fifty-yard start over open ground and I have only one shot. If you make it don't come back. Here's two hundred and fifty pounds to help you make a start in the world just in case. Invest it wisely. I'd recommend government bonds."

He handed me a wad of notes and I made some quick calculations. Normally my father was an excellent shot. In clear light I had seen him drop fleeing rabbits at one hundred yards. Now, however, there were other factors to consider. It was late evening and the autumn sun was well in decline. Shadows crawled everywhere and gave shapes and profiles an enormity they did not truly possess. Also I could see that my father's temper had begun to smolder; little things gave him away. A tremor had entered into his white-knuckled hand as he gripped the rifle and a bead of sweat had broken out under his nose. Already I was beginning to fancy my chances but I still wanted further adjustments to be on the safe side.

"How about a head shot?" I said. "You're always telling me that my head is too big for my shoulders."

"Only at forty yards, beyond that white thorn."

"OK."

"Plus ninety quid."

"That's down to four pounds a yard. It started out at five."

"That's the law of diminishing returns. Take it or leave it."

I thumbed the notes of the wad and pocketed them. "How do I know you'll only take the one shot?"

"One is all I'll need. Besides, I've only got one shell in the breech and if I have to reload you'll have gained another twenty-five yards. At that distance you'll be well in the clear."

"What happens if I only get wounded? Suppose I take it in the lung and lie there bleeding to death?"

"Then I will leave you there and the crows will make short work of you. I'll walk out every day for as long as it takes and see how your death is progressing. On the day of your death I'll dump a bag of lime over you and within two weeks there won't be a trace of you except for a small, damp pile of chalk in the middle of that field."

"A bag of lime isn't much of a memorial."

"You're not much of a son."

"Suppose I make a miraculous recovery and wake up to find that you have come and stolen my fortune? What then?"

"That won't happen. Whatever else I am I'm not a thief."

"You won't try and profit from my death? A young, smooth body like mine would fetch a fair penny from research institutes or on the organ donor market. It would have considerable freak value. You might take off to Latin America with a mistress."

"No, there will be no profiteering. This is a matter of principle not profit. Besides, there's not much of you in it and I'd prefer you to go to hell all in one piece."

"I'm glad. I don't fancy the idea of some clueless medical student with a hangover poking around in my guts. The thought of it alone would put me off my stride. Nevertheless, you'll have a lot of explaining to do."

"I'll tell everyone that you set fire to the house and took off in shame and fright. I'll dissuade any search party by telling them that you know every one of these hills and forests and that you will probably return in your own good time. I'll tell them that you were depressed lately on account of your condition."

"That's a dirty lie. I've never once been depressed by what I am."

"*You* haven't but *I* have. Every time I look at you I sink deeper into misery and despair. Right now I'm so low that if I sank any lower I'd disappear into the ground."

By now the sun was a heavy rind over the hills and the earth glowered in shadow. The terms had been set out and I could think of nothing else I wanted to add to them. I was very calm and confident. I believed that at that moment I possessed every piece of worthwhile wisdom and knowledge in the entire world, every axiom and formula and instruction that was going to enable me to live longer. Nevertheless I wondered, did my father have any parting words to send me on my way?

"You're not going to wish me good luck or anything?"

"There's no point in wasting fortune on a dead man."

"Then I guess I'll be on my way."

"We seem to have covered everything."

I jogged out to the starting post, moving at a steady lope, conserving energy. The ground was even and the going firm, a wide stretch of pasture sloping away from the gable of our house to a downhill finish running into the conifer plantation at its farthest edge, about one hundred yards distant. I had no worries that my father would cheat and shoot me in the back within the agreed range. This was his game and he had defined the terms and he would honor them with that vain integrity that only the truly wretched possess.

Ten yards from the white thorn I burst into a sprint, running in a sharp zigzag from left to right and rolling my head. I passed the bush and veered wildly into its shadow, putting it between my father and myself. Ten yards beyond the bush and I was making good ground, breathing evenly and almost in the safety zone. Then there was a massive explosion in my head, a sunburst of white light and I was cast up into the air as if by a giant hand, hurtling forward almost on the verge of flight. I pitched through the gloom like a missile and then all was darkness.

Jesus, I had to hand it to the little runt, he wasn't going to make it easy for me. There he was, running faster than I would have thought possible on those useless little legs of his and jogging that massive head from side to side as if it were some sort of beach ball.

I knew the moment I lifted the gun to my shoulder that I'd been hoodwinked. The little bastard had kept me talking just long enough for the sun to disappear beyond the hills. His head was nothing more than a blur between the ridged walls of the gunsights and he was darting from side to side, shortening and lengthening each burst at random. He was now abreast of the bush and he suddenly veered behind it and disappeared from sight. The canny bastard had put the bush between us and, with the field dropping away behind it, he would now never emerge into the open. I would have to shoot through the tree. I saw a gap in the foliage and sighted through it, waiting for his head to bob into the open space. When it did, filling the bottom of the space, I waited a split instant before the rifle boomed and recoiled heavily in my shoulder. I saw his small body come hurtling sideways out of the silhouette, swimming through the air before crashing to the ground and tumbling head over heels in an untidy mess of arms and legs. And I knew then that it was all over; I knew that my son and only child, Edward Coon the second, was dead.

Edward was neither dead nor seriously wounded, he was just out cold with barely a scratch on him. The bullet had grazed the top of his head, parting his thick hair with a terrific red lesion that cut through to the bone of his skull. He just lay there on his back breathing lightly as if he had lain down for a nap.

I saw straightaway that his condition placed him outside the terms of our agreement. He was neither dead nor seriously wounded but the danger now was that he might wake in a matter of hours and wander off into the world as an imbecile with neither wit nor memory, easy prey for thieves and malefactors. This was not what we had settled on. I wanted him either dead or alive, not queering up creation further as an idiot.

I picked him up and turned to the house. His head lolled heavily off my elbow and a thin rivulet of blood seeped through his hair. His tongue lolled thickly from his mouth. As I gazed upon him I saw for the umpteenth time how everything rank and misshapen in the world was summed up in this small bundle of flesh and bone. This child of mine seemed the very distillate of all the world's cruelty and malice. But beneath my disgust there welled also a deeper, more unspeakable feeling. It rose through my heart and leaked into my throat, swelling it and threatening to choke me. It had the same intractable presence as the rifle that lay across my son's chest.

For the first time in my life I recognized clearly that everything in my son that repulsed me was nothing more than my own mirror image.

I woke with a brutal headache; some implacable demon was working in my skull with a hammer. My room, a horrid prospect, smelled of charred timber and petrol. Shafts of light spilled through the shattered roof, settling in the room like converged lances. I walked through the ruined hallway and into the kitchen clutching my head in my hands. My father sat at the table cleaning the rifle, yanking a pull through from the barrel.

"You don't look like God and you're not forking stiffs into a furnace. What happened?"

"I creased your skull and you fell unconscious."

"And you took pity on me?"

"No, I just honored the terms of our agreement. Have a drink, welcome home so to speak." He pushed a bottle of whiskey across the table to me.

"No thanks, you know well I'm only a minor."

"Suit yourself. I would have thought that any man who had come within a hair's breadth of hell would want to celebrate his deliverance."

"I'm not in the mood for festivities, I just want to get my head together."

I pulled up a chair and watched him cleaning the gun. No matter how many times I had seen him do this simple task, the way he worked those stubby fingers of his still enchanted me. The guile and seamless grace of his movements. I had often reflected that somewhere in him there was a craftsman howling to get out, someone with patience and poor eyesight who worked with precious materials and terrifying degrees of accuracy. He laid down the rifle suddenly and stared into space for a long moment.

"We can't go on like this," he said finally. "It's nothing personal but this has got to end. People like you and me have no place anymore in the world, Edward. We'd be better off dead."

"Speak for yourself."

"That's what I'm doing. I am so lost, so lost. It's a matter of scale, I think. We're told every day that the world is getting smaller and smaller and that distances are narrowing down, bringing the peoples of the world together in harmony. But for people like you and me it just gets bigger and bigger until we've dropped right through the meshes of it and into this pit. We have no life anymore."

"Was it ever any other way?"

"Yes," he said vehemently. "Yes, it was. There was a time when we had status and valuable skills. It's hard to believe that people like us were passed down from kings to princes as part of inheritances and that we were privy to their inmost thoughts. And it's harder to believe that some of us were real artisans and craftsmen, shoemakers and fullers and spinners of gold thread, diamond prospectors even. Did you know our forebears trafficked in foundlings for depleted bloodlines and that we made ends meet with a bit of cradle-snatching? All honorable trades in their own worlds. But not anymore, that's all gone now. Now we're not even good circus material. History has passed us by, Edward, and we're dead men, dead men both of us."

"That's not unusual. The world is full of people who have been passed over by history—gypsies, tinkers, and so on."

"Yes, but none have fallen so low. We are the lowest of the low; right now we are neither men nor beasts, we're just nightmare creatures stalking a no-man's-land between myth and history."

"You're just full of self-pity."

"Don't patronize me, Edward. I've lived long enough to be able to distinguish pity from disgust. I cried for six months when your mother died and I couldn't eat for two after the first time I held you in my arms. I'm not likely to confuse the two. At this moment I'm so sickened by myself I couldn't summon up the energy to puke. And while we're on the subject of disgust, tell me, why did you burn down the left wing?"

"That was an incomplete job. If you hadn't come along I'd have burned down the whole house. I was hoping that when you came back the whole thing would be destroyed and we could go off together and make our way in the world. I wanted a new start. There was a time when I thought this house was our sanctuary and refuge. And it was, too, for many years—our own little scooped-out space in the world where we were safe and without enemies. But over the years this sanctuary has turned into our prison; there's no house around here for miles and we have no friends or function anymore. Now I think it is time to up roots and move on. Somewhere out there, in the vastness of the world, I know there is a small place where we can find our niche."

"Doing what?"

"I don't know. I was thinking in terms of adventure and destiny, taking every day as it comes, you and me facing fortune head on."

He closed his eyes as if experiencing some vast weariness.

"That's a young man's game, Edward. I'm too old for that kind of optimism."

He was right. I saw for the first time how all his years of rancor and bitterness had eaten away the fabric of his soul. He had about him now an air of utter defeat. It ran in every line of his body, coursing through his arms and legs and chest and into the curve of his blunt spine. Some terrible weight seemed to have settled upon him and it came as an immense shock to see that he was now almost shorter than myself.

By this time the gun was cleaned and he was tidying away the oil and the lint. I hadn't seen the hacksaw on the table and I noticed also that a piece of the barrel was lying loose beside it. He had sawed another inch off the stock, customizing the gun yet further. He handed it to me.

"Take it," he said. "It should handle lighter—I've shifted the balance nearer the stock. Today it's your turn. The same terms and no arguments."

I felt my eyes start in their sockets.

"I can't do that," I whispered in disbelief. "I can't. It's just crazy." I retreated a few steps from the gun he was holding at arm's length. "I can't."

"Take the gun, Edward," he insisted. "Take it." He thrust it suddenly onto my chest.

"No," I yelled, "no!" I fended the gun off wildly with my hands.

"This isn't an order, Edward, it's a request." He had me pinned against the wall now, laying the rifle across my chest. He took his hands away suddenly and I found myself holding it. A calm, solemn note entered his voice.

"I've hated you from the moment you entered the world and I've hated you all the more because you are my son. I didn't think the world could commit the same atrocity twice in the same place. But I was wrong. And worst of all I've felt neither shame nor remorse for my hatred. Now, not once in all these years have I ever asked you for anything, not once because what did a wretch like you have to offer, you who had less grace than I did? But now I'm asking you for this one thing. Take the gun and be my son, just this once and final time."

The gun burned in my hand but I could not let it go.

"Is it what you really want?" I blurted.

"Yes, it's what I really want. I cannot suffer this anymore."

He turned and made his way quickly through the back door and outside he stood facing toward the field. The day was cruelly lit; a high, unseasonable sun flared in the sky like magnesium, casting neither shadow nor illusion. My father turned into the field and I could see by the way he moved, the slouched gait and the hopeless slope of his shoulders, that he wasn't going to make it. I was filled with sudden panic.

"Dad," I cried.

"Yes."

"Run hard."

He turned without a word and continued on his way and when he got to the starting post he just kept on walking.

Blues for Emmett Ward

And so we made ready. Our last summer was at an end and by the time October came round our dope supply and nixers had dried up and the days were closing in like a corridor in the autumn gloom. Our cushy summer rituals had gone into a rut and now the signs were telling us something. We opened our eyes and read them the only way possible: go, move on, leave, fuck off somewhere else, we were being told.

And so we were ready. We bought our tickets, packed our ruck-sacks, and flew out of Shannon on the eighteenth of October, two weeks after Emmett's twenty-second birthday. The plan was construction work or bartending, whichever came first, and long enough to get money together to travel to Mexico or California. A vague plan right enough but with Emmett and myself there was never any other sort. With Emmett beside me I had no worries. He was my best friend, my right-hand man, my brother in arms since childhood. He was the steady one who spotted the flaws and pitfalls, the one who saw consequences when I saw only opportunity. Whatever happened I knew it would work out the way everything we did together worked out—me, blundering and impetuous, going the scenic route, Emmett, the steady one, taking time out to light a smoke and consider, then arriving there before me via the short cut.

I sat back on the flight and closed my eyes. I had no worries.

John Tighe, two-year veteran of a concrete gang, had a flat in Queens. He shared a room with Paul Flatley, another exile from our hometown. Both were the same age as ourselves and hungry for news of the home place. That first night we stayed up till the early hours drinking beer and smoking, laughing and piss pulling, getting steadily drunker till John got up and stretched himself, announced finally that he was going to bed. Paul stubbed his last fag and killed his bottle, announced that he was going, too. He stood swaying for a moment, frisked his pockets, and threw out a spare set of keys. He muttered a few muddled instructions on how to find our way into the city and how to avoid the no-go areas. He clasped his head and said good night.

The next day was Friday. We weren't due to start looking for work till Monday; there was no rush.

We found our way into Manhattan the next morning and came out of the subway onto 42nd Street feeling none too sure of ourselves. We passed the entire day drifting openmouthed through the core of the bad apple, spending the bulk of our time browsing in the sex shops along 42nd Street, those dank galleries with curtained-off cubicles and overhead signs warning people to keep both hands on the magazines while reading. When we'd had enough we stumbled out into the amber sunlight with our hands stuffed deep in our pockets and Emmett lit a fag and shook his head, wondering aloud how such beautiful women could be brought to do such things. We stopped again farther on, and listened to some black dude standing seven foot tall, dressed in army fatigues and speaking to the crowd through a hailer. He was yelling some garbled shit about Afro-Americans being the lost tribe of Abraham, the disinherited nation whose identity had been usurped by the Jews but who were now on their way to their lawful inheritance over the corpses of anyone who stood in their way, Paddies included. And when we'd heard enough of that we walked on farther to where a cardsharp was turning a three card trick on a tiny, baize-topped table in front of another crowd. He must have seen me coming because he suckered me into wagering my ten against his twenty that I couldn't find the ace of spades alongside the king and queen. I kept my eyes riveted to that card but he still took my ten quicker than you could say honky-assed motherfucker. We strolled on and ate at a deli, a massive, neon-lit food hall thronged with secretaries and yuppies eating at the end of the day. At the self-service counter we shoveled lasagne and side salad onto plastic plates, weighed them at the cashier, and got a bill for thirty dollars. We ate and rode the subway home in embarrassed silence, knowing once and for all that we'd some serious wising up to do.

When we got back to the flat John and Paul had returned from work. They were sitting with their feet on the table and swinging out of their chairs, drinking longnecks and eating huge sandwiches. The day's work showed in their faces: gray cement lines ran from the corners of their eyes. With a sweep of his boot John cleared off his end of the table and proceeded to roll up a smoke. He glanced up and grinned.

"Well, men, are you ready for the town?"

When we returned to the flat in the early hours we sat in the kitchen, blissed out among the ashtrays and empty food cartons, the strewn clothes and cups. The rubbish of only two days without a cleaning rota had mounted up in every conceivable corner, turning the flat since our arrival into the lair of some hibernating animal. We'd have to make more of an effort, I thought vaguely; we weren't students anymore.

Paul and myself were sprawled in the armchairs and John was at the table bent over a pouch of tobacco, struggling to fashion a last spliff before we turned in for the night. Despite our fatigue the mood was one of quiet elation.

"If I hadn't seen it with my own eyes I wouldn't have believed it," John was saying, heating a nodge between his thumb and forefinger. "Emmett Ward, our Emmett, a ladies' man. It just goes to show, there is a God after all."

"And she was a fine thing," Paul added, settling down deeper into the chair. "That dress must have been sprayed on with a power hose—she had a pair of nipples you could hang a wet donkey jacket on."

"Did you get a look at her?"

"Just a glimpse when I went up for drink. You couldn't see much of her with Emmett sucking the face off her. She looked the biz though, a pair of legs you could tie a bow on your back with."

"He came over to me at the end of the night, cool as you like, 'Don't worry about me, lads, I'm going home with this one.' And off he went without another word, a grin on his face like a Cheshire cat."

"And he was well gone, too, the same Emmett."

"Well fucking gone. A couple of cans and a few smokes, it goes straight to his head. He wouldn't have been half the playboy if he had all his wits about him."

"He'll wake up tomorrow and he won't know what the hell hit him."

Emmett had scored and scored big time. We had started the night with cans and a few smokes and then taken a taxi to a nightclub somewhere in Queens, a split-level, glass, brick, and mesh-wire affair where we'd got seats in an alcove off a dance floor that wasn't much bigger than a snooker table. Emmett and Paul went to get drinks. Paul returned in a few minutes with drinks for John but there was no sign of Emmett until he finally turned up and plunked a drink in front of me. But instead of sitting he just mumbled something about this babe and said he'd see me after awhile. And that was it—the last I'd seen of him all night till near the end when he came over and told me he was going home with her and that he'd see me the next day. I was gob-smacked. Paul had spotted him through the crowd standing at the bar giving mouth-to-mouth and returned to confirm that Emmett was indeed fixed up with a fine thing—a cross between Uma Thurman and Michelle Pfeiffer, a total ride as he'd put it. I was glad for Emmett; a good going over would do him all the good in the world.

John finally managed to skin up and he'd shifted to the couch. He was sprawled out with an ashtray on his chest, his eyes closed, luxuriating in the booze and fatigue. Suddenly he started laughing, his Adam's apple hopping and his breath coming through his nose in short bursts. He sat up spluttering.

"I'll bet she'll give him some mauling all right when she gets her hands on him. She looked like she'd be well able to go . . . he'll need both hands to pull the sheets out of his hole tomorrow morning."

"I'd say more than the sheets will go—quilt and mattress and pillow, the whole lot. I wouldn't start looking for the headboard either."

"He'll turn up on the doorstep tomorrow all dazed and bruised, his hair sticking out all over the place, saying, Lads, what hit me?"

"And we'll have to put him sitting down and give him hot, sweet tea to help him get over the shock. It's OK, Emmett, it's OK, it was only the ride, you had a good time, you had a good time. Look . . . what's this, a pillow hanging from your arse?"

"We'd have to call the Knights of Malta."

We were giggling uncontrollably now, the dope kicking in and the tears streaming down our faces. We were well pleased with our joke and Emmett's good fortune. I sat back and wiped the tears from my eyes, then passed on the spliff.

"This could be the making of Emmett, though, the beginning of something. Maybe she's a rich widow looking for a toyboy. Emmett could be set up for life."

"Jesus, that'd be the way to live for awhile. This bored, rich widow taking you on and feeding you and giving you spending money. I could go for a good long stretch of that."

"You'd get bored with it soon enough, though," Paul interjected, assuming the mock voice of morality and restraint.

"Yah, the novelty would wear off after awhile all right, ten or eleven years," John said, and we all collapsed laughing.

"All I'm saying is that my pride wouldn't let me," Paul spluttered archly. "I'd feel used and demeaned." We collapsed again and sat back in our chairs, passing round the spliff a final time.

"Seriously, Mike, it's an idea. Work isn't easy to come by anymore. You could be a long time pounding the pavements before something comes up. What you should do is take that smooth arse of yours onto 42nd Street and start hawking it up and down the sidewalk. I'd bet you'd build up a regular custom in no time."

"You could get Emmett to pimp for you," Paul added. "Now that he's set up with this wealthy chick it'd be the perfect front. I bet she'd introduce you to a nice, classy sort of punter."

I fell in with the joke. "I was thinking about it but I'd be afraid no one would want me. Imagine hawking your ass day after day and no one wanting it. All those men and women turning up their noses at you and passing you by. Try explaining that to your ego. And that's what would happen, I know well."

"Oh, I don't know, a young smooth ass like yours and all those older, frustrated women. I'd say you'd make a fortune."

"A roaring trade, I'll bet."

I just grinned. My inspiration was seeping away now. It was better to abandon the joke before the ass got tore out of it completely. This was the fag end of the day and jet lag and booze and dope were overwhelming my body, making it fifty times heavier than it really was. I was about to drift off to sleep but I had a sudden vision of Emmett somewhere in the city, straddled by this big blonde with huge tits who was bouncing up and down on his stick. Emmett was gazing up at her as she rode and there was a look of utter amazement on his face. I shut my eyes tighter and grinned, drifting off to sleep.

Go, Emmett, go, go, go.

My neck was stiff in a rictus of pain the next morning, pain flashing through to my elbow whenever I tried to move. I had fallen asleep in the armchair. I opened my eyes and saw John picking his way cautiously over the broken ground of cups and clothes, moving toward the fridge with his hand clasped to his forehead. I struggled out of the chair and stood swearing at the pain in my neck, knowing already that the day was useless if it didn't go away. John handed me a carton of orange juice.

"What time is it?"

"Half two. The day's almost gone."

"Jesus, I've one mother of a headache."

"That's the whiskey—a great idea at the time but you never stop to think."

"How did we sleep so long?"

"That's it again, up all night talking shit instead of getting to bed. Come on, let's tidy up this place and get some breakfast."

We gave the room a quick blitz, heaped everything into bags and corners, then sat at the table to drink tea and butter bread. Paul wandered in from the bedroom looking seriously gray in the face; we had heard the unmistakable sound of puking coming from the toilet. He sat down without a word and John gave me a knowing grin.

"How're you feeling, Paul—is the belly up in a heap?"

"Fuck off."

"Don't worry about it. Mike will have the pan on in a minute, rashers and sausages and runny eggs and . . ."

"*Fuck off,*" he hissed weakly, burying his face in his hands. "Whose idea was the whiskey anyway? A real fucking genius whoever it was."

"Oh yah, I have a distinct memory of tying you down and pouring it back your neck."

Paul groaned deeply. "Why do I do it, why do I fall for it every time?" he agonized. "Wouldn't you think I'd have learned my lesson, that it does my fucking head in?"

"That's it again, you see. Paddy doesn't stop to think. Plow straight ahead and fuck the begrudgers."

"Do you not feel shit?" he asked wonderingly. "I used to be able to drink you under the table."

"I did feel bad," I said grimly. "But now that I see the shape you're in I feel a lot better."

He groaned bitterly. "It's just like you, ya cunt."

I poured him tea and he sipped gingerly.

"I wonder, will Emmett call or what the hell's he at?"

"He probably needs all his time to get those sheets out of his hole. He might need surgery."

"The last thing on Emmett's mind now is ringing us. If he has any sense he'll be going back for seconds."

The rest of that day drifted by in small talk and a couple of hours poring over the *New York Times*. We made dinner and it settled our stomachs and afterward John skinned up and we passed round the first smoke of the day. There was still no word from Emmett.

"Wouldn't you think the bollocks would call?" I said. "I don't give a shit what he's doing but I hope he remembers we're supposed to go looking for work in the morning."

"Don't worry about it. You'll be long enough working. Have you got money?"

"At the present rate of expenditure, about enough for a week."

"No worries then. You can stay here as long as you like. The moment you start earning you can start putting in with the rent."

"Thanks, men."

The rest of that evening drifted away in front of the telly and by the time I went to bed there was still no word from Emmett.

And there was no word the next morning nor through the whole of that day. I spent the time alone in a kind of bewildered prowling, listlessly sorting through tapes and CDs, lying on my back with books and mags but tossing them aside after a few pages because my concentration wasn't there. When the boys finally returned from work I was startled out of the shallow doze I had fallen into beside the tape deck. When I confirmed that there had been no word from Emmett I saw their momentary disbelief turn quickly to bravura foolery.

"Now that he's got a taste the bastard can't get enough of it," John said. "Like a suck calf."

But John wasn't fooling anyone. A thin virus of anxiety had entered the room and our mood. The only subject worth discussing was now faintly unspeakable and as the evening wore on we forcibly immersed ourselves in books and the TV. Finally the tension was bearable no longer and we drifted off to our beds, silently, one by one.

I slept badly that night, surfacing from time to time through fitful dreams till finally I rose at six to eat breakfast with John and Paul before they went to work. The anxiety of the previous night had now deepened to outright worry and John, true to his nature as the decisive one, faced it head on. He banged his cup down and held up his hands.

"That's it. If there's no word by this evening we're going to the cops. I'm not spending another night like last night."

I kept my head down and groaned. I didn't want to hear this.

"That's a bit drastic. Cops won't do anything until he's been missing for three days," Paul said.

"I know that, but at least they'll have his description so they can start straight away. We have to do something."

"They'll know straight off he's illegal."

"Matter a fuck. Look, either something's happened to him and he needs our help or he's still out there poking this blond bitch and hasn't given us a thought, in which case he deserves whatever's coming to him."

"It's not his form to stay away this long without a word."

"Exactly."

Paul opened his mouth for one further objection and then shut it again. John was right—we couldn't spend another night like last night, we were freaked out.

They left for work but not before they emptied their pockets and gave me a further two hundred dollars in case I needed it. They left the flat in silence, almost bashfully, and I settled down again to my vigil beside the phone. I sat awhile in the kitchen drinking more tea and smoking. There was no doubt in my mind now that something terrible had happened to Emmett; I knew it as surely as if I were standing over his gray corpse on the kitchen floor. I tried to bury this thought within me by making more tea and clearing away the breakfast things but I gave up after a few minutes and went back to bed and slept with the phone on my pillow till noon. When I awoke I lay in bed staring at the ceiling for an age and then I got up. I blundered around and tried to clear away the breakfast things again but I found my mood had changed utterly, making any sort of chore impossible. My patience was exhausted and I could neither sit nor stand. Before I noticed it I had taken to pacing the floor. Now I could feel one of my infrequent rages building inside me, coming to a head, ready at any moment to spill out in sudden violence and verbal abuse. I was filled with an incoherent, unreasonable rage toward Emmett. Why had he gone and let this happen to him? I seethed. I had the obscene conviction that whatever happened to him had been drawn on him by his own stupid innocence. The stupid bastard, I raged, the stupid, stupid fucking bastard.

The phone rang suddenly, scattering my rage. I was on it before it rang a second time. It was Emmett, his voice all choked and barely able to speak.

"Mike, Mike, is that you?" he blurted.

"Emmett, where the hell are you?" I yelled. "We've been worried sick. Why haven't you called?"

He ignored the question. He was crying openly now, making low gulping sounds beneath his words, snuffling.

"Mike, come and get me quick, quick, I think I'm dying."

"Emmett, do you know where you are?"

He didn't seem to hear me, his pain or whatever it was seemed to overwhelm him just then, rising up in a great wave and breaking from him in sobs.

"Emmett! Emmett! Take a hold of yourself. Calm down, just calm down." I spoke to him like that for a few moments till he steadied down and then I asked him again if he knew where he was. He gave me the address and I made him repeat it to make sure I got it right.

"Be quick, Mike, please," he said again as he began to sob. "I think I'm going to die."

"Just hold on, Emmett," I implored. "I'm on my way."

I don't remember anything about that journey. It passed in a kind of slow-motion blur of whizzing glass and concrete, people and cars.

All I could think about were Emmett's words which kept hammering in my head—I'm going to die, he'd said, I'm going to die.

The cabbie stopped several times to consult a map and I drummed my feet and cursed with impatience. We drove south into Brooklyn, journeyed for an hour and turned west beyond Bensonhurst toward Gravesend Bay. Finally we spent a crucifying amount of time over the last half mile negotiating one-way and pedestrian systems, crawling through tiny streets beneath tenements that blocked out the sunlight and that teemed with black kids and lanky teenagers hopping basketballs on the sidewalks. We pulled up eventually at a gap in the tenements where one of them had been flattened and the vacant area wired off for development. I saw Emmett straightaway. A crowd of kids had gathered to one side of the site entrance and Emmett was visible over their heads. He had his back to the wire facing the kids and he was suspended from the mesh by one of his arms held high over his head, his fingers threaded in the diamond pattern. His head was hanging and his body had a pendulous motion; his arm was carrying his full weight. I burst through the crowd of kids and lifted his head. Emmett's face was gray and there was a heavy rivulet of blood draining from the corner of his mouth. His eyes were two sightless bores in the middle of his skull, the irises totally occluded by the giant pupils.

"Emmett, it's me, Mike, I'm here now. Everything is going to be OK. I'm taking you home." I'll never know why I came out with that awful platitude but it seemed to have an effect on him. He closed his mouth with a thick, rasping sound and his eyes flicked into momentary focus.

"Mike," he whispered.

"Yes, Emmett, it's me, Mike. Everything's going to be OK now."

He started to sob then, his head dropped and all his pain seemed to flow out of him.

"I'm going to die, Mike, I'm going to die."

"You're not going to die, Emmett. We're going to get you out of here and get you seen to. Everything is going to be OK."

It was a bitch of a job loosening his fingers from the mesh. The circulation had been cut off from his hand and the weight of his body had frozen his fingers in the wire. I managed to raise him up slightly and pry them loose and he fell deadweight, sobbing into my arms.

"Look, mister, he's bleeding," one of the kids called. "He's bleeding."

I saw that Emmett was holding his hand over the soft flesh beneath his ribs. Blood was oozing steadily between his fingers.

"I don't want to die," he whispered, "I don't want to die."

I picked him up from the ground and bundled him into the taxi, yelling that I needed a hospital.

"Don't let him bleed all over the seat, man," the driver warned.

"Fuck the seat! Just get us to a hospital."

Emmett tipped over in the seat, his head falling into my lap. He was sobbing quietly now, almost strangely contented in his grief. I kept my hand over his belly, hoping it wouldn't split and spill his guts all over the floor. I wanted to cry myself but I've never had a talent for that crying shit. Right then I just felt dried up and twisted in my gut, plus bitter as all hell. I knew I was going to carry this with me for the rest of my life. I could feel it entering into my bones on a tide of darkness, washing up through me and swamping my heart. Rages and outbursts weren't my thing, not those fancy volatile moods that flared up and burnt out in an instant. I was more a long-distance runner in these affairs, measuring out my anger and bitterness in daily increments, mindful of the long haul ahead—and I knew already I would have plenty of material here to see me through for the rest of my days.

We pulled up in front of a run-down brownstone. I threw Emmett's arm over my shoulder and hauled him through the door of the hospital, into the neon-lit foyer that opened out from the reception desk. The whole place had an air of incipient dilapidation about it, all paneled glass and new-laid tile but already clouded over with a recent film of grease and dust that was there to stay. The reception area itself was a study in controlled bedlam. Everything teetered on the edge of shambles; nurses sprinted down signposted corridors and trolleys whizzed by with their broken human cargo. Inside the main door two cops prowled, eating doughnuts and drinking coffee from Styrofoam cups. It looked anything but a place of healing.

I wrestled Emmett over to the admissions desk and confronted this doll-like receptionist. All hair and glossed lips, she stared at me as if a patient were the last thing in the world she expected to be faced with—I half expected her to pop gum in my face at any moment. I then proceeded to spend the worst five minutes of my life trying to make the bitch see the emergency of our situation. She couldn't seem to get it into her skull that we were only in her god-forsaken country a matter of hours and no, we weren't paying into a health insurance scheme. I had begun to scream and reach into the proscribed areas of my vocabulary when out of the corner of my eye I saw the cops put down their cups and make their way across the floor toward me. Emmett chose that very moment to draw all the attention to himself. With a low moan he slid through my arms and collapsed heavily to the floor like the stricken victim he most surely was. His arm flew outward in a stylized gesture of farewell and the blood cupped in the palm of his hand arched out over the floor, splashing the admissions book on the receptionist's desk.

There's nothing like the sight of blood for drawing attention. A dissonant chorus of shrieks went up from the other patients and all of a sudden Emmett was submerged beneath a huddle of white coats who were ripping away his shirt and calling for plasma and trolleys. Emmett was lifted onto a trolley and whisked away beneath a neon sign marked Emergency. I trotted down the hall in his wake and found myself spluttering out answers to a series of questions fired at me by the doctors—blood type, reaction to anesthesia, and so on. I blurted out what I knew, which was damn all, and then they disappeared into what I presumed was the operating theater.

Suddenly I was all alone in the hallway with not a clue what to do with myself. In my confusion I pulled out a pack of fags and made to light one. Then I remembered where I was so I put it back in the pack and walked back to the entrance and sat on the steps outside and lit up.

It was midafternoon by then and the city cowered beneath the accumulated heat of an unseasonably hot day. The sun blazed past its zenith having drained the morning vigor and I sensed a silent, pent-up scream in the concrete and metal all around. It thrilled and vibrated everywhere, a terrific ruinous tension. I felt like opening my mouth also and howling from the depths of my being; I settled instead for burying my head in my hands and grinding my teeth till my jaws hurt.

I stayed there and finished my cigarette, then went back inside to the operating theater. I sat down on a leatherette bench beside an ancient Negro with a snow-white beard and a porkpie hat. His eyes were sunk in some silent dream of ruin and when he eventually rose up out of it he regarded me with a strange complicity. For the first time since the whole shambles had begun I seriously wanted to cry; I felt the tears scorching behind my eyes and begin to flow down my face. I buried my face in my hands and sobbed quietly. After about an hour the doors of the theater swung wide and Emmett was wheeled away down the corridor, attached to drips and so on. A small, balding surgeon stood over me, peeling away a surgical mask like a second skin and mopping his brow with his sleeve.

"Have you made a statement to the cops?"

"Is he going to be OK?"

The surgeon regarded me for a long moment. "He's going to wake up in considerable pain and there is no predicting how he will react when he wakes up to the memory. He will need to be handled with kid gloves for a while. Physically speaking the prognosis is good. Provided no infection has set in yet he could make a complete recovery. He's a young man, his body should be able to cope. With a little adjustment to his diet he should be OK."

"How serious an adjustment?"

"Not too serious. He will have to cut down on his intake of alcohol and certain other foodstuffs."

"For how long?"

"I'm afraid for the rest of his life. He won't have the capacity to process all the waste that a normal person has."

"What do you mean? He was only cut, a knife in the belly."

The bald surgeon just shook his head blankly.

"It's not that simple. He's been cut all right, cut seriously. Someone has lifted one of his kidneys."

I spent most of the following week sitting at Emmett's bedside, watching and listening to the monitors and respirators as they hummed and ticked out his suffering. His tranquil body lent an almost sacral atmosphere to the room and in deference to his efforts I quickly became attuned to the rhythms of those machines. My breathing began to rise and fall in time with the respirator and my own blood began to pulse in sympathy with the peaks and troughs of the cardiograph. I willed Emmett to draw strength from this silent empathy.

Emmett hardly ever woke during those postoperative days. He surfaced infrequently for brief, disquieting moments, mumbled a few garbled words like a stoned prophet, and each time was quickly submerged by one of the fleeting nurses who administered sedatives as if they were trying to thwart some blasphemy. I stayed by his bed and listened to him breathe.

On the second day I gave a ten-page statement to one of the cops who seemed to have a regular beat in the hospital. I answered a hoard of lunatic questions about our mission in New York, our circumstances, why we hadn't visas, and so on. On the fifth day I was locked out of Emmett's room and he was kept awake just long enough to give a statement of his own. That evening I was confronted by the same cop who bluntly presented me with two choices: we could leave the country of our own volition in a few days after Emmett was discharged or we could wait, in which case we would be served with expulsion orders, thus making it virtually impossible for us ever to enter the country again. Either way it was no choice. I was coming quickly to realize that these people had no souls.

"Will there be an investigation?"

"Yes, we have your statements but I wouldn't hold much hope for it. Unless what happened to your friend can be tied to a wider circle of similar incidents then I'm afraid it doesn't have much priority, not considering your status. It might be the case that it is part of such a circle but either way your presence here isn't needed. We have your statements, that's all you can do. Take my advice and get your friend out of here and home to where he can get some proper medical attention."

"What did he say about the whole thing?"

"Not much, he can't remember anything. He got into the car with the lady and that's about it, it's all a blank from there on. He can't even remember how he made the call to you. You know as much as he does."

' ' '

Emmett was discharged the following Monday. Our bitter sojourn in the land of hope and opportunity had lasted barely nine days. The very basic terms of our travel insurance didn't stretch to the type of extended care he needed and anyway, right from the moment it became known we were illegals, he was only in the hospital on sufferance. It was made clear to us that his bed was needed for other, more needful cases.

We got a taxi to the airport and I led Emmett through the departure lounge, aware that I was getting a lot of quizzical looks from the other boarders who kept staring at the big, glazed child I was hauling by the hand. He sat beside me in the window seat, morphined out of his skull and staring wall-eyed through the tiny window as we flew between cloud levels. He had his hand clasped over his midriff and I turned out the palm every so often to check he wasn't bleeding. We didn't speak a word during that whole journey, there was nothing to say. From time to time the trolley dollies checked to see that he was OK and I answered in his stead; Emmett was miles away, floating serenely in a warm sea of anesthesia.

Both sets of parents were in Shannon to meet us. I towed Emmett by the hand into the arrivals lounge and delivered him silently over to his parents and the medics who were there to take him away. I assured them I was OK and then handed over the medical charts and stood back out of the bubble of hysteria that now surrounded him. They lifted him onto the trolley and both sets of parents followed silently in its wake as it made to the exit. I watched as they moved away, moving silently like a private cortège, and I didn't know it at the time but I was seeing Emmett Ward, my best friend, my right-hand man, my brother in arms, for the very last time.

`        `   `     `

I kept in touch with Emmett for a while after that. I called on him each time I went home. After a period of convalescence he lived with his mom and dad and underwent counseling for some sort of post-traumatic stress disorder, another fucking American ailment. Odd times he was in good form and he'd talk away and we'd go for a pint together but these were only odd times. Most times he was so full of grief and depression he would just take to his room and wouldn't be coaxed out. Sometimes he wouldn't even see me. I used to stand outside his room and listen to him making this low, whimpering sound like a whipped animal. It's the most awful sound in creation, the sound of a fractured heart.

I tried to persuade Emmett to return to college with me. The following spring I managed to bluff my way through an interview and onto a postgrad diploma and I had it in mind that he would come back with me and I'd look after him, take him under my wing, a kind of role reversal. But Emmett wanted nothing to do with the idea. "That's all over," he said quietly as if saying good-bye to a part of himself forever. "I want to stay at home for a while and get myself together." I didn't push it. To tell the truth, for all my good intentions I wasn't entirely confident of being able to do anything for him. You see, something had died in Emmett, a light had gone out in his eyes and his mind. Sometimes when I went to see him I'd look into his face and I'd see right through to the back of his skull. There's nothing in there anymore, nothing but blank space.

Now he spends most of his time tending a small garden that runs from the back of his house, a beautiful, geometrical thing with rows of veg and herbs; so many herbs that I cannot name half of them. Right now it's the joy of his life and he spends every minute of his day there, weeding and tending it. But I hate that garden, I hate it with a passion. When I saw him working in it for the first time I knew that his contentment and happiness were genuine and yet it saddened me to the core. I wanted to walk through it and start kicking and smashing the whole thing, pulling up roots and trampling stalks. Something's been ripped out of Emmett and this garden, with all its lush color and beauty, has become the piss-poor substitute for the life he should have had.

A couple of months ago I came round the gable of his house and I stood and watched him working there. He was pulling weeds and fiddling with a hoe between the ridges. What got me, though, was the way he moved, a kind of soft lumbering that threatened at every moment to topple over into disaster. But he never damaged a stalk or a plant, he just kept moving one foot in front of the other like a somnolent giant. As far as I knew he wasn't on any medication at the time but you wouldn't have thought that if you'd seen him. I stood there in the shadow of the trees and I thought of all the misery and shit and spoiled dreams that make up the world. And then I turned and walked away. The pain in my chest had got so bad I was going to cry out and I don't think Emmett would have understood.

I don't see Emmett anymore. I avoid going round to his house. I sometimes meet his old man in the street or the pub and he smiles and shakes my hand, then asks me when am I going to come over. He can barely keep the pleading note out of his voice. I tell him that I'll call soon but I never do and I never will. There's nothing I can do anymore and besides, Emmett frightens me now. My parents get on to me about it as well but I just avoid talking about the subject. All I know now is that for the first time in my life I've turned my energies to my studies and things are going well. I'm getting the grades and I'm keeping my head down, I'm beginning to see the big picture. I hope Emmett Ward understands.

Amor Vincit Omnia

Speedie Ryan didn't give a fuck. No money or job, no woman or qualifications, and no prospect of acquiring any in the near future. But Speedie wasn't worried, Speedie was laid back, so laid back in fact that if he was any more laid back he'd be a rug.

Speedie had his mother's heart broke and his father's also. Sitting around the house all day watching vids and chain-smoking, he was driving them to despair.

"Speedie, wouldn't you try and get a job?" his mother would plead. "At least put in an application for one, college or something. You're twenty-eight years old, ten years on the dole. That's a crying shame for a young man like you. One day you're going to wake up and the best years of your life will be gone and you won't have one thing to show for it."

Speedie would hold up a lordly hand.

"No rush, Mom," he'd say. "All in good time. I'm thinking."

"Thinking! What are you thinking about? All I see you do from one day to the next is sit there watching telly."

"I'm thinking about life," he'd say. "Thinking and taking pre-liminary notes. Making sure I get it right when I make a start. You wouldn't want me to start out on the wrong foot and spend the rest of my life out of step with myself, now would you?"

"No, I suppose not," she'd say resignedly.

"Well then, don't worry, all in good time, all in good time. Mom . . . are you making tea?"

But one day everything changed for Speedie.

He was coming by the dole office after scratching when he passed a young woman going the opposite way. She was one of those slight, New Age waifs, hung with pendants and anchored to the ground with Doc Martens, topped off with lank, blond hair that made her face look smaller than it really was. And Speedie knew straight away that this was the woman for him. Speedie knew that he was going to spend the rest of his life with her and that she was going to have his kids and they were going to live happily ever after. A whole future opened up for Speedie in that instant and it was as clear to him as newsreel running in his own head.

So Speedie got his act together. He went out and got a job in a kitchen. A job as a gofer, scrubbing pots and floors, making sand-wiches and emptying bins. It wasn't much of a job but it was the first he'd ever had and it pleased his old pair. It was the first step in his new life. On the evening he got his first pay he put on a clean pair of jeans and T-shirt and went in search of the waif. And Speedie had researched his quarry's habits so he knew where to find her. She was in a pub sitting alone, reading, a near-empty glass before her. Speedie bought two pints, sat opposite her, and got straight to the point.

"Hello, my name is Speedie Ryan and I'm here to propose to you. I want to marry you and spend the rest of my life with you. What do you say?"

The waif regarded him blankly.

"Thanks for the pint," she said curtly. "Now fuck off and leave me alone, I'm expecting someone."

"You don't understand," Speedie said. "I'm in love with you and if you don't accept me then my life will be worthless. I will wander the earth a broken man with a cavity in my chest where my heart should be. I know also that you will love me if you give me a chance."

"Jesus, just get out of my face and leave me in peace. Who the hell are you anyway to come here with this shit?"

"Well, I'm not going to tell you a lie. I'm not going to say that I'm the only son of some wealthy business magnate with interests in copper and timber in Latin America and I'm not going to say that I'm some stud who's hung like a donkey on steroids. I'm Speedie Ryan and I work as a skivvy. It's a job with no prestige or prospect of advancement. Also, my sexual experience is negligible. I do know, however, that given time I can make you happy."

"Oh please!" she cried with disgust.

"I'm going to pursue you to the ends of the earth," he said, "and one day you are going to be mine."

"You're an arrogant bastard," she retorted.

"No, not arrogant. I just know what I know and I know that one day you are going to be mine. I'm going to go now," he finished, "I've said all I've got to say for the moment and I can understand that it might be a bit much to take on board straightaway. Just think on what I've said." He got up to leave.

"You're not even going to ask me my name?"

"I know your name. It's Olwyn Crayn and you're twenty-one. You're from west Mayo and you study English and French. If you keep your head down you're on course for first-class honors in your finals."

"You bastard," she hissed. "How the hell did you know that?"

"Like I said, I know what I know and I know everything about you."

And Speedie left her to finish her pint alone.

Speedie worked hard in the following weeks. He worked hard at his job, about fifty hours a week, and his parents were bemused at the change that came over him. His habits changed, he was barely around the house anymore, and when he was he spent most of the time in his room. But what worried his parents most was the distracted, driven look that had entered his eyes. They could hardly get a word out of him anymore.

"Speedie, why don't you sit with us tonight and watch a video? We don't seem to see a lot of you these days."

"No can do, Mom. I'm a busy young man. I need to get my sleep, I have to be up for work." With that he would leave the room and go to his bed.

"I suppose we should be grateful," his mother would sigh.

And Speedie worked hard in pursuit of Olwyn. He sent her little presents and notes, a short poem even, and he took to stopping her in the street for conversation. But Olwyn would pass by without a word, contempt written all over her face. One time he made a show of her by turning up in a pub with a bunch of flowers and mortified her in front of her friends by telling her that he would love her till there was not a single breath left in his body. And then he overstepped the mark completely. He sent her a note that told her, among other things, it would be his dearest wish to have her coiled body beneath him with her nails raking his back.

Two nights later Speedie was walking home in the dark and he got a battering. He was walking through Prospect Hill when he was jumped from behind. Someone pulled his coat over his head and dealt him a kick behind the knees which sent him sprawling. More kicks rained in on his head and his belly and when it was done someone knelt over him and told him that if he didn't fancy wearing his balls for earrings he should leave Olwyn Crayn alone. When Speedie went to work the following day his workmates pretended not to notice that his face was black and blue and that he was holding his ribs.

Speedie should have taken the hint. Speedie should have been philosophical about the whole thing. Speedie should have consoled himself with the fact that there are many more fish in the sea or with the outright lie that in all probability Olwyn was a lesbian. These were the ruses that would have satisfied the old Speedie and sent him off in some newer, safer direction. But this wasn't the old Speedie. This was the new improved version, the focused one with a life, and these ploys cut no ice whatsoever with him. Instead, he was just inspired to greater, more desperate measures.

On the following night Speedie made his final attempt to win Olwyn. He lifted the key to her flat from beneath the stone in the garden, entered, and waited for her to return. When she got back she drank tea in the kitchen with her other flatmates and crashed onto her bed half an hour later. Speedie waited till he heard her sleeping, then climbed out of the wardrobe and up the bed toward her. Olwyn woke instantly and flailed out with both arms, screamed blue murder, and woke the whole house. Speedie tumbled down a flight of stairs and was chased from the house by the other tenants. He ran all the way home.

Speedie was pulled in by the cops the following day and held on remand pending his trial.

Speedie Ryan's in prison now, doing two years on charges of breaking and entering with intent to commit bodily harm, both sentences running concurrently. With good behavior he might get out in a year. Speedie works in the prison mess but he's a changed man now. He doesn't say much anymore. If you ask him he just shrugs his shoulders and tells you that it's all in the past, he doesn't give a fuck anymore.

Speedie's parents visit him when they can. It's a difficult journey that takes them to another province but they do the best they can. If you ask them their eyes fill up with tears and they'll tell you that their hearts are broken seeing their only son behind bars like this.

Olwyn Crayn is living in a squat in New Road, shacked up with a long-haired slacker who has no work or qualifications and no immediate prospects of acquiring them either. If you talk to him he'll tell you he's chilling out, taking it as it comes, there's no rush. Olwyn sleeps most of the day now and spends the night and early morning watching vids and smoking dope. She hasn't submitted her graduate thesis so she has yet to get her degree. She might go back and finish it next year, then again she might not, she'll see how things go. And if you ask her she'll smile and tell you she's in love.

The Occupation: A Guide for Tourists

My jeep was one of a dozen vehicles tailed back from the checkpoint. It was the last vehicle in a convoy of three other jeeps, several marked container trucks carrying emergency medical aid, and one transit van fitted with radio and signaling equipment. Up ahead, the border security were swarming over the first trucks, searching through the cabs and spilling the contents out onto the dusty road. One of the guards had disappeared into the security hut with a handful of our entry permits. An air of surly menace hung over the guards. They had the aspect of men completing a despicably menial task by way of punishment. Every one of them needed a shave and a new issue of fatigues. The thirty-year occupation showed in every filthy, frayed piece of webbing and in the corroded state of their antiquated weaponry; and this was the occupying army.

Ours were the first vehicles to gain entry to the occupation in fifteen years. We were a detail of Amnesty observers coming to verify rumors of horrific and systematic human rights abuses. During the last year details of work camps and smuggled photographic evidence of mass rape and torture had been finding their way into the

Western press. Eventually world conscience had been sufficiently moved to force a UN resolution that achieved a temporary opening of the border. We were the first entrants but, somewhere to our rear, a massive convoy of relief aid under UN guard was wending its way through the desert.

Evidently this border detail was taking the recent UN resolution as something of a personal insult. Only such lofty censure could account for the sheer sense of affront exuded by the soldier who was making his way toward me. He was a blunt hump of a man whose skin had been weathered to the texture of old leather. His corporal's stripes were barely visible beneath the mantle of dust that clung about him. He was handing back the visas to the other travelers without a word. When he stood before me I saw that he had also handed out a second document, a few xeroxed pages. I read it through and I quote it here in full. It was titled *The Occupation: A Guide for Tourists*. It went on:

1. While traveling in a foreign country you come upon a terrible scene. Atop a hill a young man is being put to death before a crowd of onlookers. He has recently been nailed to a cross. Blood streams from a wound in his side and his thin body is faced into the full glare of the sun. He does not have long to live. Do you:

   A. Feel outrage and disgust and immediately cut the man down from the cross?
   B. Pass quickly without saying a word? You will not presume to meddle in the judicial procedures of your host country. Besides, the man was obviously a notorious criminal who got what was coming to him.
   C. Admire the skill with which the whole tableau has been staged and resolve to seek out the theater company and make them a lavish contribution.

If your answer is A, then proceed to 2A, if B to 2B, if C to 2C and so on.

2A. You take the man to a small hospital on the outskirts of the city and try to sign him in at casualty as your brother. While the man lies bleeding on a trolley you enter into a sordid dispute with the hospital bursar. You finally undertake to pay the medical fees in foreign currency, American dollars and deutsche marks mainly. You also surrender your passport as security. The patient is wheeled away rapidly for emergency surgery and you spend the next few days in the city while the man is monitored in the intensive care unit.

2B. You have put the incident quickly out of your mind and spend a few days touring the outlying countryside and city. You discover terrible scenes of waste and devastation. The occupying armies have requisitioned crops and animals and the country's infrastructure is a shambles. Whole provinces have been isolated by cratered roads and demolished bridges; famine and disease are rife in the worst-hit areas. When you reach the city you find that it is crawling with paupers and wounded veterans, the thoroughfares of the commercial center are a *chevaux-de-frise* of broken glass and strewn metal.

2C. You trace the theater company to an abandoned warehouse by the railway station. They are a small company specializing in a particularly vivid brutalism. Productions of *Hamlet* and *Oedipus Rex* have taken a devastating toll on the players and their confidence is at a low ebb. They have recently had to pull out of an important production because of a shortage of funds. You make an offer to underwrite this new production and it is accepted with gratitude. You are treated as a messiah.

3A. After four days the young man regains consciousness. He is tended to by a retinue of a dozen men his own age. The surgeon introduces you as his savior but he is singularly lacking in gratitude when told of your intervention. He accuses you of having thwarted his destiny and of arrogantly meddling in things of which you know nothing.

3B. An explosion in the commercial area of the city results in many casualties. A rebel attack on an army convoy has been completely mistimed: the device goes off near a mobile soup kitchen killing mainly women and children, injuring hundreds. You sign up at a mobile blood transfusion unit and donate five hundred milliliters of blood. Pandemonium reigns in the streets and you volunteer to do relief work in one of the field hospitals.

3C. As part of the underground art movement you learn that the company has a constant fear of infiltration by the authorities: it has been rightly identified as the source of resistance propaganda. Several productions in the past have been shut down by the security forces.

4A. After ten days your relationship with the patient has not improved. He is incommunicative and evasive. No one will reveal his identity and local police have no record of him having committed any crime. You decide to persevere with your efforts of friendship for a few more days.

4B. You are contacted at the hotel by the transfusion unit who inform you that you have a developed case of HIV. You spend the rest of the day drinking heavily at the hotel bar. Outside there is a heavy military presence. Patrols move continuously up and down the street, never resting except to disperse small gatherings and send people on their way with a cuff of their gun butts. Overhead, helicopters cross the sky and when night falls searchlights probe the streets. Everyone suspects that there are several more incendiary devices triggered to go off.

4C. The company has planned a final production of an ancient morality play. It will be a public performance with an overtly political theme; it is hoped that it will incite the city to all-out, unified resistance against the invaders. You are sworn to secrecy and at their request you take on a minor but significant role in the production.

5A. Psychological tests have shown that the patient suffers from a complex of neuroses ranging from severe paranoia to extreme credulity in occult and New Age religions, healing crystals, and tarot cards. The psychologist remarks that this condition is not unusual, the character of the occupation has given rise to several such cases. He has treated several men, all with undocumented pasts, who claim to have healing and regenerative talents. He will not venture a prognosis.

5B. After four days wandering through the city in a drunken stupor you sober up near a brothel. It is the middle of the night, in heavy darkness, but your mind is now clear. You enter the brothel and promptly engage in several acts of anal intercourse with underage boys. You then refuse to pay. There follows a tense moment when a search by bouncers reveals that you are carrying no currency whatsoever. You calmly await the arrival of the police.

5C. Rehearsals are continuing smoothly and you are now enjoying a privileged status within the company. You realize that there is an unspoken effort among the players to court your goodwill. They bring you small gifts of hard-to-get coffee and local craftware. Furthermore you have discovered a talent for acting and your performance has drawn genuine praise from the other players.

6A. The patient's attitude has now developed to outright hostility. You narrowly escape serious injury when he attacks you with scissors in the recreation room. You are rescued by four male nurses. The psychologist explains that you have now assumed demonic status in the patient's imagination. Not only are you responsible for a salvation he did not need but also for the political failure of his death. He suspects that you are an army spy.

6B. You cooperate fully with your interrogators and admit to having no funds whatsoever. You astonish them further by confessing to six attempted murders via the sexual act. Your captors are in a quandary; they need to prosecute but are unsure of the grounds on which to proceed: the emergency laws have no provisions for dealing with aliens. On a sheet of paper you outline the charges against yourself and draw up details of an emergency bill covering the crime of murder by sexually transmitted disease. You advise that the bill be made law as quickly as possible and waive the right to a preliminary hearing. You are scheduled to stand trial in three days.

6C. You have begun to covet the lead role in the play. The principal player is a buffoon whose every word and gesture grates on your soul. As a method actor he has immersed himself totally in the role. He has assumed a facile air of wisdom and his speech has become littered with anodyne, pastoral anecdotes. Several of the female players have begun to attest that he has a cure for menstrual cramp. You resolve to turn him over to the authorities. You begin to circulate information about him in various bars and cafeterias.

7A. You now have misgivings about the wisdom of your intervention. It is revealed to you that the patient is one of the leaders of the resistance and that you have interfered with a mythopoeic event essential to the salvation of the city. Your responsibility for the fate of the people weighs heavily on your conscience and after a night of soul searching you resolve to make amends.

7B. Your trial begins in the ruins of a religious museum. The witnesses testify from the pulpit and the judge is seated behind the altar.

At his back, the door of the tabernacle has been recently shattered. The jury is made up of outpatients from a nearby infirmary. You conduct your own defense but limit your examination to apparently pointless questions on the history of the occupation. In your closing speech you plead guilty and urge that the maximum sentence be handed down. In his summative speech the judge congratulates you on the skill and clarity of your defense. He speaks at length on the groundbreaking nature of the trial and assures you that your name will merit a chapter to itself in the judicial history of his country.

7C. On his way home from rehearsals the principal actor is picked up by the security forces. After interrogations and beatings he signs a detailed confession outlining various subversive activities and connections. Morale in the company plummets when several more members are implicated. The company is now gutted of a large part of its artistic and administrative talent; its future is in real jeopardy. You move quickly to take charge of the production, promptly casting yourself in the principal role and allocating the lesser ones in such a way as to throw light on your performance. There is a feeling of renewed confidence.

8A. You outline your plan to the patient and after consultation with his cadre it is decided that it will go ahead. You are issued with a new identity that places you immediately in the pantheon of resistance heroes who have kept the flame of national salvation burning. Within days you are being greeted surreptitiously as the hidden king.

8B. After only two hours' deliberation the jury files back into the pews and the foreman returns a guilty verdict. You congratulate yourself on having conducted a successful defense. The judge commends the jury on their verdict and then draws a black cowl over his head before delivering the sentence. You hear that your execution will be expedited immediately and that there are no provisions for an appeal.

8C. The day of the production is drawing close. Flyers have been distributed and a large crowd is anticipated. The dressmaker works long into the night preparing your costume; there are numerous alterations to be made before it will fit. You spend the rest of the evening at a small restaurant with the rest of the cast.

9A. The patient briefs you on the details of your mission. Initially overcome by crippling fear, you surmount it with the knowledge that a whole nation is depending on you. Besides, events have now taken on a momentum of their own. You are robed in a regal gown and a makeshift crown is placed upon your head. You are paraded through the slums of the city to a summit on its outskirts, the site of your ascension. On your journey various thugs take the opportunity to indulge in indiscriminate violence, and there are several scuffles with your minders. By the time you reach the summit you have sustained injuries to your abdomen and your cloak has been ripped away.

9B. You are led from the museum into sunlight wearing a sign that details your crimes. When your eyes have adjusted to the sunshine you are taken through the streets where the crowds are gathering to view some sort of pageant. Upon reading your crimes they grow incensed and start to attack you. They seem to have a ready supply of whips and chains and start to rain blows down upon you. By the time you reach the execution summit your body is running with blood.

9C. The routes are lined by heavy crowds conspicuously armed with whips, chains, and sticks. You move serenely at the head of your supporting cast and the production is going smoothly. Suddenly the onlookers play the part of persecutors. They work your body in passing and by the time you reach the summit your torso is a tracery of lacerations and you have begun to hallucinate. You try to hold your focus on the lines of your parting speech.

10. Beneath the cross you are given a final moment in which to address the crowd. The soldiers stand aside and an expectant hush descends upon the multitude. You have their full attention. You begin haltingly, it is your first public address, and your voice lacks resonance. Gradually, however, you gain in confidence and your speech becomes a ringing affirmation of life, the sacredness of resistance through arms and art, and the necessity of justice. The murmur of assent grows until a wave of applause breaks over you; it is sustained while the soldiers take you bodily and hoist you onto the cross. As the nails are driven in you feel no pain; your ecstasy has lifted you beyond sensation. From your perch you can see out over the crowd down onto the ruins of the city. Columns of smoke billow in several parts and food queues are visible in every quarter. This is your kingdom and auditorium, your panopticon, and it remains fixed in your imagination until consciousness, like the daylight, drains away to darkness.

I gazed past the checkpoint into the occupied country. The dirt road beyond the sentry post curved past an isolated grove of cedars, wending its way to the top of a low summit. Halfway up the slope a woman led a donkey carrying a huge bundle of kindling. Beyond the hill the city cast up a gray pall of smoke, shrouding the summit. Beneath the smoke vague shadows moved. I took my binoculars and gazed into the fog; I saw that the joiners were already working on the crosses.

Getting It in the Head

I suppose, looking back on it, there were easier ways of getting our hands on those bottles. We could and should have used a hacksaw to cut our way past the iron grid that covered the window and then got a stone to smash through the glass into the store where we knew those bottles of Coke and orange were stacked up to the roof. But the hacksaw never even dawned on us. Right from the beginning we knew it had to be an explosion or nothing. Isn't that strange, the way your mind fixes on something and you cannot see anything but that one thing? Now that I think of it we could have limited the damage by using a screwdriver to unscrew those grids. It would have probably taken a lot less time than a hacksaw as well. But it's too late thinking of hacksaws and screwdrivers now; we didn't think of them then and that's all there is to it. They were no fun, not when the alternative was a good, roaring explosion. Besides, we had been disappointed by the fire when it hadn't given us an explosion—the world had let us down, we had felt hard done by. There was nothing for it then but to have an explosion of our very own.

A few nights ago I woke in the middle of the night to find my room filled with a queer, orange, jerky light. The night seemed full of crashing noises and raised voices. From my second-story window I saw down the street that Coen's bar and nightclub was ablaze and that it had been for some time. Already the first timbers from the roof were crashing down inside the building. Through the blown-out windows I could see them hitting the floor with a great gush of sparks. It looked as if at any moment the whole roof was going to fall in. I began to dress in a real hurry, pulling on two pullovers, my jeans, boots, and baseball cap that had come all the way from America and that I never went anywhere without. I had already seen my parents in the crowd on the street, looking at the fire with their mouths open, so I knew there was no one to hold me back. In a minute I was legging it through the back garden and over the fences that separated my house from my friend Jamie's.

I was hoping Jamie wasn't in too deep a sleep. If he was I might never wake him. Last year when we went camping in the football pitch outside the town (we had wanted to go to Clare Island but our parents said, "You're too young, you're only ten") a bull had wandered into the pitch during the night and raised such a racket bellowing and roaring when it saw our red tent that I didn't get a wink of sleep the whole night. But Jamie never knew a thing about it: he just snored his way through the whole thing. I never saw anyone like him for sleep.

Anyway I had to rap hard on the window before he pulled back the curtain. He didn't look his best standing there in his pajamas with his hair sticking out like he'd been electrocuted. He pushed up the window, wiping the sleep from his eyes.

"What is it, Owl? It's the middle of the night."

"Come on quick, get dressed. Coen's pub is on fire." Being so full of sleep he wasn't so quick on the uptake.

"On fire?"

"Yes, on fire. The roof is about to cave in any minute. Pull on your clothes, we'll go for a look."

"Wow," he said. "Hang on a sec."

He was fully awake now. It probably took him just a minute to dress and he was still tucking in his shirt when we rounded the alley-way by the firehouse and came into the main street, which was now lined with fire hoses connected to the water main. Four or five men from the local fire brigade were standing in a clearing in front of the pub, jetting water onto the roof and through the windows. But they looked like they were fighting a losing battle: the roof looked just ready to fall in. To get a better view me and Jamie climbed onto one of those right-angled direction signs that stood by the wall at the back of the crowd. It was real comfortable up there, dangling our legs from the round bar and the wall nicely to our backs. The night was warm as well. We could see everything, all the people milling around in a semi-circle and the local cops with their arms out keeping them back from the fire. Between the cops and the building were the firemen. They looked great in that weird light with their helmets and long, black coats and heavy hoses tucked up under their arms. They looked real cool even though I knew every one of them and knew they were only part-time firemen, really shopkeepers and barmen. Everyone's eyes were on them like they were gladiators in some sort of contest, willing them on to win. Just right then they seemed to lose the fight. With a great roar, the sort you imagine a dragon makes, a huge section of the roof caved into the middle of the pub. Flames leaped high and a mushroom of sparks bloomed from the pub. A huge wave of heat drove the crowd back. Now the fire really raged and all the firemen could do was contain it until it burned itself out in its own good time.

"It's just like a movie," said Jamie.

That was the truth. Right at that moment I was thinking the whole thing would be perfect if I had a tin of Coke and a packet of crisps to eat while I watched.

"Yah," I said. "Just like at the cinema."

Into the golden light, from around the corner, my older brother showed up under the signpost. He looked the way he always looked, sorta cool, sorta wrecked, long black hair, leather jacket, and a fag sticking out of his pale face. Jamie and I admire that leather jacket of his a lot. It's one of those biker ones with brass buckles and zips. Sometimes when he's in bed I pull it on just to see what it looks like, but of course it's far too big for me. Anyway Jamie and I plan to buy one like it when we get older. But Jamie doesn't think it will work for me. He says you never see a fellow with specs wearing a leather jacket; it looks daft. I think I could be different though, I could set a new trend. Just to be sure, though, I'm on the lookout now for a fellow with specs wearing a leather jacket. So far my luck hasn't been good.

"How are the men?" my brother said. "The men they couldn't hang."

I hated that joke and he knew it. He looked pissed, as he always did this time of night. Even on our signpost we could smell the beer coming off his clothes. He was smoking a rollie, a really long one, sucking deep on it with his eyes closed.

"What do you men make of this little conflagration?" he mocked suddenly. "You there, Owl, at the head of the class, have you any light to throw on the subject? All those books you read, there must be something in them about the significance of fires and pyrolatry in primitive communities—discussions and analysis and so forth."

He was laughing now, leaning heavily on the wall and sucking his fag. I was wishing he'd go away. He was pissing me off and getting in the way of my movie. He couldn't even stand straight now;

he had one hand on our signpost. He pulled the fag from his mouth and gesticulated across the street with the red tip. Then, for the first time in his life, he said something interesting.

"There'll be one hell of a bang if those petrol pumps go up." He was pointing to the garage a few doors down on the opposite side of the street.

"Those pumps," he said. "They'll have more to put out than that little blaze if all that petrol goes up. There won't be two bricks on top of each other in the whole friggin' town." He stood shaking his head in disbelief for a moment and then pushed himself off the wall and staggered away. Jamie was thinking the same thing I was.

"Imagine if there was an explosion." The fire danced in his eyes like tiny demons as he spoke.

"Yah," I said. "It'd be brilliant. The whole town going up in one big fucker of a bang."

I could see the whole thing already, the collapsed buildings, the smoke drifting over the charred timber, the corpses everywhere. I wondered what it would be like without my parents. I decided quickly enough that I'd get over it, I'd often thought of killing them anyway. I'd have the house to myself—that would be a good thing—no one to tell me what to do. I could read all night if I wanted to—another good thing. I'd have ice cream for breakfast. There'd be no school so I could educate myself as I wanted to. I'd read up all about wars and plagues and dinosaurs and things like that. It would be heaven.

Jamie was speaking. "God, the whole town would be wiped out. There would be nothing left but a black hole like you see in a Road Runner cartoon."

It was then that I began to wish with all my heart for that explosion. I could even hear it already in my head, a deep roar that filled out the night with nothing but itself, a huge light and rushing wind. Jamie must have been thinking the same thing.

"Let's go to the Protestant church," he said. "It'll be safer there if anything happens and we'll have a better view."

We sprinted by the back of the crowd to the end of the street and into the church grounds, weaving through the trees and headstones. Even at this distance, about a hundred yards, the church walls danced with the shadow of flames. We climbed up the yew tree and moved on our bellies out onto the branch that allowed us to reach out and pull ourselves through the narrow, slitted window into the bell tower. We came here sometimes when we were looking for bats and things like that. We climbed up the stairs into the belfry, ducked under the huge bell and out onto the window ledge where we could sit side by side. We were comfortable then and I knew that if the town went up we were at a safe distance. We could see over the heads of the whole crowd and almost down into the blazing pub itself—we were that high. We could see the floor plan of the pub and the flames really raging up off the timber floors. The wooden bar, running along the wall backward into the nightclub, was throwing up a wall of flames curtaining the whole inside. By this time the firemen seemed to be concentrating their water on cooling down what was left of the roof so as to stop the fire spreading. I was beginning to have second thoughts about those firemen. If they kept jetting water like they were doing then there wouldn't be any explosion. Already with the water falling down inside from the roof the flames along the bar seemed to be dying down a bit. Jamie was having his doubts, too.

"Those firemen will ruin everything," he said. "Any more of that water and there will be no chance of any explosion."

And that was exactly what happened. More and more water went in over the walls and down from the roof and bit by bit the flames died down. By the time we came down from the tower there was nothing but a dull glow somewhere in the middle of the building and the firemen were walking in and out through it as they pleased.

I imagined the dragon lying there in the middle of the building groaning, just about to die from some massive wound. All I could think of as I ran home was how bitter I felt toward those firemen. They had stolen something from us and even though I knew them and knew that some of them were my friends' dads I would gladly have killed all of them right then.

II

My father's always said that my temper would get me into trouble some day. He knows everything, my old man, or at least he thinks he does. I guess it's this self-assumed omniscience that makes him my old man. Well, I have to admit it, he was right, my temper has got me into trouble. But what he doesn't know is just how much trouble it is and how seriously it's going to affect him. It just goes to show that no matter how much you think you know, you ultimately know damn all.

When I was a kid, younger than Owl, my old man had to make several trips to the school because my teachers were always ringing him up, complaining about all the fights I got into. I was having problems with discipline, he was told. It was true I got into a lot of fights but none of them were my fault. I just wanted things done fair and square, that's all, games played without any cheating and so on, and I was prepared to fight to see that it was done.

I remember one really vivid incident. I was playing football in an under-twelve match and I was being marked closely by this lanky kid who was stronger than me but not as quick. All through the game I had half a yard on him but it was no use. He kept pulling and clinging to me and holding my jersey and the ref must have been blind because he blew for none of it despite all the abuse he was getting from the sideline. Late in the game I was running to the ball, one stride ahead of him, and had it nearly in my hands when I felt my jersey stretching out behind me and my legs losing ground. He was hanging out of me again and I could take no more of it. I spun round with my boot swinging upward and it caught him clean in the groin. If anyone tells you that kids don't feel that kind of thing they're talking shit because that kid just stood there in shock, with the color draining from his lips and his eyes clouding over with something milky before he toppled forward, facedown on the grass. The ref grabbed me by the neck and called me a little bastard under his breath and I saw a woman come shrieking out onto the pitch, all flying skirts, yelling, "My baby, my baby!" I was so blind with rage I lashed out again, this time with the other boot, catching the ref under the kneecap. He went down, too, and all of a sudden there was a big crowd around us shouting and cursing and throwing punches over my head as more and more parents spilled in from the sidelines. There was now almost a full-scale riot. The ref and a few others got a bad beating and the match was eventually abandoned. The organizing committee set up an investigation that evening to find out what the hell had happened.

The next day a lawyer's letter was delivered to our house and the old man received it at the front door. I didn't know what it was at the time but I had a fair idea it wasn't exactly singing my praises. When Dad came in from the hallway he looked like he could chew iron. He kept looking at me and I was sure he was going to deliver one of those long speeches about good manners and doing the right thing. But for some reason—maybe even then he sensed I had stopped listening to him—he just cut the whole thing down to a few words.

"Before you do something like that again, think, just think."

That was all he said and it was enough. I didn't care to hear any sermons then because I was adamant I'd done nothing wrong. That evening I was called to the town hall to answer questions from the investigating committee. They had to submit a report to the Mayo GAA Board. I knew all the old men asking the questions so I wasn't a bit afraid. I just told them what happened, that I wanted to play football but that the other kid wouldn't let me and that I'd had to do something, because the ref was doing nothing at all and that no, I wasn't sorry about the whole thing. I was dead proud of that testimony at the time and even today my composure and cockiness impress me. I don't know, however, if I feel so proud of the whole thing now. I think I may have castrated that kid. But my most vivid memory of the whole thing is the blind rage in which I had struck out, how the whole world suddenly darkened and I became a lashing knot of fury. Well, that was what I started talking about here, my temper and how it was going to get me in trouble. Now it finally has and it's trouble of a real serious sort.

It all started at that fire a few nights ago, the night Coen's pub went up in flames. That was a dangerous fire, too, so near those petrol pumps and gas containers. The whole town could have gone up. It was a bit of excitement though, the biggest since those Hell's Angels pulled in here two years ago. Now that was a piece of real excitement. No one ever knew who invited them or why they came here but for three days in September our little town was overrun with hundreds of bikers in long hair and chains. Why they should choose Louisburgh I'll never know. Louisburgh's only a built-up crossroads and so far west against the coast we don't even get tinkers. The most glamorous thing about it is the name. Mention it to someone and they invariably say that it sounds like somewhere in America. There is a Louisburgh in Pennsylvania, I think, but I know nothing about it. All I know is that Louisburgh in west Mayo is one of the unlikeliest places on the planet for six hundred bikers to dock up in for no good reason.

They came in bunches, a few at a time from early morning swelling to a steady stream during the day. By late evening there were six hundred bikes lined up throughout the town, taking up every inch of parking space so that any locals who chanced coming to town for a pint that night had to park beyond the bridge at one end and the church at the other. They seemed to bring the good weather to an end also. The warm days of July and August had lingered on until the schools had opened up but right from the appearance of the first bike the sky had darkened and the rain began to fall. It would piss continuously for the whole of that weekened.

Everywhere you looked for those three days there was wildness and freedom. Heavy bikers with beer bellies sat astride customized hogs—none of that production-line shit—and every one of them, despite their greasy looks, carrying a horny-looking girl in tight jeans and T-shirt. I remember one especially big biker steering a trike with a single arm—he had left the other one in the Falklands two years previous. He stopped his trike in the middle of the square and stood up in the saddle with his head thrown back, letting out a big, strangled howl at the sky for no reason it seemed to me other than the sheer hell of it. I thought it was the most eloquent and sensible thing I had heard in my whole life and I envied him being able to speak it out like that. For those three days I never took my eyes off him. He enthralled me as if he were some sort of barbarian prince. Everywhere he walked a crowd seemed to gather about him and now and again he would leap onto the roof of a parked car, the armless sleeve of his jacket flying, and stand there howling out his soliloquy or whatever it was and all those about him seemed to have a perfect understanding of what he was on about. On the Monday morning he rode out of town at the head of one hundred bikes with two yards of heavy chain manacled to his wrist at the end of which was the prettiest girl of the whole weekend, the winner of the wet T-shirt competition that had been held in the open rain.

While they were here the bikers rigged up two massive Marshall amps to the backs of trikes and bludgeoned the town into submission with nonstop heavy metal. It seemed a deliberate policy to subdue the town. They were peaceable enough, however, their numbers and appearance so terrified the town they had no need of strongarm tactics. They reminded me of those northern hordes that streamed down on Rome in the fifth century and brought in the Dark Ages. But these bikers didn't rape or pillage or anything even though they could have; the whole place was wide open to them. They could for instance have declared a separate state, the People's Independent Republic of Louisburgh, and no one would have raised a finger against them. But they didn't. By ten o'clock Monday morning they were gone, lifting camp like some nomadic tribe and leaving in their wake a lot of broken glass and a small town that breathed easily for the first time in three days. I was sorry when they had gone; they had left a real impression on me. I bought a leather jacket as soon as I could and some day I'm going to get a bike of my own.

But that fire was the biggest thing in this town since those bikers. It was the early hours of the morning and I was walking from the bridge end of town, having come out the back entrance of a pub selling after hours. Walking up the street I saw that the sky was already orange with the fireglow and that a big crowd had gathered before the pub. Going round the corner I ran into Owl and Jamie sitting on a signpost at the back of the crowd. Owl's my younger brother and I swear there's not a weirder kid in the whole of creation. It was me that put Owl on him. Right from when he was an infant he was reading books. It seemed to damage his eyesight because he was only four when he was fitted with his first pair of specs, a big pair that made him look like a professor. But they also made him look like an owl and that's the one that stuck. Right then he and Jamie were held rapt by the fire. They seemed to be concentrating hard, like they had to submit a report on it to someone.

The sight of Owl maddened me, everything about him maddened me. Just him sitting there on the signpost in his cap and T-shirt, all golden-haired and clear-skinned, an identikit angel, made me sick. I never liked him. I loved him, he being my brother and all that, but I never liked him. You see, Owl did things to me, all sorts of things. I don't mean torturing things and shit like that. That wasn't Owl's way. Instead he just filled my head full of things, dark crazy things. There were times he would say something just to madden me and I could feel the bones beneath my flesh straining out to hit him or do him some lasting injury. In moments like that I could easily picture him standing there bawling in pain and fright, a red mark on his face where I'd struck him. That was the kind of thing Owl inspired in me and I hated him for it. No one else could make me think that way.

I looked up at him on the signpost and said something to him, something I can't remember, I was that drunk. Owl didn't bother replying. That was his way with people he knew were not as smart as himself and, as he was never slow to point out, there were plenty of those. I couldn't argue with him there, his gifts were obvious. He kept getting glowing reports from school, reports that seemed to be always read out in the kitchen whenever I was near.

"He is an excellent pupil with exceptional abilities. It is a pleasure to teach him," my mom would repeat, smiling cozily at Dad.

That was the kind of thing I heard twice a year, Christmas and summer, ever since Owl started school. He would be there in the kitchen with Mom and Dad listening to the report being read out, basking in their pride and wearing that smirk on his face he used specially to madden me, making me itch to hit him. He knew that the reading out of his reports, which were a foregone conclusion anyway, was only an underhand rebuke to my own average efforts. Owl could do no wrong; he was the blue-eyed boy, literally. Mom would comment on those blue eyes of his, telling us wistfully they were a sure sign that he lacked iron. Owl lacked something all right but it was something more fundamental than iron. I think myself it was humanity or mercy or something like that, something you can't quite put your hand on but if you don't have it you're not human.

And it constantly amazed me that I seemed to be the only one in the whole world who saw this. No one else saw that there was something wrong with him, everyone seemed to believe that he exuded nothing but light and cheer. Was he really that beautiful that he blinded everyone to his real self? Whatever it was, most people thought that I was just plain jealous of him. "If you were more like Owl, worked hard like him, you would have no need to be giving out or be jealous of him." That's what my mom said any time I talked of Owl to her. But she's wrong. The last thing in the world I want to be is like Owl, I want to be as different from him as possible.

Owl was real happy looking at that fire, just like I knew he would be. Anywhere there was a chance of death and destruction I reckoned that was where Owl belonged, gazing out of those glasses with that grin on his face. Sometimes I thought he belonged in a different age than this, in some age where death and destruction were daily catastrophes. Maybe Europe during the world wars or during the plague years was where he belonged, walking through devastated cities, a beautiful and untouchable angel of death surrounded by corpses and the sound of shutters clattering in the breeze. That was the way I pictured Owl and despite how young he was I have no qualms admitting that he frightened me. He should have frightened other people as well.

Once when he was an infant, about two or three, we had relatives visiting us. One of them was a nun. Owl was playing on the floor and they were making a big deal of him, how gorgeous he was and how good his talk was. Then this nun starts rubbing his head and asks him, "And what does the little man want to be when he grows up?" I suppose she was expecting some guff about driving trains or being a fireman or something. She got some shock when Owl looked up from his toys with those blue eyes of his and said out clear as day, "When I grow up I want to be an executioner." Man, I could have sworn the temperature in the room dropped a few degrees when he said that. The nun was real stunned. Everyone tried to laugh it off, giggling, saying wasn't he a great boy to know such a long word. But it didn't work. Owl just sat there looking up with those blue eyes. He'd spoken and there was no unsaying what he'd said.

That was the moment my parents should have seen into him, into his heart. But they didn't. Even in those early days they were blinded by his beauty. I used to wonder, too, did they ever guess the type of books he read? Most twelve-year-olds are stuck in Enid Blyton or Roald Dahl or such like. But not Owl. Owl's two principal books were Daniel Defoe's *Journal of the Plague Year* and John Hersey's *Hiroshima*. I asked him lately how he got his hands on those books and he told me blithely that he got them in the local library. I knew he couldn't have got them checked out because they weren't in the kids' section and he said he hadn't had them checked out, he'd stolen them and thrown them out the window. He would read these books at night underneath the bedclothes, and I swear I could hear him laughing grimly as he turned the pages. I don't know how many times he'd read them; he'd had them for about three years but a week barely passed without him taking them out just once. He would hunker down under the bedclothes with his torch, reading and laughing, surfacing now and again to test me with the meaning of some gruesome word he'd come across. That used to frighten the fuck out of me.

"I'll bet you don't know the meaning of the word *septicemia?*"

He would speak that out of the darkness like a ghoul and even in my bed it would strike me with a chill.

"Septicemia is the deadliest of the three forms of plague; it has a hundred percent fatality rate. It can be transmitted by the human flea, *Pulex irritans*, or the human louse, *Pediculus humanus*. A rash develops within a few hours of infection and if you are not dead within one day you certainly will be within three."

He would speak that out with slow deliberation, savoring the Latin terms as if they were delicacies.

"It was one of the forms of plague that in the middle of the fourteenth century wiped out a third of the population of Europe; ten million people."

"Shut up, you fucker, and get to sleep." These were the moments in which I ached to hit him. I never did though. I felt sometimes that that was what he wanted. Another of his preoccupations was hanging.

"Guess how long it took for the quickest hanging in the history of the British penal system? How long did it take to get the prisoner from his cell to the scaffold and hung? Seven seconds. Isn't that amazing, seven seconds? Imagine the speed and the panic of that."

He would laugh then and settle back to reading again but my sleep would be gone for the night. It was incidents like this that left me with my most vivid image of Owl, a golden head with blue eyes looking up from some grisly book to see how the world was squaring up to the bloody word he was reading.

Anyway I stood there beneath Owl and Jamie watching that fire rage on and on. The building was now totally devastated, the roof having fallen into the center of the building, and sending up a tower of flame. I got to wondering what would happen if those petrol pumps and the gas store opposite blew up. The explosion wouldn't leave a living soul or a building standing in the whole area. Human torches would reel out of the darkness and bodies would litter the streets in every direction. All the emergency services would be mobilized to no effect. Politicians would come wringing their hands, bemoaning the loss of life and talking of the need for sterner safety measures. A full public inquiry with accountability would be promised. This whole vision, all its death and hypocrisy, made me weak and nauseous. I couldn't handle it. I wondered why the town hadn't been evacuated and why all those people stood looking up at the fire like it was some sort of show or something. They were just standing there, a couple of hundred of them rooted to the spot without talking, except for now and then someone raising their hands like a zombie to point out some detail in the midst of the flames. I wondered why they were so fascinated with it, all these ordinary people moved to leave their beds in the middle of the night to watch this disaster. I wondered, would they have been so quick to come in such numbers if, instead of a fire, word got out that a public exhibition of lovemaking was taking place here on the square? I doubted it. Probably the only people to turn up would be there to put an end to it. They would speak of public decency and the need to protect family values. But the real difference is that lovemaking wouldn't give the same thrill as this fire; it's not death-centered like disasters and killings and fires and that's why it wouldn't rivet the minds of these people. They would walk away muttering about morals and decency but in their hearts they'd be pissed off because their minds hadn't been gripped by some image of death.

Anyway my mind began to wander thinking these thoughts. It didn't help either that the heat and the fresh air was making me feel the effect of all that drink I'd taken. I decided to go home and leave those people to their fire-gazing. That way if the whole town went up I'd know nothing about it in my sleep. I staggered home in the lamplight, my head reeling, fighting down an unbelievable desire to puke.

When I got in the house was empty. Like everyone else in town my parents were on the street watching the fire. I went straight to the bathroom and spent ten minutes on my knees in front of the toilet, puking up my arsehole. I had drunk too much again. This was becoming a habit recently, a habit I badly needed to get under control. I gripped onto the bowl, fighting to keep my eyes open. I didn't want to fall asleep beside the bowl and the old pair coming in finding me there, giving me grief. That's all I seem to get from them recently, misery and grief. I don't care to stay around the house much anymore. I just get up in the afternoon and leave for the pub and stay there most of the day drinking, playing pool, and backing horses. I only come back in the evening to eat and they start giving me grief about returning to university and resitting those exams I should have done in early June. I didn't want to hear anything about it that time of night nor about how much I was drinking and how much I was letting the family down. I'd heard enough of that shit lately.

I staggered out of the bathroom and along the hallway to the bedroom I shared with Owl. I flopped onto the bed fully clothed and into the type of coma that only too much drink can bring on.

III

The next day at school we were the only two kids to have seen the whole thing. We told the whole story at lunch break and there was a lot of talk as to whether the fire has been accidental or an insurance scam. Some of us thought that maybe someone had come in the night and torched the place in some sort of revenge mission none of us knew anything about. This was the best idea and we hoped hard that it was true.

Anyway, when we went home that evening, the charred husk of the nightclub was sectioned off with caution tape and crawling with detectives. They didn't look a bit like the detectives you see on telly. There wasn't a sharp suit in sight and I'll bet they hadn't a shoulder holster between them. They were wearing sensible anoraks with hoods and were walking carefully over the steaming timbers so as not to get soot on themselves. They looked more like auctioneers who were going to buy the place and rebuild it than detectives; they definitely didn't seem too interested in fingerprints and that sort of thing. The two local cops walked up and down outside the caution tape shooing away anyone like ourselves who came too close. So, after we had our tea and changed, Jamie and I sneaked up the back way to the pub from the river. We lay on our bellies in the long grass like two snakes, about fifteen yards from the building. The detectives were still prowling around inside or standing about pointing at the walls and the blown windows and the roof that lay on the floor like a shipwreck.

"Those fuckers are going to be there all day," Jamie said. He spat into the grass. "I'll bet if a clue fell out of the sky and clocked one of them on the head they wouldn't recognize it."

That made me laugh. I could just see a clue falling out of the blue air and clocking one of them on the head. The clue didn't have any shape and it wasn't made of anything I knew of but I thought of it as one of those rocks you see lying nice and tidy on the side of the road in a Road Runner cartoon. I saw that rock falling out of the sky with a whistle and burying one of those detectives beneath it so that all you could see were two legs kicking out from underneath it. I got a fit of the giggles then and I had to bite a mouthful of grass to stop laughing but some of it went with my breath and I started coughing and choking and I thought I'd die for lack of breath but Jamie started thumping me on the back and telling me to keep quiet. It was a close thing but I stopped choking eventually and I must have been crying or something because my sight was blurred with all the tears in my eyes and I had to take off my glasses and wipe them.

"Christ, don't they give you anything to eat at home?" said Jamie. "You must be fierce hungry when you try a feed of grass. If you'd told me I'd have brought a handful of hay."

He was my friend and I was grateful to him for saving my life but I told him to fuck off anyway. "Look," I said. The detectives were leaving the back of the building and going through to the front. We leaped up and ran through the grass to the back of the pub. The back door, or what was left of it, was wide open so we entered quietly, a bit awed. I had read a lot about fires and explosions and the damage they left behind them and the inside of this pub was just as I had imagined it would be. It looked great, all blackened timber, blown glass, and the roof open to the sky. Even the light inside the building looked strange, hanging there kinda sooty, a piece of darkness from the night before. Oddest of all I saw that the bottles on the shelves behind the bar had been melted down to smoky blobs and some of them had even run over the edge in long, black icicles. I was just going to cross to the shelves and break one of them off—they looked so sharp—when Jamie started calling me from outside. He was standing on a pile of blocks looking into the store, a square lean-to running straight off the back with an asbestos roof. The whole structure was blackened with smoke but seemed to be fine otherwise.

"Come here and have a look at this."

I pulled myself up on the blocks and gripped the iron grid over the window. It took me a second to see through the cobwebs and dust on the window but gradually I could make out the red and yellow crates that were stacked in columns up to the roof. I had seen them several times out front, stacked on the sidewalk, waiting to be brought in here so I recognized them straight off. They were bottles full of Coke and lemonade and orange and stuff like that. We both must have had the same idea at the same time because we looked at each other with wide grins all over our faces.

"There's thousands in there," Jamie said, "thousands. If we could get our hands on them they'd be worth a fortune."

I checked out the door, a heavy teak one, but it was locked with a padlock. The grids over the windows weren't moving either.

"Come on," I said. "Let's go back and have a think about it."

We ran down to the end of the garden and sat in the long grass chewing stalks.

"If we could get our hands on those bottles we'd make a fortune," Jamie was saying. "If we don't get them they'll only be given out to the other pubs in town."

"We could sell them on the Reek." Like all my best ideas that came to me out of a mixture of deep thought and a sudden flash of inspiration. Reek Sunday was just three months away and if we could set up a stall halfway up the pilgrim path we'd make a fortune.

"A bottle of Coke sells for one fifty. That's one fifty clear profit on every bottle. We'd be set up for the summer if we could pull it off."

"Yah," said Jamie, his eyes opening wide. "I'd buy a leather jacket with the money."

I couldn't think right off what I'd buy but a leather jacket sounded daft. He'd need a new one in two years' time when he'd grown a bit. I was thinking maybe I'd buy a pile of books. What I really wanted was a set of *Encyclopaedia Britannica*s, my favorite books. I wondered how much they'd cost.

"You could get a set of contact lenses and then get a leather jacket."

"You can't get contacts until you're a bit older," I said. "Your eyesight has to grow like your body and your mind."

"That's a pity," Jamie replied. He spat lengthily to show his disgust. "I'd get one of those biker jackets with brass buckles and zips. I don't care for the silver ones; they're a bit tacky."

"How are we going to get into the store?" The problem had just occurred to me and it put a stop to Jamie's waffle. "The door is heavy and so are those grids."

"Shit," said Jamie. "I hadn't thought of that." I knew he hadn't. It was just like him. "Well," he continued, "you're the genius, the man with all the ideas. Out with it."

This was the moment I should have thought of the hacksaw and cutting the lock or, better still, unscrewing the bolt or the grids with a screwdriver. But instead of that my mind skipped clean over them and started thinking on that explosion we had been done out of the night before and how this door could be the chance we needed to have one of our very own. I got real excited thinking about it. I could see it already in my mind.

"We could blow the door off the hinges," I said. "An explosion."

"How? We know nothing about explosives and even if we did where would we get them?"

"Bolt bombs," I said. "There has to be some way we could rig up a massive bolt bomb to the door." All us kids at some time or other had made bolt bombs. They're simple enough to make. All you need is two long bolts and a nut plus a carton of red matches. Just thread the nut onto the top of the bolt and fill it with red sulfur from the matches. Then screw in the other bolt as tightly as possible and you're ready. All you have to do then is throw the whole thing at a wall or whatever and it explodes with a bang and a flash. It can be dangerous enough because the bolts come apart with terrific force and have been known to land fifty yards away. I reckoned if there was some way of containing and directing the force of the explosion, then the door would be no problem. I explained it to Jamie and he saw the beauty of it. For once he also saw the flaw in it.

"But how do we rig it up? It's no use throwing a bomb at it from a distance, no matter how big. It'll go all over the place. We'll have to be quick with an idea as well; those bottles won't be there forever."

He was looking at me, putting it up to me and that worried me because right then I was stuck for ideas. My brain just wouldn't work, it seemed to have seized. It shouldn't have been like that either. I was the one who read all the books, the one who knew things. Jamie was disappointed when I shook my head. He stood up and spat, doing his hard man bit.

"Not good," he said. "Not good at all. We'll have to think harder."

"All I know is that it will have to be fixed in place and it will have to be a lot bigger than any we've ever used before."

We walked along by the river and came out at the end of town. I didn't speak; I was too busy thinking and I was still finding it hard to come up with ideas. I knew that the bomb would have to be fixed to the door, taped like I'd seen it done in movies, and I knew it would have to be a tubular one of some sort. But the most difficult detail of all was the triggering device. That was the thing that had me really stumped.

I left Jamie at the back of the house, told him I'd see him the following day after I'd had some time to think. He told me to think hard because we hadn't much time. I walked on without saying anything and came up the back garden to our house. I went straight into the garden shed. This is where I do any thinking I have to do. It's an ordinary timber shed full of tools and plastic drums with weed killer and so on. But the main thing is that it's quiet. My parents rarely come here and my brother never comes here—he's too busy getting drunk.

I sat down on the lawn mower—I had plenty to think about. I began to run through several experiments in my mind with tubular piping. This was the best I could come up with—copper piping, about one and a half inch diameter packed with sulfur and sealed at both ends with brass fittings. I reckoned that would do the trick but it still left the problem of the trigger mechanism. I began to think of how easy it looked in those Westerns I'd seen on television when the outlaws came to blow up a safe, how they fed out a slick-looking length of black fuse connected to five or six sticks of dynamite that looked like those sticks of rock you get on school tours with "A Present from Knock" running all the way through them. The outlaws lit the fuse and it buzzed along nicely while they hunkered down behind a table in the next room with their fingers in their ears. I would have given anything for twenty yards of that fuse then.

On the floor was a ball of brown string my mom used for tying up bean plants. I took it up and played with it for a while. It was very fine, hopeless for anything I had in mind, but it gave me a clue. I ran out of the shed and straight through the house and into the street. I had a feeling I could get exactly what I needed.

I was running toward Francie Doyle's pub, the smallest and oldest pub in town, a tiny place with wooden counters running parallel to each other, a place where you can buy beer or a pair of those nailed boots he keeps hanging from the ceiling or a pair of those long drawers I had seen my grandfather wearing. It's a treasure trove of all sorts of things. Francie was the only one in the bar when I walked in, behind the counter mopping it with a not-too-clean cloth.

"Well, young man, aren't you a bit young for places like this?"

Francie was a strict old man, he didn't like kids in his pub, but I liked him anyway. Sometimes when the door to his sitting room was open you could see through to a big cabinet that was packed tight with books; big, serious-looking ones with black covers. I had seen them several times when I had come here to get Dad for his dinner on Sunday afternoons. I itched to know what those books were about. Dad had often said that Francie was real smart, that he could talk about anything. But right then I had more than talk on my mind.

"Can I borrow some twine, Francie? I'm making a kite and I need some of that white twine to tie the struts."

"A kite, by God. Well, we'll have to see what we can do." He walked over to the opposite counter and was rummaging underneath it. "How much do you want?"

"Oh, a good bit, it's going to be a big kite."

He came up from beneath the counter with a big ball of white hemp twine. He began looping it from elbow to palm. He stopped after a few loops. "Is that enough?"

I scrunched up my face. "I think I'll need more than that. It's going to be very big and I need it to be strong."

"Are you sure it's a kite you're making and not some class of an airplane? You're not thinking of leaving us altogether—flying away and never coming back?" He was now winding the loops on his elbow back onto the ball and when he had it all wound in he tossed it to me. "Have the lot. It mightn't work the first time."

I hugged the ball. "Thanks a lot, Francie, this'll do the job."

"Think of me when you're flying," he called as I shot out the door.

I ran down the street with the ball under my jumper, straight through the house, just stopping long enough to pick up a box of matches from the kitchen, and into the shed. I cut off a few feet of twine and dipped it into the fuel tank of the lawn mower. There was good soakage in the twine. When I pulled it out it had changed color to a light brown and was real limp. I stretched it out on the ground and lit the end of it. The flame traveled along it nicely, not one of those busy demon flames sputtering and fizzing like you see in Westerns but with a blue peak that moved quickly enough to take it where it had to go. I must have been grinning back to my ears. At last I had the triggering mechanism and the whole thing figured out. I did a small war dance to celebrate, shaking my fist and howling like a dog. I had been worried there for a while. I thought I had run clean out of ideas. But it wasn't like that. My brain had just got stuck in neutral for a while. It happens to the best of us.

Jamie came over next day and I explained everything to him, the bomb and its triggering device. He looked at the ball of twine dubiously.

"Does it work? It looks a bit rough."

I cut off a few feet and ran a demonstration for him. The flame ran as smoothly as before. Jamie had a grin on his face.

"I think we're ready to rock," he said.

"We need lots of other stuff as well. Can you get hold of a piece of copper piping about this thick with brass fittings on the end? About a foot long?"

"No problem, the old man has plenty in the shed."

"We need it drilled as well. Two holes opposite each other, one bigger than the other. We need the fuse knotted in the small one and run out the big one through the sulfur."

"The old man will do that for me. I'll tell him I'm doing some project for school."

"OK, those are the easy bits though. We're going to need an awful lot of sulfur to fill a pipe that big. Both of us will have to go to every shop and pub in town and buy a carton of red matches. That'll be twenty cartons, nearly ten thousand matches."

"Christ, we'll be stripping the heads off them till Christmas."

"It's the only way we can get that amount of sulfur. It has to be done. We have to be careful we don't turn up in the same shops and pubs too soon after each other. You do it this evening after dinner, I'll do it tomorrow evening."

"Sound. When do you think you'll be ready?"

"If we have everything together by tomorrow evening, the matches and the pipe, and if we get five cartons done tomorrow and the day after, we should be ready by Monday night."

"That's what I was thinking, too. After the weekend the town should be nice and quiet."

"That's right. This tape"—I held up a roll of white insulating tape—"can be used to fix the bomb to the door. Just above the bolt."

"You have it all figured out, Owl. You're a smug git."

I was grinning again. I could see in my mind all the pieces of the bomb—the pipe, the fuse, the sulfur, and tape—lying there waiting to be put together so that they could come apart with a big bang. I began thinking that if this explosion went well I might move onto bigger things like remote-control devices or one of those plunger explosives you see in Westerns. I'd have to read up about them and the materials would be hard to find but right then I had no doubt that if I put my mind to it I would be able to do it. It was a great feeling, knowing you could do these things. I felt like I could live forever.

Jamie was laughing to himself on the lawn mower.

"This day next week Charles Coen will be minus one door. Not that the fucker will miss it with the insurance coughing up." He rose from the lawn mower. "I'd better go. Mom will have the dinner ready and I have a lot of matches to buy."

"OK, it's time for me to eat as well. Call round again tomorrow evening."

He left and I went inside, washed my hands, and sat at the table. My brother was there, his head bent over the table, rolling a smoke. His black hair was hanging in his food and his leather jacket was hanging from the chair. He lifted his head and I could see that he was just up even though it was well after four. He seemed to be a lot paler these days, even paler than he usually was. Not that he was ever the picture of health. But today his eyes looked like burnt holes in a blanket. I decided to get the first word in.

"How is the waster?" I asked. The table was full of food so I started to tuck in. Mom passed behind me and ruffled my hair.

"Eat up, good boy," she said.

"And what has our resident genius been studying today?" He finished rolling his smoke and was clearing the tobacco off the table into his pouch. "Was it perhaps some study on the migration of rats from central Asia to the Mediterranean in the fourteenth century? Or was it something on the occurrence of leprosy in Paris during the Age of Reason? Or was it something local, Owl—a short comparative study of indigenous snake venoms before the arrival of our patron saint?"

"Fuck off, you waster." I had to hiss that because Mom didn't like me using bad language. My brother was pulling lazily on his fag. His eyes seemed to glow blackly.

"You didn't happen to see any anacondas on your travels today, Owl? You'd want to watch yourself in that long grass in the garden. You'd never know what might be lurking in it." He was talking about a nature program I'd seen last week about snakes. It had shown this boa constrictor strangling and eating an ass. When I had told him about it he hadn't believed a word of it.

"It wasn't an anaconda, you ignorant fucker. It was a boa." He was trying to make me look stupid now. I wanted to ignore him but he kept on.

"Three months it took for this boa to digest this ass." He was laughing now, using that hooting laugh, hoo hoo hoo, he used specially to make me look foolish. "Three months and nothing but digesting. No time to look for women snakes or read a book or even an hour's sleep. Every minute of his day taken up digesting this ass. Christ, nature is a fright, hoo hoo hoo."

Mom reentered the room. "Can't you leave the child alone and not be persecuting him? Let him eat in peace. Why do you always have to be at him?"

"Some child. All he ever talks of is diseases and plagues and misery." He did a perfect mimic of me. "Did you know that the bubonic plague wiped out a third of the population of Europe in the mid-fourteenth century? Imagine that—a whole third."

"At least he has an interest in something." Mom was patting down my hair again. Mom always took my side and so would Dad, too, if he had been there.

"Oh yes, he has interests all right. His mind is full of destruction and death and misery. A nice, polite boy is our Owl. What do you want to be when you grow up, Owl?" He put on the childish voice again. "When I grow up I want to be an executioner."

"I never said that," I roared.

"You did say it, you young fucker." Now he was roaring, too. "I was here in the room." He put on the childish voice again. "When I grow up I want to be an executioner."

"For God's sake can't you leave the child alone." Now Mom was roaring. "He's a good boy and he does what he's told. If you had half the interest he has you might make something of yourself."

"Yah," he said with disgust, grabbing his jacket from the back of the chair. "I've had enough of this shit. I'm going out."

"You can't go out without your tea."

"Fuck the tea," he roared from the hallway. The door slammed behind him and the house was quiet. I buttered a slice of bread with a smirk. I'd beaten him again.

I went to get the matches the following evening. That was a job in itself. I started at one end of the town and went into every pub and shop. Some of the shopkeepers wanted to know why it had to be red matches; weren't brown ones just as good? I just shrugged and said that I was told to get red ones. That set some of them muttering and grumbling and shaking their heads but I managed to get them anyway. Half an hour later I was back in the shed with ten cartons of matches. Jamie was there waiting for me. He was holding the length of copper piping with brass stops neatly fitted. It was drilled, too, and whoever did it had done a real neat job. There were two holes opposite each other, one twice as big as the other so as to let the flame into the sulfur. The twine threaded tightly into the smaller one.

"Are you sure this will work?" Jamie was asking again. "Are you sure it will explode?"

"It should do. When the flame goes in the sulfur ignites. Because it's contained and pressurized it should explode. It should work, the principle behind all explosives is much the same. Have you done many matches?"

"About four cartons. I did two yesterday and a couple before I came here. If I get three done this evening I'll be well ahead. It's a pisser of a job though, it takes ages."

"I know, I have to start yet. I hope to get a few cartons done before I go to bed."

"How are we fixed? Have we nearly everything done?"

"We've just the matches to do. If you bring your lot over tomorrow evening we can put it together and be ready. I should be ready by the evening. We'll make a check of everything tomorrow evening, make sure we're not missing anything, and then hide it here till bedtime."

"OK, I'll let you get on with it. You'll need all the time you can get to do those matches. Don't forget to hide the pipe, too."

He pulled the door after him and I started on the matches. It was awful work. I sat on the lawn mower engine scraping the heads off those matches into a pea can. I threw the waste matches into a shopping bag; I was going to stuff it in the rubbish bin when I'd finished. I was thinking on one detail as I worked, one small detail that worried me. Everything now hinged on the sulfur exploding under pressure. I knew about black powder explosives, that they were a mixture of sulfur and nitrates and that those nitrates could be found in compost and dung heaps if they were left standing long enough. But it would have been impossible to get those nitrates in this little town. No one had compost heaps, no one had any gardens at all, and the farms outside town had slurry pits, which were no good. Even if there were dung heaps outside the town it would be just a chance that there was potassium nitrate crystallized in it. I was just hoping that the sulfur would go off like an explosive as I'd said it would. I was praying it would—I'd look really stupid if it didn't. All my good ideas would be for nothing. If my brother heard about it he would never let me hear the last of it.

Bit by bit the tiny red pieces filled up the bottom of the pea can. I calculated that when we had done the twenty cartons we would have over two pea cans. That would be more than enough to fill the pipe. We would probably have some left over. Better to be safe than sorry. Two and a half hours later, coming up to tea time, I had four cartons done, over two thousand matches. The sulfur filled the tin over halfway. It looked real innocent stuff, red and gritty like heavy sand. I wondered was this what Semtex looked like; I'd heard a lot about it on the news lately. My wondering came quickly to an end. Mom was at the back door yelling for me. I tidied away the stuff quickly. It was time to eat again and I was hungry.

I was up early the next day before school making a start on those matches. I had done two more cartons after tea the evening before and now the whole day was ahead of me for the last four. The pea can was about three quarters full. I was sure we would have more than enough. I spent an hour before school and three hours in the evening and then suddenly they were done. As if on cue Jamie walked in with his sulfur, a whole tin plus a handful in a plastic bag. We had nearly three tins full. I took the pipe down from the shelf and unscrewed one end and began packing in the sulfur till it was half full. Threading the fuse through the holes and knotting it was a cinch. I packed in the rest of the sulfur over it and screwed back the stop end. At long last it was ready. It was heavy and really solid. With the twine coming out of it, it looked like something you swing around your head when charging into battle. I handed it to Jamie.

"Our suspect device. Let's check now and make sure we have everything ready. We need to be organized tonight when the time comes."

We laid out everything we needed, the bomb still connected to the ball of twine, a roll of insulating tape, a small can of petrol, a box of matches, and a penknife. We racked our brains for a minute and then reckoned we had all the angles covered. I packed the lot into a bag and put it back on the shelf. We were ready.

"What time will you call at?" Jamie asked.

"About two o'clock. The pubs will be closed and the town will be quiet. And for God's sake don't sleep too deep, I don't want to be waking the whole town hammering on your window."

"I won't be able to sleep tonight, too excited." His eyes gleamed. "This time tomorrow we'll be set up for the summer. It'll be all ahead of us and we'll be rotten with money."

"That's if you're awake."

"I'll be awake, don't worry."

I lay with my eyes open wide after twelve o'clock that night. I didn't need to force them wide. I was too nervous to go to sleep but I thought I'd better be safe than sorry. I kept urging the time to hurry up and get to two o'clock because I was all jumpy. It felt like those times when I was a kid at Christmas and believed in Santa Claus, lying awake and not being able to sleep and the time taking forever to pass into morning. But I don't believe in Santa anymore, I just pretend to—it's more profitable.

At last I saw on my watch that it was coming round to two o'clock. Another twenty minutes. I used my flashlight to dress in the dark and I was just about to lace up my boots when I heard the front door slam. Damn, I was hoping I would have got the job done and been back before my brother came home. Usually he didn't turn up until five or six in the morning. Now I would have to wait until he fell asleep. I strained my ears to hear him moving around the kitchen. I heard the radio come on and the kettle being filled and then all was quiet. I cursed him darkly. I couldn't leave while he was in the kitchen; I had to use the back door into the yard. I wouldn't be surprised if he was down there doing this on purpose, smoking and grinning, knowing well that I had to pass through the kitchen.

It was two o'clock now and I was thinking of Jamie. He had probably fallen into one of those comas of his and I would never wake him. Would I continue on my own and do the job without him? I didn't think so. Explosions, especially one like this, needed witnesses, people who could talk about it among themselves when it was over. Just then the door opened and my brother came in. He was going to bed after all, and he was too lazy even to turn on the light. He bumped off the end of my bed with a curse and then I heard his leather jacket hitting the floor and his boots and the buckle of his belt. The bed creaked as he got into it and then the room flared up in a weak orange light—the fucker was going to smoke one last fag before he went to sleep. I could hear his breath wheezing in his chest as he inhaled. He'd had asthma since he was a child, one of the reasons he was so pale. Smoking as much as he did didn't help either. He finished the fag and stubbed it out eventually. It was now twenty past two and I would need another half hour to make sure he was asleep. I was curled up tight, fully clothed under the bedclothes, looking at the watch face like it was the only other thing in the universe. My ears were straining to hear him breathing in the opposite bed. Eventually he started making that piggish breathing noise that told me he had dropped off; it was a quarter to three. I rose out of the bed and took my boots in my hands; I would put them on in the kitchen. From the kitchen to the shed to Jamie's window it couldn't have taken me more than a minute. Jamie poked his head from behind the curtain. He was fully awake and dressed.

"What the hell kept you?" I could tell he was anxious.

"I got held up—that stupid brother. Are you ready?" I held up the bag. "Let's go."

In another five minutes we had made our way to the river and were running up the back way to the pub. I could see the town street lighting through the blown-out windows and a big moon hanging over the town like a white plate. We would have plenty of light. We drew up panting before the door of the shed. In the blue light it looked a lot heavier than I had remembered. It was made of heavy, brown teak and was locked in the middle with a single bolt and padlock. I began to have doubts about the bomb. Maybe I should have made it bigger, used more sulfur. Jamie didn't seem to have any doubts though. Already he was holding the copper pipe to the door, checking it for size. He had the masking tape out, too.

"Below the lock," I instructed. "We want to be sure we get the bolt off."

He began prizing out the tape with his teeth but I halted him.

"Hold on till we soak the fuse first. Hold the pipe to the door till I run it out."

I ran with the ball of twine to the sod ditch about twenty-five yards away, cut it, and gathered it back to Jamie. He had the can of petrol open. I dropped the whole of the twine into the can and shook it up, careful not to get the opening into the sulfur wet. It was just another minute's work to tape the pipe to the door and run the wet fuse behind the ditch. We hunkered down. The box of matches lay on the ground between us.

"Who'll light it?" I could see the whites of his eyes like cold marble. He was blowing in his hands like he was cold, but he couldn't be, this was early summer.

"I'll light it, it was my idea." I was sure of myself again and Jamie didn't seem to mind. In fact he looked pleased, I had a feeling his nerve might be failing him. I lit the end of the fuse and watched it take off. For the first time in the whole plan I thought about what would happen when the explosion went off. Were we going to walk into the store, and walk out with those crates of bottles under our arms? I didn't think so. It dawned on me for the first time also that the explosion was going to wake the whole town. I knew we would have to make a run for it. That made me grin. I knew that this was what we had both secretly decided to do once the bomb went off— run like hell. All that guff about selling those bottles and making a fortune had only been an excuse. All we were ever really interested in was making a big bang.

I watched the blue flame make its way steadily along the fuse. It moved like a dream, steadily and not too fast. Lying so near the ground it looked like a tiny ghost. I don't think I could have stopped it now even if I had run forward and thrown myself on it. It would have just shrugged me off and kept going with a life of its own. It was now about two yards from the pipe and I held my breath as it disappeared over the final length and into the darkness of the pipe. I was going to suffocate if it did not go off then. For one hollow moment, when it felt like some heavy weight was plummeting in my belly, I was sure it wasn't going to happen. Then, with a dull yellow flash and a roar of things coming apart, the door heaved backward into the lit-up shed and the concrete over the door showered upward with the asbestos sheeting. Jamie let out a great cry and jumped back in exultation. I was going to start one of my war dances but all of a sudden this rubbish—timber, stone, and asbestos chunks—came falling out of the sky all over me. I had to bend over with my arms over my head for protection. I don't think I've ever had a happier moment than that one, bent over and laughing like an idiot with all that debris falling onto me. When I eventually looked up at the shed I felt a real deep swelling in my chest. You didn't need to know much about explosives to know that a pretty impressive one had just gone off in the vicinity. The door was lying in pieces all over the inside and most of the asbestos roof was all over the garden. But what really impressed was that on the side of the door where the bomb had been taped, the whole front wall had been blown out and you had a clear view right into the center of the shed. I was never so proud of my abilities. It had worked beyond my wildest dreams and I knew I would do it all again.

I seemed to be on my own. Already I could see the lights come on in the backs of houses along the street. I turned to run but straight away I tripped over Jamie who was lying on the ground. I came up with my face beside his, straightening my glasses, and I nearly got sick with fright. Jamie's breath was coming in short jerks and he looked like he'd just walked out of a slash and hack movie.

Jutting from his left eye was the bolt of the door. He was still alive, barely. I could hear a whimpering sound and another thick, gurgling one coming from his throat. I had to concentrate my whole mind to keep from reaching out and shaking him even though I knew that no amount of shaking was going to rid him of that bolt in his head. I was going to shit myself with fright if I stayed there much longer, I could feel my ass beginning to twitch. I got up to run and I could hear myself crying. My legs didn't seem to want to carry me. They seemed to be going in two directions at once. But after what seemed like an age I was running in the back door and up the stairs to my room. I was going to get my brother.

I V

What I really want to talk about is Owl because in every way Owl is the beginning, middle, and end of my world. That'll bring me to this trouble I'm in and maybe through talking it through I'll be able to make some sense of the whole thing.

The day after the fire I went to have a look at the pub. I was amazed at how the blackened shell looked like all those other gutted buildings I had seen in newsreel footage of bombings from all over the world: Dresden, Coventry, Hiroshima, Beirut, Belfast. This charred and blasted pub could have belonged to any of those cities of ruin and disaster. I half expected to see fire wardens in Home Guard uniform walking among the rubble organizing a cleanup and carting away the maimed and the dead. But it was more low key than that, just a few detectives and a couple of plainclothes pigs walking around looking for clues. They stopped to ask me had I nothing better to do than hang around and when I pretended not to hear them they told me to fuck off. Before I fucked off I caught a glimpse of Owl prowling through the building, walking over the charred timber and broken glass with the surefootedness of a rat, the confidence of one who had finally come into his inheritance. It must have been during these moments that he got the idea for that explosion. If ever I saw a kid in his element it was Owl right then. He had that big grin on his face, like someone who has returned after a long journey and recognizes everything about him. He wasn't doing anything, just walking and grinning, keeping out of the cops' way, almost serenely contented.

I watched Owl over the following days and there was definitely something on his mind, he seemed preoccupied with some mysterious project. When I came in at night his bedclothes were no longer up in a heap with him reading beneath. In fact for those few days he never mentioned his books at all, he just became sunk down in thought behind those glasses of his, which seemed to grow bigger and bigger, making him look more and more like a bird of prey. When I got him alone I tried to pry it from him.

"You're thinking those heavy thoughts again, Owl. Share them out to me. I might learn something."

"I doubt it. If brains were dynamite you wouldn't have enough to blow your nose."

"That's right, I'm not as smart as our little genius."

"You said that, not me."

And that was as far as I got.

Monday night I was proved right. I couldn't have been sleeping more than one hour when he burst into the room and started waking me, pulling my quilt and yelling at me to get up. I mumbled something incoherent and tried to curl up tighter on the bed, which by now had no clothes. He just kept on shaking me and yelling at me, his voice rising higher and higher and then pulling my hair harder and harder until I could take no more of it. I rose from the bed, my arm uncoiling from beneath me, and I caught him clean on the mouth with the back of my hand. It drove him a few feet across the room and put him sitting on his bed. I didn't mean to do it, it was just another of those thoughtless moments. I just stood there shivering, in more shock than he was. He at least had the sense to straighten up his glasses and keep on yelling at me like nothing had happened. I hadn't a clue what he was yelling about; my mind was totally taken up with how I had risen up like some animal, hitting and screaming. Mom came into the room then and seeing Owl's bloody nose went to him with a shriek. Soon everyone was shrieking.

"He hit the child, I swear to God he hit the child."

"He was pulling the fucking head off me. I had to hit him." I was nearly in tears.

"Listen to me, listen to me," Owl was yelling. He was trying to break out of Mom's embrace, doing some complicated swimming stroke to get out of her arms. When he eventually did his voice climbed over our shrieks.

"Listen to me!"

He had summoned up all his strength to get our attention and I willingly gave it. For the first and only time in my life I was grateful to him for something. I wanted nothing more than to forget how I had hit him and most especially how I had enjoyed it. It had thrilled and horrified me at the same time, my whole body tingled with pleasure, and now that I had started I wanted to continue on battering him. But I didn't want to think like that, that was madness. Instead I focused my mind on how, for that small moment, I was grateful to him for not making a big deal. That seems important now, that moment of near decency rescued from a relationship that did nothing but make both our worlds darker and uglier places.

It took me a few seconds to focus on what he was saying; some sort of cloud was having difficulty rising from my brain. But when it did and my head was clear I couldn't believe what he was saying. So this was his mysterious project, rigging up an explosion that had gone off and killed his best friend. I began pulling on my clothes straightaway and, amazingly, issuing instructions. I told Mom to stay there and wake Dad and then I pushed Owl ahead of me out the back door. I followed him through the gardens and over fences till we came up the back way of the pub from the river. We were beaten to it by a small crowd. The local doctor was bending over Jamie in the light of two torches held by the cops. I could see straightaway that Jamie really was dead—he was lying on his back with the door bolt jutting from his eye. I could feel myself wanting to heave. My legs weakened and I had to clench my belly to fight down the nausea. One of the cops swung his torch on us.

"What are you two doing here?"

"We heard a bang, we came to see what happened. Who is it?" I was taking the first step toward covering for Owl. I moved closer to him. "Who is it?"

"Jamie Harkin, the poor child, dead to the world. God help his parents." The doctor had now draped the corpse with a white sheet. The cop continued looking at us.

"He was a friend of yours, Owl. Do you know anything about this?"

He was shining the torch full into Owl's face, lighting up his gold hair and big specs. Owl was just staring blankly, he didn't look like he was going to speak. I wondered if for once in his life he was stuck for words. I did something really weird then: I put my arm around him in a gesture of brotherly comfort. I wondered, did Owl notice what I did? I doubt it. Warm human things were not the sort of things that captured his imagination. It was the only time, other than the wallop I'd given him, that I could ever remember touching him. I was amazed to feel that he was skin and bone like any kid his age, like myself in fact. That shocked me. I had always thought that there was something less than human about Owl, something synthetic. I had expected to feel some sort of atrocity, a cyborg perhaps, partly flesh and bone and partly synthetic skin stretched over a structure of aluminum rod and plate powered by some internal

source. If this had been the case I might have been able to accept
Owl, maybe even understand him. Instead I felt a deep revulsion at
finding him so ordinary and, what was worse, finding him so like
myself. I removed my hand from him as if it had been burned.

"Owl's been at home all evening. We just heard a bang in bed
and came here to see. Is there anything we can do?"

"No, we're just waiting for the ambulance. You'd better go home."

I walked ahead of Owl keeping a distance between us. I wanted
to be as far away from him as quickly as possible.

Mom and Dad were waiting for us in the kitchen when we
entered. Dad was up now, on his feet, just wearing trousers, his hair
sticking out all over the place. Mom sat on the chair, fiddling dis-
tractedly with the hem of her cardigan. Both were looking at me for
the story. I started to make tea instead, holding onto it on purpose.
They'd know all about it soon enough. Mom put her arms around
Owl, cuddling him up close and patting his hair down, whispering
to him. That little gesture reminded me of a story Owl had told me
once, one of those stories he'd got from God knows where. It was
about this Brazilian girl whose belly began to swell up like she was
pregnant. But she was very young, thirteen or something, and
protested she was a virgin. X-rays showed that she was not carrying
a child but that she was definitely carrying something. When she
went under the knife a six-foot snake, albinoid but in perfect health,
was removed from her stomach. Seemingly she had eaten something contaminated by fertilized snake eggs. The only difference I
could see at that moment between Owl and that snake was that
because of the benign environment of the girl's womb the snake,
unlike Owl, had never developed a venom.

Looking across at the three of them then I suddenly got real
depressed. It welled up in me like vapor and I could feel the tears
burning at the back of my eyes. There was my mother, a miserable,
deluded thing, and my father, trying hard and always failing to

assert control. And then there was my brother, Owl, the center of the world since the first day he'd happened into it. I hated every one of them then, hated them for being there and for being what they were and for bringing me into the world and for bringing Owl into the world also and making it a worse place. And I hated myself for hating and in short I hated the whole world and everything in it.

I could see Dad was getting impatient. At last he came out with his single-word question.

"Well?"

"Well, it seems that Owl has gone and done it this time. Jamie's dead. He's lying out back of Coen's with a bolt in his head."

Mom let out a wail, a sound like a door hinge needing oil, and clasped Owl closer to her.

"My baby, my baby."

Dad moved behind them to embrace them both. I drank tea on the other side of the table. Owl began to struggle from Mom's grasp, doing that complicated stroke again, a swimmer coming through mire.

"Do you think they'll get me?" His face was lined with worry.

It crossed my mind to frighten the shit out of him then, to tell him that it was only a matter of a few days before forensics traced him and the cops came to haul him away and send him down for a good long stretch in a place where there was no Mom or Dad or books. For the first time in my life I could have taken the upper hand over him. I could have had him dangling like a worm on a hook. But I was tired of the whole thing, so tired I hadn't got the heart.

"Even if they find out it was you, and they probably will, they can't do anything. You're too young; besides, it was an accident." Why did I make it so easy for him then, why did I not torment him? Was it just fatigue or somewhere deep in myself did I sympathize with his awful misfortune? Despite myself, did some mysterious blood affinity come to hand and lend real gentleness to my attitude?

I didn't want to examine it. Maybe I was just plain scared. Owl was looking at me like he had never seen me before and I just wanted to get out of his way.

"I'm going to bed. There's nothing more we can do tonight."

"We're all going to bed," Dad said resolutely. He had picked up Owl out of Mom's arms. Owl's head had begun to loll to one side and his eyes were closed already. How could he have fallen asleep so quickly?

Dad carried him up the stairs behind me and laid him on the bed. He was like a rag doll, soggy with sleep. I helped take off his boots and jeans just so that Dad would leave the room and leave us alone. I didn't want to talk, I just wanted to go to sleep as quickly as possible. Eventually he took off Owl's glasses and pulled the quilt over his still body. He stood looking down at him for a few moments. I pulled off my jacket and T-shirt over my head. I was sitting on the bed unlacing my boots, purposely ignoring him, when he turned to me.

"Do you think it'll be all right? I mean, Owl, he'll be OK?"

I looked at him in disbelief. I couldn't believe he was looking for an opinion from me or that he could be interested in anything I might have to say. But he looked real shaken, uprooted even, slumped and with his hair all over the place. His whole appearance was that of a man left out in a strong wind. I wanted to tell him to fuck off there and then, tell him that it had nothing to do with me. He was my father, our father, he could cope with it, that's what fathers were for, that was why they got to make speeches about good manners and achievements and shit like that. Now was *his* time to be a real father. Part of me wanted to say all these things and another part of me just felt sorry for him. He looked kinda pathetic standing there in his vest and trousers. He looked slumped, like his center of gravity had slipped. I didn't like seeing him like that. I preferred him when he was ranting and raving and giving out. I knew where I stood with him then; I could understand him, not like now. This pathetic version of my old man had me completely wrong-footed. I just wished he would leave me alone quickly.

"It'll be OK," I said finally. "There's nothing anyone can do to him. The whole thing was an accident." He just stood there looking at me for a moment, then nodded his head solemnly.

"I suppose you're right, things will look better in the morning. We'll be able to think straight after a few hours' sleep. God rest poor Jamie." He paused for a moment and then shambled from the room. "Good night."

I lay staring at the ceiling. It must have been getting on toward five then, the first rays of sunlight had begun to glow in the window. I began to think of Jamie lying there in the grass with the bolt through his eye and the trickle of blood running into his ear. I wondered, how did he feel at the moment of death? Were there fireworks and brilliant lights like we are led to believe from the telly, and then a sudden shutdown to complete darkness? Or was there a slow fade of images to a gray, blank screen that just buzzed on and on and on till it made you want to scream but couldn't? One thing was certain now; in spite of him never having completed his schooling and despite how few books he'd read, Jamie now had more answers than I or anyone else alive. Right now there wasn't a wiser man on the planet than Jamie Harkin. That struck me as a funny sort of deal. You could have all the answers you needed, the only problem was that you paid for them with your life, the very thing you needed the answers for in the first place. Talk about giving with one hand and taking away with the other. I remembered reading somewhere that life is a sort of trap, it gives you cancer and it ends in tears but try leaving home without it. But now I know that life is a joke, a joke we've heard a million times before with death as the punchline we can see coming a mile off.

I began to have a vision then of Jamie being welcomed into his own death. There was this stage and a comedian in a suit and frilly shirt, his elbow resting on the mike stand. He puts his arm around Jamie, full of bonhomie, playing to the gallery. But Jamie's bewildered, he's looking around him, wondering where he is, asking all the time, "Where are the answers? That's what I'm here for—the answers." Silence descends on the auditorium. This is not supposed to happen. Jamie is supposed to show his teeth, grin, and bear with the farce but obviously he knows nothing about it or he hasn't taken the time to read his lines before being called from the audience. There's this funny querulous look on his face. And the comedian is pissed off big time. Once again the volunteer from the audience has refused to cooperate. With his arm still around his shoulder and grinning all the time, the comedian leads Jamie back to his seat, whispering in his ear as he does, "Fuck you, kid, if you can't take a joke."

I must have fallen asleep thinking these thoughts because next thing I was awake, looking across the room and seeing Owl's head on the pillow. Straightaway my memory filled up with images of the night before. I leaped out of bed. I needed fags and my mouth ached for a drink. Going downstairs and moving through the house I knew that it was deserted but for me and Owl. My watch read half eleven: Mom and Dad would be at work. I grabbed my jacket and checked it for money. It yielded twelve pounds and some small change, enough for fags and a few pints. I was set up for the day.

Outside, our little town was filling up. It was Tuesday, dole day, and the square was full of cars from the surrounding area bringing in farmers to sign on. Burly men with tanned faces walked through the streets in shirt sleeves, laughing, throwing wisecracks back and forth. Some were obviously in a hurry to sign on and return home to silage-making or turf-cutting while this good weather held. Others were more anxious to get their money and have a few quick pints before leaving. The whole town throbbed with life.

I bought fags and stood outside the shop, unwrapping them in the sunlight. I couldn't get them out fast enough, my hands were shaking, a nicotine fit first thing in the morning. I lit one and sucked deep and it sickened me, the way the first one always does. I closed my eyes and gradually my body soaked up the nausea. The rich smoke filled out my lungs, stiffened my whole skeleton, and within moments I was ready to meet the day. Mom keeps on at me about smoking, telling me my clothes reek and my hands are stained and I look like shit. Then she tells me that I have to look after my heart— there have been a handful of casualties on both sides of the family who have been stricken down with dodgy hearts. She keeps telling me about some documentary she's seen on how Ireland has the third highest rate of heart disease in the developed world with a way higher than normal rate here in the west. Seemingly we eat too much food, drink too much drink, and smoke too much smoke. I'm glad she didn't see the one on the rate of mental disorder here in the west. Now that was a sorry story. Anyway I'm going to keep on smoking for as long as I can. It's one of the few things I enjoy. Fuck the heart is what I say, try and enjoy life. Stay alive when you're alive and make sure people can tell the difference when you're dead.

I stubbed out the fag. My mouth felt like sandpaper. I thought I might chance a pint. Normally I wouldn't drink so early in my hometown—I wouldn't be up, for one thing—and besides it draws too much attention. Drink a pint before twelve o'clock here and people are giving you a subscription to the Betty Ford clinic. But now there was a crowd in town I thought I just might get away with it. Besides, it was near twelve; after the angelus was thought to be a respectable time.

I walked across the street, into the pub facing me. I was lucky. There was a nice crowd, not too packed and a few vacant stools.

Most of the men drank standing up, trying to give the impression that they were just there for the one and on the verge of leaving, their conscience not fully at ease. I took a stool at the far end of the bar facing the door and called for a pint. The pub was full of talk, a gale of words followed by squalls of laughter, a kindly turbulence. The topics of conversation were simple ones: the weather, its beauty and unpredictability; the wetness of the bogs and the difficulty of bringing machinery into them; football, Mayo's tradition of spectacularly gifted but temperamentally fragile players; cattle, the likelihood of poor prices for them in the autumn and the probability of our whole area being rezoned as an EC disadvantaged area. Apart from the football I hadn't much interest in any of it, but I sat listening to their words anyway. These men were a different species to me. They seemed so full of a substance I would never have a fraction of. They were real men, full of real certainties and preoccupations, full of strength. I had a desperate feeling of incompleteness among them. I felt like a fragment left over from some disaster or a sketch toward some future project. I had none of their wholeness. As I listened to their words I had an urge to finish my drink and leave. But I didn't. I hoped that the longer I stayed in their midst hearing their words and their laughter, the closer I would come to having some of their completion. Maybe some of their secret would rub off on me. I was hoping, too, that Owl would be up and out of the house when I got back to get something to eat. I didn't want to see his face any sooner than I had to.

Without my noticing, the conversation of a few men with their backs to me had changed. They were talking about Jamie. One of them was telling how he'd heard about his death in the cop station when he'd left in his dole form.

"Christ, it's shocking what can happen, even in a small town like this. The poor child hadn't a clue what hit him." He spoke with real wonder in his voice. "How the hell did a young child know enough to rig up an explosion like that? Seemingly a big piece was blown out of the wall along with the roof and a couple of windows." He was a thin man with long sideburns and he had suddenly become the center of attention in the whole pub. The attention didn't seem to rest easily on him. He shrugged his shoulders quickly. "That's what I'm told anyway." He slugged his pint and sought to disappear into the background of those about him. The pub was filled with words again, everyone expressing the same disbelief.

"Someone other than a child had to be responsible."

Another agreed. "No child would be smart enough to put something like that together."

"That's for sure."

"It had to be someone older and smarter."

I was suddenly disappointed with the whole lot of them. They were just like my parents: tenants in a fools' paradise, totally blind and without imagination to see that the world could puke up something like Owl, a creature ready-formed with his own venom. This was what you got for spending your life here in the west of Ireland, on the edge of the world—a thin imagination, a narrow mind that had huge chunks of the world falling down each side of it. Owl was one of those chunks, something so outlandish that even if they saw him rigging up the explosion with their own eyes they would not have been able to believe it. Owl was outside the compass of their imagination and that's all there was to it. I could listen to no more. I took my jacket and passed through the throng into the street.

V

When I woke there was no one in the room but myself. I walked through the house and it, too, was deserted. I made breakfast and sat at the kitchen table eating a bowl of cereal, wondering what I was going to do with the day. I badly wanted to go back to the site of the explosion and have a look at the wreckage in the plain light of day. I decided against it though. In fact I decided against going outside at all that day. It seemed best to stay inside for a couple of days and lie low till the panic of Jamie's death blew over. Try not to draw any attention, that was the thing.

It seemed funny to have a whole day ahead of me that wasn't in some way concerned with my bomb. A whole day seemed such a huge length of time, white and empty, waiting to be filled. It was like a big hole stretching down and down into the day. If I wasn't careful I might fall into it and never be seen again. I had to bring all my concentration to bear on the problem. I decided that after breakfast, which was coming to an end but which I was going to stretch out with a glass of milk, a banana, and a comic, I was going to look at the telly. It would be open now and there would be cartoons on for a few hours. That would pass some time until Mom and Dad came home. They would have news for me and I would be able to plan my day after hearing it. I was beginning to feel like some sort of outlaw holed up in his hideaway, waiting for news and supplies from his outlaw friends. That thought pleased me and just to add to the effect I went to the window and looked out on the day through a chink in the curtains. The town was full and I remembered it was dole day. That worried me. For some reason I wanted the town to be deserted, no people at all, just blank streets. If these people stayed around all day I would not feel safe leaving the house. I thought about that for a while, about how I would never be able to leave the house and how my parents would have to tell the neighbors I had gone away somewhere. I would get older and bigger, never leaving the house and reading all the time just to keep myself educated and abreast of things. Then one night, when I was big enough and had read enough, I would walk out in the dead of night to make my way in the world, a tall, white giant whom the sun had never shone on. That was all rubbish and I knew it but it was good fun thinking it for a few moments.

I got my milk and banana and sat on the couch to watch telly. When it came on it was a Road Runner cartoon and as usual the coyote was laying a trap for the Road Runner. He had a wooden crate of explosives with ACME EXPLOSIVES stenciled on the side. He was going to use them to blow up a tunnel and trap the Road Runner inside. But as usual the Road Runner was too fast and the coyote was plain stupid. The explosives didn't go off until the coyote went into the tunnel to check. Tons of rock came down on him and he had to dig himself out all bruised and battered, only to have the Road Runner laughing at him and making that stupid beep beep noise. That coyote sickens me. All that hardware and explosives and no brains. What I would have done is brought a shotgun with me into the tunnel and stayed under the pile of rubble until curiosity got the better of him and he came in to have a look. I'd rise up then out of the rubble with both barrels blazing; that would put an end to that stupid beep beep noise.

I turned off the telly; it was boring me. I began to wander through the house in the semidarkness, drinking more milk, looking for something to do. I thought how empty a house is when you are looking for something to do. I thought about reading a book, I hadn't done that in a few days. But I didn't feel like it. What I really wanted to do was to go to the shed and have a look at what our explosion had done to it. I regretted that I hadn't stayed a moment longer after the bomb had gone off to take in all the details. I couldn't remember much about it now; the panic of seeing Jamie lying on the ground seemed to have done something to my short-term memory. All I could remember was the bang and then Jamie lying there and then legging it through the garden.

What a waste. All that work and planning and I couldn't remember a thing of it.

I was in a huff then, pissed off with the whole situation. I decided to go to the cupboard under the stairs and get out my favorite game. I needed some way to pass this terrible time until my parents came home and this game seemed just the thing. The game is called Axis and Allies and it's the best game in the world. You play it with two to six people and it's very complicated, lots of rules and so on, but basically what you do is, using dice and strategy, you move your ships and armies around the board, which is a map of the world, in such a way as to capture the enemies' cities—London and Washington or Berlin and Peking. I've been playing this game for nearly three years now and I still like it. What I like about it is the mixture of luck and strategy. You have to use your head but even if you do you never know when your luck will run out. One bad throw of the dice and it could be all over no matter how smart you are. Besides, it's the only game my brother will play with me now. We used to play cards and other games once but I used to beat the crap out of him always. He just hasn't got the concentration for games. For some reason this is the only game he's stuck with. There must be something in it that he likes. Whatever the reason, over the last few months he's become damn good at it. I used to be able to beat him with my eyes closed. But not anymore. These last few games have been neck and neck. Some have gone on for days and some have had to be abandoned in stalemate. He seems to enjoy playing me now that he has the measure of me.

I set out the board and symbols on the table. I planned to just have a look at the game, set up a few trial moves to pass the time and sharpen my skills. I was doing that for ten minutes, had the game set up against an imaginary opponent, when the front door slammed. My brother entered the kitchen.

V I

Those few pints left me feeling dazed in the sunlight. I needed to go home and make myself a cup of coffee, that would clear my head. When I got into the kitchen Owl was kneeling on a chair at the table playing his game of Axis and Allies. With his baseball cap on his head and his face scrunched up in concentration he looked like some military tactician planning out some maneuver. I greeted him.

"Hello, cunt."

"Hello, bollocks." He didn't even raise his head.

I plugged in the kettle and buttered a piece of bread. I was watching Owl playing the game, playing against himself, probably trying to perfect his skills. I marveled at how easily he had taken to that game. It had been in our house a couple of years; Mom and Dad had given it to me for a Christmas present but I had never taken much interest in it till Owl started to play it. That was over two years ago and had really amazed me. One day I came in and he was sitting there at the table, same as now only younger, with the whole game set out before him, dice, symbols, atlas, charts, and IPCs—Industrial Production Certificates—all ready to go. It amazed me that he'd got even that far with it because this is one difficult mother of a game. Believe it or not, there are thirty-three large pages of rules and instructions to be read before you can start. That's a fact, thirty-three pages and it's still possible to come up against a situation not covered in the rules. What you do then is write away to some place in Massachusetts where the game is manufactured and someone there will give you arbitration after a couple of days. Can you believe that? Sometimes I hear something like that and I wonder, is the world off its fucking head or, more likely, did it ever have a head to begin with? Imagine, somewhere in Massachusetts there's this dude with a load of qualifications the length of your arm, someone a lot smarter than you or me, and all he does is answer queries from young fucks like Owl the world over who are stalled and waiting patiently to hear from him because the very game he invented does not have a complete set of rules. My head goes into a spin thinking about things like that. I begin to wonder about the world's sanity.

Anyway the game's difficulty didn't stand in the way of Owl. In fact playing it seemed to be one of those times when he was in his element. I remember hearing a story once about one of those young composers who was brought to St. Paul's Cathedral and shown its massive organ. This organ was so complicated that young men had to undergo an apprenticeship to learn how to play it. But this young prodigy, who wasn't yet ten years old, sat down and played away on it with an intuitive knowledge of how it worked. That was how it was with Owl and this game. When I came in that day he had the game set up, an achievement in itself, and he asked me to play with him. After he'd explained the basics he went on to beat the shit out of me in about ten minutes. He overran all my territories, captured London and Washington, my armies, and IPCs before I could figure out what the hell was happening. He kept on beating me for a good time after that. It took me a few months to figure out the complexities of the game but gradually I got a clearer picture of how it worked. I became better at it and in these last few months I've clawed back most of his advantage. The last few games have dragged on for days, most of them ending in stalemate after both of us have negotiated and haggled and then settled the issue by carving up the whole world between us. We would be exhausted after these negotiations, negotiations that left neither of us satisfied because we were both back where we'd started. He would negotiate with real tenacity and quickness of mind, dodging and weaving and stalling, making me feel like the blunt instrument bludgeoning up the bright young kid. That was one of his craftiest tricks. He would stall and stonewall, feign indecision until I could take no more and lost my temper and stood up roaring and swearing and thumping the table while he sat there with a smug grin under the peak of his cap, gathering up the pieces because he knew then that he'd won a moral victory, a second-rate victory admittedly, but the only one possible in the circumstances. I wondered for a while, was this some plan of his to humiliate me, playing for a draw so that he could expose me like that? But I don't think so. In the beginning, when he beat me at will, he had a choice of victories. Either an economic one, where he took all my IPCs and brought my armies to a halt because without industry I couldn't keep it supplied or maintained. A good enough victory but not militarily comprehensive. Or a military victory, where he advanced his armies so far that he captured my two capital cities. This was the triumph that appealed most to his imagination. He usually ended his final move, when the game was obviously well won, in a maneuver that was totally superfluous, a piece of heel-grinding on an epic scale. When I had conceded defeat he would align together the separate components of his armies and deploy them simultaneously over the whole of my territory in a massive sweeping movement that left nothing in its wake but a landscape of crippled war machines and razed buildings. He did it with such loving elaboration you could only assume that the move was a tight paraphrase of awful, greater design in his head.

The kettle boiled so I poured coffee and buttered a slice of bread. I took an apple from the fruit bowl and began eating it with a steak knife. Those few pints had me ravenous. Owl raised his head from the game and looked at me dully, with an almost languorous distaste. I wondered how someone his age could summon up such a depth of contempt. Kids are supposed to be simple beings, with simple passions like pain, pleasure, disappointment, hatred, and so on. But contempt is no simple emotion. It is a complex feeling, a refinement of those base feelings of disappointment and hatred, an emotion that is the cool, clear distillate not of the heart but of the imagination. I was suddenly aware of just how gifted Owl really was. Even in his attitude toward me he was a genius. He was speaking now.

"Are you going to stand there all day like a zombie or are you going to play me?"

He had the whole game set up now, the board and symbols divided into two, his Allied army neatly ranked and ready to go. Sometimes we tossed to see who took which side—me, if I got the choice, preferring the Allied one. If he won he took the Allied side, too, simply because he knew that I wanted it. But in truth it never seemed to bother him which side he took, he didn't see any difference between being head of the Allied forces powering east toward Berlin or Peking or commander of the Axis forces marching west on London and Washington. It was all the same to Owl which side he was on; right or wrong or politics or historical allegiance didn't come into it. Whereas I preferred to be the Allied commander for reasons I was not too clear on, Owl found that his imagination was equally at home on either side.

I left the coffee and food on the table, ready to play. I was going to beat him this time, I could feel it. You know those rare moments you have when you're absolutely sure something is going to happen and the only surprise is when it happens exactly as you had anticipated. That's how I felt just then and I knew I would go on the offensive straightaway.

"I suppose it's right and fitting that you should take the Allied side, all those books you read and you knowing so much about explosives and that sort of thing." Despite my words I didn't feel too coherent. That's what comes from smoking and drinking on an empty stomach. I'd feel much better when I got the coffee inside me.

"I know more than you, which isn't saying much. Are you going to play me or are you going to keep talking shit?"

"OK, little man. Toss for start."

He flicked the coin onto the back of his hand, calling heads, and heads it was.

"I'm glad you got a head start, you little fuck; you're going to need it."

"I've never needed a head start playing you. Still, if you want to be foolish." He rattled and threw the die. "There's a six to begin with."

VII

So there he was, sitting at the table ready to take me on, my older bro, my smug protector of last night.

He hadn't hope of winning the game. I could smell the beer off him from across the table and I knew his concentration was shot to hell. He should've known it, too; it'd happened before and I'd kicked his ass easily. But he never seems to learn. He was wearing that look on his face, that slightly doped look that told me he was neither drunk nor sober but somewhere in between. When it came his turn to move I could see it taking him that split second too long to focus on the board, that tiny delay telling me his brain is coming out of the starting blocks a split second too slow. He was probably trying to sober himself up before Mom and Dad got back but that coffee and apple weren't going to do it.

I was going for a military victory, a complete and utter humiliation of him, letting him know once and for all my complete superiority over him. When I had my armies massed I was going to move for it as quickly as possible, lure his forces out into the open, and destroy them quickly and completely, leaving him in no doubt that I never wanted anything from him again, not his protection nor his constant moralizing nor his I-told-you-so silences nor, most especially, his you-are-my-brother-so-I-forgive-you arm around the shoulder that he was so quick with last night. I was thinking that I was smarter than he is, I was greater than he'd ever be, I knew things that he couldn't even guess at. He was going to find all this out once and for all.

This die was running real good for me. It was coming up fours, fives, and sixes, attacking dice, giving him no option but to defend. But I was biding time for the moment, hoarding IPCs, building up wealth instead of going for an all-out attack. My plan was to develop special weaponry, long-range bombers, jet power, nuclear subs, and so on. I was playing cagey, soaking up his attacks and committing just enough forces to hold my positions. He hadn't the brains to guess what I was up to. It was going to come as one big shock to him when I unleashed all this weaponry on him, when this blanket of ruin hit him. It was going to come at him from all sides and he'd be in no doubt that this finally was the end, the end of his smug moralizing, the end of his bitching, the end of his baiting, the end of his smartness, the end of his head, the end, the end, the end, the . . .

VIII

How did I let that happen?

I'd been playing the game fairly well, as well as could be expected with Owl throwing such attacking dice—fours, fives, and sixes time after time. Was this another side of his genius? Had he some influence even in the world of chance? Whatever about that, I was doing OK, holding his armies, riding out my bad luck till it turned. But it didn't turn. My dice kept coming up defensive numbers, giving me no chance to take any kind of initiative. I began to wonder, was I missing something, was I playing the game to my best even within the limits of my desperate luck? I ran through all my possible options insofar as I could remember them. No, there was nothing else I could do. What was wrong with the die then, why was it so bad? I could see that Owl was biding his time also, playing cagey even with such good dice. That was sensible. It wouldn't do so early in the game to try for the spectacular, not now when there was so little between us. This bad luck had to change some time.

My mind began to wander. I began thinking about stupid things—throwing the dice and making the complex moves like a robot while all the time I was picturing Jamie lying on the ground as dead as a doornail with the bolt sticking from his eye and thinking how little it all meant to me and to Owl and to the world except to show again how death can stalk down even the most unsuspecting just to keep the rest of us on our toes. Jamie's body, "the remains," was probably at home now in one of the front rooms with the lid of the coffin tightly screwed down. He wouldn't have an open one, not with one of his eyes gone. That was death grinding the heel, Jamie not even allowed to look his old man and lady in the face because he might only see half of them. My mind was wandering like that when suddenly I snapped to just in time to see Owl throw another six. My mind scrambled for focus, trying desperately to clarify what was going on.

And then I saw it, the bastard, I saw what he was going to do. Here it was again, another of those military victories of his. His whole army was ranked and ready to move, armed beyond all recognition; one of those total maneuvers that was going to overwhelm and crush me. And there was nothing I could do. He had duped me into deploying my armies to parts of the world that were of no consequence. I had Japanese naval and airforce units tied up in bloody sideshows in the Pacific, off the Aleutian Islands, waiting to get devastated by Owl's American forces limbering up off Midway, heavy aircraft carriers with escort and support weaponry. Already he had thrown to move out of the North African desert, across the Mediterranean into southern Europe; troop carriers and landing craft were already beaching in southern Italy and Normandy. My own forces, decimated and near ruin after a disastrous campaign on the eastern front, would never return in time to defend their backs. I was about to be destroyed. The whole disaster was shaping up on the board like an organic growth, a kind of cancerous flower that threatened to envelop everything. I was beginning to smother, a real tightness in my chest was making it impossible to breathe. I was reading Owl's triumph in his face; those laugh lines around his mouth were an obscene end-of-world calligraphy that spoke nothing but the end and that were saying now, "Well, brother dear, it seems as though you lose yet again." He had thrown a six, his last die, enabling him to move all his forces at once. A tension snapped, I was unleashed. Through a blur of motion I saw my hand, the focus of my whole being, grab the steak knife and swoop across the table, the point splitting the air and landing up to the hilt in Owl's neck, just to the left of his Adam's apple. It seemed to hit something vital, the small wound immediately started to pump rich blood and flow stickily off the handle onto the table. Owl began clutching his throat, gurgling, his whole body jerking like the chair was electrified. One hand reached across the table and started clawing the air in front of my face. Was it a pleading gesture or was he trying to claw out my eyes? His own eyes showed nothing but blind panic, popping, just about to spring from their sockets. He didn't seem to have the sense to pull out the knife and I remember thinking the crazy thought that this was no time for Owl's brain to have deserted him. The board was now covered with blood, a huge puddle forming over the whole playing area, a heavy rivulet moving with the incline toward the edge of the table. With a thick groan Owl crashed forward, facedown onto the table, twisting the knife in the wound with a terrible ripping sound.

All was quiet then, a horrified silence except for a small ticking sound, blood trickling off the table and falling steadily into a pool on the floor. My mind filled up immediately with an unbelievable thought. I thought that if I were ever going to kill someone again I would use a knife without a serrated edge. A smooth blade next time. I don't know how long I dwelt on this, turning it over in my mind—smooth edge serrated edge, smooth edge serrated edge. It seemed to give me some kind of comfort. I had the vague notion that I should get up and do something, make the room more presentable, tidy up or wipe away the blood. But that would have been pathetic; here was a disaster beyond any cleansing. I even had the insane idea that if I grabbed Owl I could shake some life back into him. I seemed to believe that his life had just retired into some deeper part of him and all it needed was a good shaking to bring it forth again. It is amazing how rubbish like this fills up your mind in a crisis. But I didn't dare touch him. You don't go prodding monsters, not even dead ones.

Soon the kitchen was rank with the smell of death and shit. The blood was thickening to a black scum on the table. Owl's baseball cap was still on his head, back to front, keeping his head out of the blood. I knew it would fit me, you just know these things. I pulled it quickly off his head, like I was snatching something hot, and his forehead popped into the blood. It fit me snugly just like I knew it would. Not only did it fit but it seemed to belong there. Without it Owl looked naked, incomplete. Only in bed was he ever without this cap. I began thinking of Jamie then and Owl and our little town out here in the west of Ireland, out on the edge of the world, throwing up these two fresh corpses in the space of two days. It just goes to show you that even in this little town, where there are only ordinary people with ordinary lives and visions, here, too, there is time and place enough for death to be spectacular, for it to come with drama and fireworks and lay low two kids who by rights have no business knowing anything about it.

The boy Jamie, apprentice to my brother, Owl, explosives engineer and death angel, both dead. May they rest in peace.

How long have I been staring across at Owl's slumped body? I don't know, I can't seem to get a focus on the passage of time. I cannot seem to move either, some rictus has entered into my own body. I do know that for as long as Owl's body is across the table from me I will be unable to move, I will be sitting here, rigid, gripping the table with both hands while rigor mortis stiffens out his limbs. If Owl were to be left there till the end of time, his corpse petrified, I would be here opposite him, staring at him without blinking, some sort of guardian over him, some sort of vigilant. Time would pass and the days would mount to eternity but I would still be here, I will always be here.

Even in death he works his magic.

—